www.alohalagoonmysteries.com

ALOHA LAGOON MYSTERIES

Ukulele Murder
Murder on the Aloha Express
Deadly Wipeout
Deadly Bubbles in the Wine
Mele Kalikimaka Murder
Death of the Big Kahuna
Ukulele Deadly
Bikinis & Bloodshed

BOOKS BY ANNE MARIE STODDARD

Aloha Lagoon Mysteries:
Bikinis & Bloodshed

Amelia Grace Rock 'n' Roll Mysteries:
Murder at Castle Rock
"Caper at Castle Rock"
(short story in the Killer Beach Reads collection)
Deception at Castle Rock
"Sleighed at Castle Rock"
(holiday short story)

BIKINIS &
BLOODSHED

an Aloha Lagoon mystery

Anne Marie Stoddard

For Leslie, Sally, Jean, Beth, Mary Jo, Aimee, Catherine, & Dane: Thanks for welcoming Kaley home to Aloha Lagoon!

ACKNOWLEDGEMENTS

A lot of work goes into writing and releasing a book, and thankfully, I get to do the fun part (which mainly entails drinking copious amounts of coffee, daydreaming, and talking to characters in my head while typing away on my keyboard). However, this book wouldn't be possible without all the amazing people who gave their time and expertise to help polish my story until it shined. First and foremost, thank you to my mentor, Gemma Halliday, for offering encouragement and excellent writing advice, as well as for continually giving me the opportunity to share my stories with so many readers. Thank you also to Kim Mulkey Griggs and Dori Harrell for getting to know my characters and providing invaluable editorial feedback. Thank you to all of the other Gemma Halliday Publishing authors for being the most incredibly talented, kind, and supportive group of women I've had the pleasure of working with. I'd also like to thank anyone who reads this book. Kaley, Noa, Aunt Rikki, and the others wouldn't exist without your support!

CHAPTER ONE

———

"I don't get it," said the petite redhead in front of me. Through the sliver of space between the airplane seats, I watched her swivel to face her friend, a curvy brunette with an unfortunate acne problem. "'Aloha' means 'hello' *and* 'goodbye'? How does that even make sense?" She scrunched her nose. "Why would you say the same thing regardless of whether you're coming or going?"

The brunette flipped the page of the magazine she'd been browsing. "I think that's a common misconception, actually," she said. "I read that people do say it as a greeting sometimes, but it actually means 'love and peace,' or something like that. It really describes the Hawaiian way of life."

"The Hawaiian way of life?" The first girl snorted. "What is that—like, actual sex on the beach? Or shaking your booty in a grass skirt and chugging mai tais all day long?" She seemed to think that over for a moment, and a grin spread across her freckled face. "You know, that actually sounds pretty great. Where can I sign up?"

I rolled my eyes. *Silly mainlanders.* At least the brunette had done her homework. Tourists were always so quick to mimic our culture and expressions for their amusement. I turned in my window seat to stare at the vast ocean below and caught a glimpse of my reflection. A blush crept into my cheeks. I had no room to gripe.

Despite being born and raised in Kauai, I was as pale as the two women seated in front of me. My father had been Maoli, a Native Hawaiian, but my mother had been a blonde, blue-eyed New Yorker with skin whiter than the sand of the local beaches. Though I'd inherited my father's dark brown hair and eyes, my lighter complexion was a gift from Mama.

For the most part, I didn't even talk like an islander either, having spent the past five years managing a clothing boutique in Atlanta, Georgia. Words and phrases like "y'all," "darlin'," and "bless your heart" had found their way into my vernacular. I'd spent a truckload of money maintaining the golden highlights that accented my naturally dark hair. Even my name, Kaley, was a mainlander's abbreviation of my Hawaiian birth name, Kalani. I'd transformed from a proud half-Native Hawaiian to Southern Belle Barbie. Love makes you do some pretty crazy stuff.

What did all that effort get me? My wispy bangs bounced as I puffed out a frustrated breath. *A one-way ticket back to the islands and a pasty tan line on my ring finger.* I'd completely reinvented myself to please my husband only to have him leave me for someone "more exotic" (his words, not mine). Actually, it was more like *several* someones.

As if to rub saltwater in the wound of my recent divorce, a little boy who'd also been on my connecting flight from Atlanta scurried up the aisle wearing an oversized Falcons jersey. The name and number stitched to the back of his shirt were like a dagger through my bruised heart. *Colfax, Fifteen.*

Bryan Colfax was the star running back for Georgia's beloved pro football team. Despite the fact that it was the end of June and the first kickoff was a couple of months away, I couldn't walk more than five feet in any direction of downtown Atlanta without seeing his face on a billboard or passing some fan wearing his jersey. Apparently, I couldn't even escape him on a cross-country flight. Here I was, somewhere miles above the Pacific Ocean, and my ex was *still* everywhere I looked.

Up until a few weeks ago, I wouldn't have minded. I used to swell with pride every time I introduced myself as Mrs. Colfax or overheard someone gushing over Bryan's last-minute, game-winning touchdown run against the Saints last season. Of course, that had all changed when I'd come home from work early last month to discover Bryan holding private auditions for the Falcons cheerleading squad in the bedroom of our penthouse condo. Nothing ends a marriage faster than seeing your husband beneath three hot twenty-two-year-olds in naked pyramid formation. Bryan and I had been having trouble connecting over the past several months, but that had been the game-ending play.

After telling the ladies where they could shove their pom-poms, I'd given Bryan *my* spirit finger and kicked him out of the condo. Unfortunately, that hadn't lasted very long, considering the property was in his name and our prenup hadn't included an infidelity clause. One expedited divorce later, all I had left of my life in Georgia was public humiliation, a broken heart, and an oversized Prada duffel full of clothes and shoes. I'd even dropped that two-timing jerk's last name. *Goodbye, Kaley Colfax*, I thought as the pilot announced our descent toward Kauai's Lihue Airport. *Hello again, Kaley Kalua.*

* * *

"Aloha! Welcome to Hawaii." A young stewardess in a navy blue blazer with a pink hibiscus flower pinned in her hair stood just inside the airport terminal, greeting travelers and placing colorful flowered leis around their necks.

The two young women who had been seated in front of me on the plane rushed toward her, squealing in delight. "Aloha!" the redhead cried, ducking her head so the stewardess could place the flowers around her neck. She straightened and turned to her friend. "Been here five minutes and I've already gotten laid," she said, bouncing her eyebrows. "Quick! Take a picture." She struck a pose in front of a wall-length mural of the nearby crescent-shaped Kalapaki Beach.

I shuffled past the women, shifting my bag from one shoulder to the other as I struggled under its weight. Once outside, I set it down and scanned the pickup area for any sign of my aunt. I spotted her almost immediately. Rikki Kalua was my dad's baby sister, and at forty-seven, she was only twenty years my senior. Though petite in size, her style was larger than life. When I'd last seen Rikki on her visit to Atlanta three Christmases ago, her raven hair had grown down to her waist. She'd since shortened it to shoulder-length and added electric blue highlights. The wacky hair, paired with a deep magenta maxi dress, made her stand out even in a crowd of flowery prints and aloha shirts.

"Kalani! My *ku'uipo*," Rikki exclaimed, calling me sweetheart in our native tongue, just as she had my whole life. She opened her arms and squeezed me when I stepped into her embrace. "It's so good to see you."

A mixture of emotions melted together and flowed through me like lava. I was happy to see Aunt Rikki, who had raised me after my parents had been killed in a boating accident off the coast of Maui when I was twelve. Still, I couldn't help but feel guilty for losing touch with her over the past few years. Daily phone calls had turned into monthly emails and then just the occasional Facebook message. When my marriage had fallen apart and I'd had no place to go, my aunt had not only insisted I move back in with her, but she'd also offered me a job. Rikki owned a clothing and accessory shop, the Happy Hula Dress Boutique, which was located in the merchant area of the town's luxury resort. She'd insisted that I accept the position as her new store manager and wouldn't take no for an answer. For that, I was eternally grateful.

"Thanks for letting me come home," I said, feeling my eyes mist.

Rikki pulled back to hold me at arm's length. "Of course, honey." She gave me a warm smile. "We're *'ohana*." The word meant family. "And we take care of our own."

I breathed a sigh of relief. I wasn't sure what I'd do without her.

"Come on." Rikki stooped to grab my bag. For a tiny woman, she was in excellent shape, making the task of hauling the fifty-pound duffel look easy. We made our way through the throngs of tourists boarding hotel shuttles and entered the short-term parking lot. "I'm just a few rows down," Rikki called over her shoulder as she walked briskly past a line of SUVs. Though I no longer had the added weight of the bag across my shoulders, I still struggled to keep up with her in my black pumps and tight canary yellow pencil skirt.

I stopped short as Rikki placed my bag down beside a bright purple Vespa. I blinked at the scooter. "What happened to your Jeep?" I asked, wondering what had possessed her to downsize to something that looked like one of those Power Wheels kids' toys from Fisher Price.

My aunt grabbed the two helmets hanging from the handlebars and handed me one. "Sold it. I've always wanted a Vespa, and I told myself, 'Rikki, you only live once.' Plus, I can practically park this thing anywhere, and I love feeling the wind on my cheeks." She grinned. "If you ask me, there's no better way to get around the island."

Lips pursed, I looked from the eggplant-colored scooter to the black headgear in my hands. I wasn't looking forward to the serious case of helmet hair in my near future.

"Come on," Rikki coaxed, mistaking my disdain for worry. "No need to be scared. I'm an excellent driver." She used a bungee cord to secure my bag just below the rear of the seat cushion and then put on her own helmet. She climbed onto the bike and gestured for me to follow suit. "Hold on tight to my waist, and you'll be just fine."

I reluctantly removed my heels and stuffed them into a pocket on the side of my bag before padding barefoot around the side of the Vespa. Hiking up my skirt, I swung my leg over the bike and settled in behind Rikki. After strapping the helmet over my wavy hair, I circled her middle with my arms and held on for dear life.

Rikki and I clearly had different definitions of "excellent driver." She zipped the Vespa in and out of traffic, cutting off at least half a dozen other drivers. I couldn't even enjoy the breathtaking view of the turquoise waters as we sped around the cliffs of Kauai. I was too busy squeezing my eyes shut and praying I'd live to stand on solid ground again.

When we finally reached the employee parking lot at the Aloha Lagoon Resort twenty minutes later, I practically lunged off the bike. I lost my balance during my hasty exit and toppled sideways off the scooter, hitting the ground in an untidy pile of tangled limbs.

"Are you all right?" Rikki asked, crouching beside me.

Bright pain stung my knees. "Ow." I moaned and rolled over on the pavement.

Rikki examined the scrapes on my legs and then clucked her tongue. "Just a few scratches. You'll get the hang of it," she promised. "Give it a week, and you'll want to buy one for yourself." Her face lit up. "Ooh! Maybe we can find you a pink

Vespa! I'll call the dealership in Lihue tomorrow and see if they have one on the lot."

"That's okay," I insisted. "I think I'd prefer something with four wheels and a little less wind in my face."

Rikki rolled her eyes. "Where's your sense of adventure?"

"In Atlanta," I said dryly. "It wouldn't fit in my carry-on bag."

My aunt chuckled. "Anyway," she said, gripping my arm as she helped me to my feet. "I just need to drop by the boutique for a few minutes to sign for our Saturday delivery. Then we'll head home, and I'll whip up some dinner," she promised.

"Whoa. That was quite a wipeout," a voice called from across the parking lot. "I've got a first aid kit if you need it."

My heart nearly fluttered out of my chest. I knew that voice.

Rikki gave me a sidelong glance, an impish smile curling her lips. "Did I mention that Noa Kahele is back in town?" Before I could respond, she turned and waved him over. "*Mahalo*, Noa. I think we might need that first aid kit."

Heavy footfalls moved toward us across the pavement. I removed my helmet and twisted around, squinting in the sunlight. My childhood best friend, Noa Kahele, was striding toward us.

"Sure. It's in my car, if you want to—" His words died away. Noa halted, his gaze fixed on me. He blinked. "Kaley?"

I gulped. "Hi," I said softly. I struggled to force down the sudden rush of guilt as I recalled the last time I'd seen Noa. He and I had been close nearly my entire life, but that had changed the night before I'd moved to Atlanta with Bryan.

I'd harbored an intense crush on Noa Kahele for years. At times I'd suspected he felt the same way about me. Unfortunately, though the chemistry between us had been downright explosive, the timing had never been right. We'd both drifted in and out of relationships with other people, never single at the same time.

After ten years of being stuck in the friend zone, our romantic tension had come to a head on the eve of my flight to Georgia. Noa confessed that he did have feelings for me, and he'd begged me not to marry Bryan. By then it was too late—I'd already made up my mind and had begun planning my new life across the country with my fiancé. I could still remember with painful clarity the dejected look in my best friend's eyes when I'd told him I was leaving. Judging by his pinched expression as he looked at me now, I was pretty sure he hadn't forgotten either.

Noa stared at me for several moments, his jaw clenched. Slowly, the muscles in his face relaxed, and to my surprise, he offered me a boyish grin. "I can't believe it," he said, moving to stand next to me. "How long has it been—like, five years? Six?"

"Five and a half." My cheeks warmed. *Not that I've been counting.* I subtly looked him over. Noa had been the chubby, awkward boy when we were kids, but puberty and years of surfing in high school and college had changed that. Now he was roughly six feet and three inches of lean muscle, dimpled cheeks, and caramel skin. His eyes were the color of dark chocolate, with tiny flecks of gold in them. A light dusting of stubble covered his cheeks and chin, and his long black hair was piled atop his head and knotted in a bun. In his board shorts and tight-fitted shirt, Noa looked like a model for a surfer clothing catalog.

All of a sudden, I was painfully aware of my own unkempt appearance. I chewed the inside of my lip, unable to believe my luck. Of all the people I could've run into after my grueling cross-country trek, gorgeous Noa Kahele just *had* to be the first. I glanced down at my bleeding knees, bare feet, and wrinkled silk blouse, wishing I could sink through the concrete.

"I didn't recognize you with the helmet on," Noa said. Lips quirked, he reached out to gently tug at a strand of my golden highlights. "What's with the blonde? Do all the girls in Atlanta look like Stepford wives?" he teased.

I felt a smile pull at the corners of my mouth. *He's still the same old Noa.* "Oh yeah? Well, the hipster barista from the local Starbucks called—he wants his man bun back." I gestured to his knotted hair.

Noa chuckled, and the sound of it warmed my insides. He'd always had an infectious laugh.

Rikki cleared her throat, pulling my attention back to her. "I need to drop by the boutique for a few minutes." She squeezed my shoulder. "Why don't you two catch up for a bit, and then you can head over there? You can meet some of your new coworkers." She gave us a little wave and then started toward the lush man-made lagoon that separated the employee parking lot from the resort's main building.

Noa's eyebrows lifted. "You're working at Happy Hula? So you're here long-term—not just visiting?"

"Yep." I put down my helmet and bent to retrieve the black Jimmy Choo pumps from my bag, which was miraculously still strapped to the back of Rikki's Vespa. I slipped the shoes on my feet and straightened again. I might have also stuck my chest out just a little. "You're looking at the new manager of the Happy Hula Dress Boutique *and* Aloha Lagoon's newest permanent resident." I silently willed him not to ask about Bryan. After my long day of traveling and ugly crying on the plane, I didn't have it in me to relive the heartache all over again right then. *If he owns a TV, then he's probably heard all about it anyway.*

"What about you?" I asked to change the subject. "What happened to California?" Noa had studied website and graphic design while we were in college. A few weeks after I'd moved with Bryan to Atlanta, Noa had left for Los Angeles to take a job at a technology start-up.

"I came home almost a year ago," he replied. "The job didn't work out." His good-natured smile faded.

I ducked my head. If I'd stayed in touch, I would have already known that, but Noa and I had lost contact after I'd moved away. Rather than try to salvage what had been left of our friendship, I'd convinced myself that he wouldn't have wanted to talk to me. After that, my life had centered around my job, Bryan, and his high-profile career. I'd become so wrapped up in being the perfect, supportive football wife that I'd eventually pushed away everyone else I'd cared about. Now I was going to have to work hard to repair my old relationships. "I'm sorry," I said softly.

"It's okay. It just wasn't meant to be." Noa turned away, and I wondered briefly if he was talking about the job or us. "Come on," he said, motioning for me to follow him across the parking lot. "Let's get you patched up."

"Why do you think the job wasn't meant to be?" I asked, wincing as the strap on one of my shoes dug in to my skin. *I guess these things really weren't made for walking.*

Noa slowed his pace so that I could keep up in my heels. He shrugged. "The job itself was fine, but the city, not so much. LA is just too intense for me. All that traffic and smog. Everyone is always in such a hurry." He gestured to the frangipani trees that lined the parking lot. "I've always preferred the beauty and laid-back lifestyle of the islands. I'm still able to line up lots of freelance design work from clients all around the world, but I get to make my own schedule. I also work as a part-time lifeguard for the resort."

Noa stopped in front of a familiar black vehicle, and I did a double take. "You bought Rikki's old Jeep Wrangler."

He nodded. "I needed a set of wheels when I moved home, and Rik said she wanted to keep it in the family." Noa had spent so much time at our house growing up that my aunt had treated him like one of her own. "Plus it's got sentimental value. I had my first kiss in this car," he added, not looking at me.

My face flushed. It had been my first kiss too—the only one I'd ever shared with Noa. I dropped my gaze to the asphalt.

Noa produced a first aid kit from his glove compartment and patted the seat cushion. "Sit right here. I'll have you bandaged up in no time." After spraying antiseptic on my scrapes (which stung like a mother), he gingerly placed bandages over each wound. "All better, right?" he asked.

"Yeah," I lied. "Thanks." The pain was even worse now, but I wasn't about to tell him that. I swallowed the lump in my throat as we stood next to the Jeep, an awkward silence stretching between us. I probably didn't deserve another chance at our friendship, but I was certainly going to try to earn it. "I'm sorry for disappearing like I did," I said quietly. "I hope you'll let me make it up to you someday."

Noa avoided my gaze, and the hurt in his expression sent another stab of guilt through my middle. After what seemed like an eternity, he looked up, a polite smile smoothing the lines on his face. "Hey, no worries," he said, his tone surprisingly casual. He held up his fist with the thumb and pinkie finger extended and wiggled his hand in the *shaka* sign. "Life happens. People grow apart." He shrugged. "Now that you're back on the island, maybe we can catch up some time," he added, though his tone was insincere.

"Totally," I said, forcing a smile despite feeling a pang of disappointment. I had the impression he was only saying that to be nice. Noa and I probably wouldn't be best buds again anytime soon. Not that I could blame him. If our roles had been reversed, I probably wouldn't want to have anything to do with him either.

I said goodbye to Noa and made my way toward the main building of the Aloha Lagoon Resort. A feeling of nostalgia crept over me as I crossed the bridge through the beautiful man-made lagoon. I'd spent many days here as a child, peering over the railing into the fish pond as I'd tried to spot Harold the Turtle. Harold was sort of the unofficial mascot of Aloha Lagoon. He'd been around for as long as I could remember—possibly even longer—and he'd probably be around long after the rest of us were gone. The resort guests had a soft spot for the old tortoise. I couldn't help but smile when I passed two little girls as they stood at the center of the bridge, pointing out into the lagoon. "There he is," I heard one of them whisper. Sure enough, the old turtle was sunning himself on a rock that peeked out just above the water's surface.

Good old Harold, I thought. I inhaled the floral fragrance wafting from the nearby plumeria and gardenia shrubs, and some of the day's tension eased from my shoulders. It was hard not to feel at home in a place like this.

Once through the lagoon, I entered a massive cream-colored building with a tiled terra-cotta roof. While the Aloha Lagoon Resort was surrounded by an island paradise, the interior was a veritable utopia all on its own. The lobby boasted an elegant granite flooring with enormous area rugs that designated sections for lounging or sitting. Gorgeous potted plant arrangements highlighted entrances to hallways, shops, and the elevator lobby. I edged past a line of guests at the concierge desk, toward a pair of sliding doors. The large glass panels parted, allowing me access to one of the resort's several courtyards.

Several smaller buildings were grouped just beyond the crystal-clear swimming pools, each looking like a miniature version of the main structure. The colorful courtyard tiles sparkled in the late afternoon sun as I moved toward one of the little shops. A familiar purple placard hung from the awning, and a dancing woman with a flowered crown and grass skirt was painted on the sign below the words *Happy Hula Dress Boutique*.

A wind chime made of seashells clinked as I stepped into my aunt's shop—and my new place of employment. The small building had an open floor plan, with a rainbow assortment of beach towels, bathing suits, sarongs, maxi dresses, and more hanging on racks all over the sales floor. Revolving display stands near the front boasted jewelry made from shells, shark's teeth, obsidian, and olivine, and shelves of funky flip-flops and colorful sandals lined the walls. I glanced down at my blistered feet and back up to the shoe racks, staring longingly at a cute and comfortable-looking pair of gold sandals.

The boutique was teeming with activity. Customers milled about on the sales floor, some perusing the clothing racks and others carrying items toward the row of changing stalls along the back wall. A young woman with long black hair stood behind the front counter, emptying a roll of quarters into the cash register. She looked up as I approached. "Aloha and welcome to Happy Hula Dress Boutique," she said politely, meeting my gaze with brown almond-shaped eyes. "How can I help you?"

"Hi." I smiled at her. "I'm Kaley, Rikki Kalua's niece."

The girl grinned back at me. "It's nice to meet you, Kaley. I'm Sara Thomas." She set down the roll of quarters and shook my hand. "I hear we're going to be working together."

I nodded. "I start tomorrow."

"Cool." Sara picked the up the roll of change again and dumped the last of the quarters into the drawer.

I sent my gaze around the crowded shop. "Have you seen my aunt come into the shop yet? I told her I'd meet her here."

The young cashier gestured with her free hand toward the back of the store. "She got here a few minutes ago. I think she's in the stockroom with the assistant manager, Louana."

"Great. Thanks." I gave Sara a little wave before turning to wade through the aisles of clothing racks, making my way toward the rear of the shop. I passed the row of changing stalls and walked down a short hallway, coming to a stop in front of a green door marked *EMPLOYEES ONLY.*

I raised my hand to knock but let it fall back to my side as the sound of muffled shouts filtered through the closed door. I frowned. Rikki rarely raised her voice. Leaning forward to press my ear against the wood, I realized that it wasn't my aunt doing the yelling.

"I don't care if she's your niece, your daughter, or a freakin' Kardashian," a woman's angry voice exclaimed. "That job is mine, fair and square."

"Come on, Louana." Rikki sounded vexed. "Be reasonable."

The other woman snorted. "'Reasonable' flew out the window when you hired your stupid niece for a promotion that should belong to *me*. I earned it."

Hey! I felt my face grow hot. *Watch who you're calling stupid.* I disliked this Louana chick already.

On the other side of the door, Rikki sighed loudly. "Lou, you've been a wonderful assistant manager, but Kaley ran a store on her own for two years in Atlanta. She's simply more qualified—"

"I'll sue." Louana's breath came out in an angry hiss. "What you're doing is nepotism. I'll sue you for every penny you're worth. I'll own you *and* this shop by the end of the summer."

"It's not nepotism," Rikki protested. I could hear her patience wearing thin. "Kaley has more experience than you. She's the better candidate. It doesn't matter that she's family. With the way you've been botching product orders lately, I just don't think you're ready for more responsibility."

"You know what I *am* ready for?" Louana's tone was low and menacing. "Some respect."

Without warning, the stockroom door flew open and knocked me backward. I staggered down the short hallway, my arms flailing in an attempt to regain my balance. I found my footing as I reached the edge of the sales floor, and the customer at the nearest clothing rack turned to give me a curious look.

A curvy woman with fiery red hair stomped through the stockroom doorway, heading straight toward me. "Get out of my way," she snarled. She pushed her way past me and stalked across the shop. "This store is the worst!" she called over her shoulder. "I'm out of here."

By now, others were taking notice of the woman's tantrum. Everyone in the store, customers and employees alike, stopped to gawk as she barreled past, pulling clothes from their hangers and tossing them onto the floor.

"Louana, stop that!" Rikki cried, chasing after her. She caught up to the disgruntled woman and grabbed her wrist, preventing her from ripping another blouse off the rack.

"No," Louana growled. She whirled to face my aunt, and her narrow face turned as scarlet as her long, curly hair. Gritting her teeth, she wrenched her arm free of Rikki's grasp. "I quit," she seethed. "But this isn't over. You're going to regret the way you've treated me. I'm going to ruin this place." Spinning on her heel, she marched out of the shop.

CHAPTER TWO

———

Tension hung thick in the air for several moments after Louana's dramatic exit. As if sensing the excitement was over, customers gradually resumed browsing the clothing racks. Sara busied herself behind the counter, attending to a woman who wanted to buy a lavender satin sarong and a black bikini. I saw the customer murmur something to the young cashier, and they both darted sympathetic looks in Rikki's direction.

My aunt didn't seem to notice. She remained in the center of the sales floor, her jaw clenched and her dark eyes fixed on the shop's entrance. Judging by the look of trepidation on her face, I suspected she was waiting to see if Louana would return to cause more destruction. It was a valid concern. If our brief encounter was any indication, the woman was nuttier than a macadamia farm.

I came to stand next to Aunt Rikki, placing a hand on her shoulder. "Are you all right?" I asked her gently.

She didn't answer right away. Instead, my aunt turned toward me and closed her eyes. She took a deep breath, and I felt the tension leave her shoulder as she pushed the air back out. When she opened her eyes again, her expression was serene. "Yes," she insisted, pulling out of my grasp. "I'll be fine. I suppose that little outburst has been a long time coming. I only wish Lou hadn't been so destructive." Rikki looked past me to the mess the angry former assistant manager had left behind. She grimaced. "I should clean this up. Hopefully none of the clothes are damaged." She stooped to collect the fallen garments, and I quickly joined her.

"Need help, Rikki?" called a young woman. I looked up in time to see a slender, busty brunette heading toward us from the changing rooms. Our eyes locked, and my stomach did a barrel roll. I knew her.

And I *hated* her.

I'd known Harmony Kane since we were kids. Don't let the sunny-sounding name fool you. Harmony had been Aloha Lagoon's resident mean girl when we were growing up. Seriously—she made Regina George look like Mother Theresa. Coming from a wealthy family, Harmony had been royally spoiled, and she'd always looked down on me. She had mercilessly mocked me when I'd shown up to school in my aunt's hand-me-down outfits. Though I'd adored Rikki's flowy skirts, bright pants, and cute peasant tops, being picked on constantly by Harmony and her friends had all but crushed my confidence.

Harmony had also loved to pull cruel pranks, usually on yours truly. Once, when we were in high school, she and her boyfriend had filled my car with dead jellyfish. Even though Rikki and I'd had it professionally cleaned, the upholstery had still reeked for months after.

Rikki and I rose to our feet as Harmony reached us. To my dismay, she was still as gorgeous as she'd been in high school, with flawless skin and not so much as an ounce of body fat. Harmony's brown eyes narrowed briefly as she looked me over. Then her lips spread in a wide smile. *Ugh.* Even her teeth were perfect.

"Oh my gosh! Kaley Kalua," she exclaimed, throwing her arms around me. "It's *so* good to see you. How have you been? You look fantastic," she gushed.

I blinked at her. *Did my plane crash on the way to Kauai? Because this totally can't be happening.* "Hi, Harmony," I replied, my tone wary. "What are you doing here?" I lowered my gaze to the shiny name badge pinned to her pink off-the-shoulder top and felt the muscles in my face go slack. "Hold up," I said, taking a step back. I stared at her, thinking I had to be mistaken. "You *work* here?"

"Harmony is my top sales associate," Rikki replied. She smiled warmly at the girl who'd made my teen life a total nightmare.

I turned to face my aunt. *Is she for real?* Rikki *did* know this was the same Harmony Kane who had put gum in my hair during tenth-grade biology class, didn't she? At the memory, my mood shifted from disbelief to anger. Thanks to Harmony, I'd been forced to chop off six inches of my long locks. My eyes narrowed. *Rikki and I need to have a chat about her hiring practices. For starters, don't put snobby, malicious skanks on the payroll.*

"You and Harmony will be spending a lot of time together," my aunt said, ignoring what I could only imagine was a sour expression etched on my face. She beamed at my rival. "Because I'm promoting her to assistant manager." She arched an eyebrow. "If you want the position, that is, Harm. Now that Louana has quit, we have an immediate opening."

"Wow. Really?" Harmony's face lit up like she'd just won another beauty pageant. She rushed to my aunt and took her hand, squeezing it. "Thank you so much!" she exclaimed.

"You've earned it," Rikki replied. "I'll announce your promotion to the rest of the staff on Monday morning." She shifted her gaze to me. "I just need to handle a few more things in my office, and then we can leave." Rikki handed Harmony the pile of clothing she'd picked up off the floor and then excused herself.

I watched my aunt flounce toward her office, her magenta maxi dress swaying around her ankles. I still couldn't believe what had just happened. Not only would I be working alongside my worst enemy, but Rikki seemed to adore her. I was right. This wasn't Aloha Lagoon. It was hell.

Harmony cleared her throat, jerking me back to the present. I turned to find her watching me through narrowed eyes. "Oh, you're still here," I said dryly.

Her lips curled in a spiteful smirk. "So, Kaley," she said in a snide tone. "I hear your hubby traded you for a younger model—no, wait. It was three cheerleaders, right?"

Her words lit a fire in my belly. "Still as bitchy as ever, huh?" I retorted. "I guess some things never change."

Harmony's smile vanished. "Time for some real talk," she said. "I don't like you, and you don't like me." A customer walked past us, pausing to browse a nearby rack of bathing suits.

Harmony plastered a fake smile on her face. "So as long as you stay out of my way, we won't have any problems," she said, her voice low. "Got it?" She turned on her heel and walked off before I had a chance to answer.

I glared after her. That was a tall order, considering we'd be working in the small shop together. The fact that she was employed at Happy Hula gave me second thoughts about taking the job. I couldn't stand to be in the same room as Harmony Kane. If the boutique had belonged to anyone other than Aunt Rikki, I would already be out the door, applying for a waitressing gig at one of the resort's restaurants. I couldn't back out on Rik though. I was just going to have to grin and bear it—and make sure that my schedule overlapped with Harmony's as little as possible.

Rikki was on the phone when I dropped by her office, so I returned to the sales floor and killed time by browsing the shop. I perused several racks of skirts and tunics, marveling at the selection of designers my aunt carried in her store. The shop specialized in what I liked to call island couture: trendy clothing in bright colors and tropical patterns from some of the world's top fashion icons, as well as several popular local designers. When Rikki had first opened Happy Hula on the luxury resort, she'd only carried two or three different brands. Now the little clothing boutique boasted an impressive roster of more than twenty different designers—from Alexander McQueen to Zac Posen and everything in between. Rikki had even secured exclusive tropical-themed lines from several brands.

By the time my aunt emerged from her office a half hour later, I'd splurged on a sleeveless navy and gold Lily Pulitzer tunic, a pair of gold teardrop earrings, and the sandals I'd been eying when I'd first arrived. I was just taking my credit card back from Sara—and silently vowing to cut it into a hundred little pieces—when my aunt approached the front counter.

"Sorry that took so long, sweetie," Rikki said, coming to stand beside me. She glanced down at my shopping bag, and a knowing smile curled her lips. "Indulging in a little retail therapy?" She craned her neck to see inside the little bag with the purple and white Happy Hula logo. "What'd you get?"

I pulled the tunic out of the bag. "You like?"

Rikki squealed in delight. "I love it! I was actually thinking of you when I ordered that."

I grinned. "I thought I could wear it on my first day at work."

I waited patiently while Rikki, Sara, and Harmony set to work closing down the boutique for the day. Harmony pretended to try to engage me in amiable conversation, though as soon as my aunt's back was turned, she dropped the act and shot me dirty looks. I did my best to be polite, which took about a metric ton of willpower.

The Kauai sunset painted a breathtaking mural across the sky as Rikki and I crossed the courtyard on our way back to the employee lot several minutes later. Dozens of resort guests were scattered about, some taking photos in front of the picturesque surroundings, others swaying to ukulele music being performed by one of the island's resident musicians. I paused to listen in admiration of the beautiful, sunny melody.

My aunt leaned in close. "That's Nani Johnson," she said, pointing to the young brunette strumming the uke. "She's the most talented musician on the island. Even studied at Juilliard, from what I've heard."

"She's remarkable." I closed my eyes and moved to the music for a few moments.

"I start my own lessons with her next week," Rikki told me.

I reopened my eyes to find her grinning with excitement.

"She's going to teach me how to play. Now that you're around to help out at the store, I'll have more free time to pursue some new hobbies."

"That's great." I squeezed her arm, thinking that perhaps I should get a new hobby myself. Maybe I could take up knitting. *Or napping on the beach. Does that count?*

When the song ended, Rikki and I joined in the applause before continuing on our way. We reached her Vespa a few minutes later. I climbed on and shut my eyes again, not opening them until I heard the familiar crunch of gravel in my aunt's driveway.

Rikki lived in a cottage on Kalapaki Drive. The little house had teal siding with white trim and a seahorse theme throughout its decor. Two seahorse statues carved from driftwood stood on either side of the entrance to the front porch, and a third, smaller one was fixed to the door, just below the peephole.

I managed to maintain my balance this time around as I climbed off the scooter. For a few moments, I stood still in the driveway, childhood memories flooding through me as I stared wistfully at the front porch. With a small sigh, I unstrapped my belongings from the back of the Vespa and followed Rikki into the house.

Little had changed since I'd last been home. The living room was still outfitted with the same set of wicker furniture with overstuffed green cushions, and a lead and stained-glass lamp shaped like a palm tree illuminated my aunt's bamboo desk in the far corner. A smile tugged at the corners of my lips as I spied a crack in the glass that constructed one of the palm fronds. My father had made the lamp as a gift for Rikki's thirtieth birthday. Not even two hours later, I'd knocked it over as I chased one of the neighbor kids through the house. My aunt hadn't even been mad; she'd told my parents not to punish me and had even thanked me for giving the piece "more character."

"Home sweet home." Rikki sighed with contentment.

She fluttered into the kitchen to make dinner, and I set my bag down and joined her. After a meal of seared mahi mahi and rice, we lounged on the lanai with an open bottle of wine between us.

"Why did you hire Harmony Kane?" I asked after a while. I turned in my seat so that I was facing her. "Don't you remember how horrible she was to me when I was younger? Is this a 'keep your enemies close' kind of situation?"

Rikki smiled at me in the moonlight. "I'd like to think I have a positive influence on her. Plus, she was just a kid back then, *ku'uipo*. People grow up. Harmony has been a model employee—literally." Her lips twitched. "She's posed in most of the outfits in our inventory for some ads in the *Aloha Sun*."

I groaned. Of course she had. I was getting the impression that Rikki had a penchant for hiring wayward employees, myself included. Maybe she thought she could fix us all. "What about that dreadful woman that quit this afternoon?" I asked next. "What was her name again?"

"Louana," Rikki replied, her smile fading. "Louana Watson."

"Oh. That's right." I chewed the inside of my lip, recalling the conversation I'd overheard outside the stockroom. Guilt wound its way through me. "I'm sorry for all the trouble she caused. I feel like it's sort of my fault."

"Your fault?" Rikki lifted a brow. "Why would you think that?"

I was glad she couldn't see my cheeks burning in the dark. "I heard your argument. She was angry that you gave me the manager position."

My aunt waved her hand dismissively. "Don't you feel bad about that for one minute," she said. "You deserve it, and I know you're going to do an excellent job." She rose from her chair and stretched, staring up at the starry sky. "You know, it's such a perfect night. I could really go for a swim right now." She looked down at me, lips stretched in a devilish grin. "Sometimes I like to go skinny dipping at Coconut Cove. Want to join me?"

I gave her a wry smile. "Thanks, but I think I'll pass." Swimming naked with my aunt in the middle of the night wasn't exactly my idea of a good time.

"Are you sure?" she pressed. "It's so peaceful out there at this time of night. And the moon over the ocean…" She trailed off, a happy sigh escaping her.

"Maybe next time." It wasn't *that* moon I was worried about seeing. I yawned. "I'm pretty beat." Even as I said the words, I could feel the exhaustion taking over. My body was still operating on Atlanta time, which was nearly three in the morning.

"Suit yourself, dear." My aunt blew me a kiss and then started toward the double doors that led back inside the house. "Rest up," she called over her shoulder. "You've got a big day tomorrow, Ms. Store Manager."

I heaved myself out of the chair and retrieved my bag. Through the living room window, I caught a glimpse of the Vespa's tail lights leaving the driveway. Slinging my duffel over my shoulder, I climbed the stairs and pushed open the door to my old bedroom. I was greeted by the same canopy bed, purple gossamer curtains, and bamboo vanity set I'd had when I was younger. With the exception of an easel and a set of watercolor paints that Rikki had set up in the far corner, everything else about the room was exactly as I'd left it. I crossed the hardwood floor and sank down on the thin comforter, weariness from travel and the time difference seeping into my bones.

It was the first time I'd been completely alone since I'd left our condo—*Bryan's* condo—to fly from Atlanta to Los Angeles, where I'd boarded the plane to Kauai. A wave of fresh pain rolled over me at the thought of my now *ex*-husband, and the dam holding back my tears broke. I had moved clear across the continent and had pushed away everyone else I cared about just to be with Bryan. In the end though, that hadn't been enough. He'd dropped me for two Nicoles and a Puerto Rican pole dancer named Valentina.

Bryan and I had been having problems for months leading up to his cheating scandal. I was over him, but I wasn't over the pain and humiliation he'd caused me. Thanks to his celebrity athlete status, every news outlet from ESPN to *Entertainment Tonight* had covered the story. My failed marriage had become a late-night talk-show punch line. I'd even had a literary agent from New York call as I was boarding the plane in Los Angeles, begging me to sign with her whenever I decided to write my tell-all memoir about my famous ex-hubby's sex addiction. Not that I was planning to do any such thing. I wanted to forget my marriage to Bryan Colfax had ever happened.

I never should have left Aloha Lagoon in the first place, I thought, wiping the moisture from my eyes. *I shouldn't have married Bryan.* I'd really thought I'd loved him, but doubt about whether or not I'd made the right decision had been eating away at me for years—and I could pinpoint the exact moment it had all started: the moment that Noa had told me he loved me.

I'd tried to convince myself that going through with the wedding had been the right thing to do, but deep down, I'd known that I was making a huge mistake. I'd loved Noa. *I should have chosen him.*

I sighed and rested my head against the pillow, pulling the purple comforter up to my chin. *It's too late now*, I thought glumly, recalling our strained reunion in the resort parking lot that afternoon. I'd seen the thinly veiled hurt behind his eyes. Things between us would never be the same. I'd blown my shot.

My second chance at happiness doesn't revolve around Noa Kahele, I reminded myself. Now that I was home in Aloha Lagoon, I finally had my life back. No more planning my entire year around Bryan's schedule. No more being polite to those catty football wives and girlfriends who gossiped behind my back. I closed my eyes and burrowed deeper under the covers. *Starting tomorrow, everything is going to be better.*

* * *

The next thing I knew, the Sunday morning sun was shining through my bedroom window. I squeezed my eyes shut more tightly and rolled over. Out of habit, I stretched my arm across the other side of the bed and found that it was empty. I cracked my eyelids open and stared at the space where Bryan used to sleep. It took my mind a moment to reconnect the dots of the past few weeks. *We're not together anymore...and I'm not even in Atlanta.*

I rose slowly from the bed and opened the curtains to see Kauai's majestic volcano in the distance. A feeling of calm filled me, and I smiled at the mountain and the expanse of lush greenery below it. *I'm in paradise.*

After a quick shower, I dressed for my first day as the Happy Hula Dress Boutique's store manager. I shimmied into the new tunic that I'd bought from the shop the day before. Then I applied a fresh coat of makeup and straightened my hair, carefully clipping it back so that Rikki's spare helmet wouldn't ruin it on the ride to work. Last, I slipped into my new gold sandals and completed the outfit with new gold teardrop earrings and an Alex and Ani bangle bracelet with a pineapple charm. I stepped back and admired my reflection. *Cute? Check. Professional? Totally.* I grinned into the mirror. *Let's do this.*

Rikki was waiting for me in the kitchen with a steaming cup of Kona brew. "Looking good, sweetie," she said. She pushed the Styrofoam coffee cup and a brown paper bag toward me from across the kitchen table. "I brought you breakfast. I jogged over to the Blue Manu Coffee House while you were in the shower."

My mouth watered as I inhaled the rich aroma of the hot drink. "Thanks." I gripped the to-go cup and brought it to my lips. *Mmm.* It was heaven. Opening the brown sack, I found a fresh macadamia nut muffin inside. I quickly polished it off before following Rikki out to the driveway. I grudgingly strapped on the helmet and climbed onto the back of the Vespa. I'd have to get a car of my own—hopefully sooner than later. If I sold my wedding band and engagement ring, I was sure I could afford a down payment on something reasonable. *Anything but a Vespa*, I thought, flinching as we shot down the street on the little scooter.

A short drive later, we parked in the employee lot of the Aloha Lagoon Resort. When Rikki removed her helmet, I saw that she was frowning. "Louana's car is here." She gestured to a green Corolla a few spaces over. My aunt chewed her lip. "She stormed out without returning her shop key yesterday. I hope she's not here to stir up more trouble."

My gut tightened as I stared at the little green sedan. It would be just my luck that the angry woman would show up to cause another scene before I could even clock in for my first shift.

As Rikki had suspected, the front door to Happy Hula was already unlocked when we arrived. She cautiously pushed it open, and we both peered inside. The shop was empty. We did a quick search of the sales floor, and then Rikki checked the cash register. Thankfully, nothing seemed out of place.

My aunt blew out a breath. "I was half expecting to find the place ransacked," she admitted, sounding relieved.

"Maybe Louana went to one of the bars on the resort last night," I suggested. "She might have been too toasted to drive and decided to call a cab."

"It's possible," Rikki said, but she didn't sound convinced. "If that were the case though, why would the shop be unlocked? You, Sara, and Harmony were all with me when I locked it last night." She stared at the shop door for a few moments, a frown wrinkling her forehead. "I'm going to pay a visit to Summer at the front desk in the lobby. I'm pretty sure she's got the number for the locksmith that the resort uses. It couldn't hurt to change the store locks, just in case."

"Good idea," I agreed. "Is there anything I can do while you're gone?"

Rikki gestured to the wastebasket behind the counter. "If you wouldn't mind collecting all of the trash from the bins around the store, that'd be great. There are bags in the supply closet beside my office. Once you've emptied all the bins, you can carry the bag out to the dumpster behind the store. I'll be back in a few minutes," she called over her shoulder as she started for the door.

I made my way to the supply closet and retrieved one of the large trash bags. The shop's wastebaskets were located behind the register, in both dressing rooms and bathrooms, in Rikki's office, and in the storage room. I emptied the contents of each bin and then tied the large trash bag closed before heading toward the store's back exit.

The rear door to the boutique was located through the stockroom and opened to a small alley behind the row of courtyard shops. I carried the bags into the alley, wrinkling my nose as the sour odor of garbage hit me full in the face. I held my breath against the stench emanating from the trash bin and walked toward it as fast as my sandals could carry me. After heaving the bag into the dumpster, I dusted off my hands and turned to hurry back inside.

Something glittering in the sunlight caught my eye, and I spun on my heel, curiosity drawing my attention downward. A sparkly green blouse lay on the ground near the corner of the dumpster. Frowning, I took a step toward it. I recognized the top from one of the racks near the front of Happy Hula's sales floor. Lying several feet away was another garment: a pair of red and white striped bikini bottoms.

I crinkled my nose as another wave of the putrid scent of garbage lifted past my nostrils. Holding my breath, I moved toward the clothing, halting when I spied a woman's flip-flop on the ground. It was black with silver rhinestones on the strap. Something about seeing the lone shoe without its owner gave me the creeps. A finger of dread tickled my spine, and I shivered despite the warmth of the June morning. I shook off the weird feeling and stepped around the corner of the dumpster to collect the blouse and bikini.

A light blue Happy Hula shopping bag was overturned on the ground next to the garbage bin. Several other dresses and sarongs were scattered about, littering the alley. My back stiffened. *Who would throw away all these clothes?*

I stooped to retrieve the sparkly green blouse, pinching it between my thumb and forefinger as I lifted it. I immediately dropped the shirt back to the ground. The other black flip-flop was beneath it. The shoe itself didn't startle me—it was the fact that it was still attached to a foot that sent me scuttling back a few steps. Alarm bells went off in my head as my gaze traveled the length of a woman's bare calf and then up toward the side of the dumpster. A horrified scream clawed its way out of my throat.

Louana Watson's lifeless body was slumped against the garbage bin, a hot pink bikini top wrapped tightly around her throat.

CHAPTER THREE

———

Rikki closed the boutique for the day in the wake of Louana's death. After calling the police and resort security, she reached out to the other shop employees who were scheduled to work that day and asked them to stay home. A crowd of curious guests began gathering near the front of the store when law enforcement arrived, and the alley behind the store was cordoned off by crime scene technicians. Rikki and I were ushered into her office, where we were told to wait for someone to take our statements.

A plump dark-haired man in slacks and a flowery Hawaiian shirt entered the room after a while. He studied us both silently as we huddled together in a couple of chairs behind Rikki's desk. The man took a seat across from us, a sympathetic expression on his round face. "I'm Detective Ray Kahoalani," he said. "But you can call me Detective Ray." He inclined his head toward Rikki. "I'm terribly sorry about Miss Watson. She was your employee?" His tone made the statement sound more like a question.

"Yes," Rikki said. "Former employee, actually," she quickly corrected herself. "Lou quit yesterday afternoon."

"I see." Detective Ray bobbed his head and then wrote something down on his notepad. "Why did she quit?"

Rikki's cheeks turned pink, and I felt her stiffen beside me. "She didn't agree with some of my recent decisions regarding the boutique." The defensive edge to her tone felt out of place coming from my aunt's lips. She was always such a gentle, laid-back person.

The detective lifted an eyebrow. "What kind of decisions?"

Rikki cast a sheepish glance toward me. She sighed. "Louana was upset that I gave Kaley a job as Happy Hula's new manager. She wanted the position, but Kaley has more experience. When I wouldn't budge on the decision, Lou got frustrated and quit."

Ray scribbled down a few more notes and then turned his attention to me. "You were the one who found Miss Watson in the alley, correct?"

I gave a shaky nod. I hadn't stopped trembling since my grisly discovery. It was the first time I'd ever seen a dead body in the flesh—not an actor in a movie or rerun of *CSI*, but an actual corpse. I wanted to scrub my brain with bleach to erase the image of her that I saw every time I closed my eyes. Louana had been slumped against the side of the dumpster, a terrified look permanently frozen on her face. A purple bruise had circled her neck where the bikini strap had been pulled tight enough to strangle her. The wound had been accented by little red crescent-shaped marks. I assumed they were made by her fingernails, as if she'd been trying to claw her way free.

A feeling of nausea overwhelmed me, and for a moment, I sensed my coffee and muffin from breakfast threatening to make a reappearance. I reached for the empty wastebasket under Rikki's desk and clutched it to my chest. I breathed hard for a few beats, struggling to keep my food down. My aunt rubbed her hand in soothing circles on my back, and gradually the nausea passed. I set the wastebasket down and glanced at the detective, unable to meet his eyes. "Sorry about that," I mumbled.

"It's all right," he said. Though his tone was gentle, his probing gaze made me nervous. "Did either of you see Miss Watson again after she left the store yesterday?"

Rikki and I both shook our heads.

"What time did you close the shop?" he asked Rikki.

"I locked up a few minutes after eight last night."

Detective Ray made another note. He looked at me. "Where were you for the rest of the night?"

"Home. At Rikki's. I just moved back to Aloha Lagoon from Atlanta yesterday, and I was exhausted." I fidgeted under his gaze. "My body hasn't adjusted to the time difference yet. I was in bed by ten."

His attention shifted to my aunt. "Can you confirm that?"

Rikki nodded. "Kaley was asleep when I got home last night," she replied.

"You weren't home with your niece the whole night?" Detective Ray's brow furrowed. "Where were you?"

"I went for a moonlight swim at Coconut Cove."

"Was anyone with you?" he questioned. "Do you have any witnesses that can confirm they saw you at Coconut Cove last night?"

My aunt quirked her lips. "If anyone saw me, they sure got an eyeful."

Detective Ray's forehead wrinkled. He pursed his lips and jotted something down on his notepad. I was thankful that he didn't ask her to elaborate—the last thing Rikki needed right then was to be busted for public indecency. Instead, the detective continued with his current line of questioning. "What time did you come home from Coconut Cove?"

Rikki's expression turned thoughtful. "Just after midnight, I believe."

"And you didn't make any stops on the way home?" His lip curled. "No late-night trip over to the resort?"

Rikki shook her head.

Why would he ask that? My palms began to sweat, and a kiwi-sized lump formed in my throat. I didn't like way the detective was looking at my aunt, his eyes narrowed in silent accusation. *He can't think she had anything to do with Louana's death, can he?*

As if in answer to my question, Detective Ray leaned forward in his seat. "You had an argument with Miss Watson just hours before she was killed," he said to Rikki, his words stained with suspicion. "Interesting."

The lump in my throat grew even larger.

Detective Ray pocketed his notebook and rose from his seat. "I may have a few more questions for you later on," he said, his eyes boring into hers. "I'll be in touch." It almost sounded like a threat.

The detective told us we were free to leave and then excused himself to join his team in the back alley. As soon as he was gone, I swiveled in my seat and faced Rikki. "I've got a bad feeling about him," I said, inclining my head toward the doorway where the burly homicide detective had just disappeared.

Rikki shrugged. "He's just doing his job, *ku'uipo*," she said, putting a reassuring hand on my shoulder. "I don't want you to worry. The police will find out who did this." Rikki gave me a small smile that didn't quite reach her eyes. I got the impression that she was putting on a brave face for me, which only fueled my worry. The detective's line of questioning had made it sound like he thought she was involved in this somehow.

But Rikki has nothing to hide, I told myself. *She's right— the police will catch the real killer.*

Rikki and I left her office and found a beast of a man waiting for us just inside Happy Hula's entrance. My aunt introduced him as Jimmy Toki, head of security at the resort.

Towering above us at over six feet tall, Jimmy had to look down to meet my gaze. "Come on," he said, giving me a compassionate smile. "Let's get you two out of here."

Rikki quickly locked the door, and Jimmy used his large frame to shield us from the crowd of curious onlookers in the courtyard. I kept my gaze fixed on the patio tiles, not looking up until we reached the main building. Word of Louana's murder had already spread beyond the resort, and according to Jimmy, a news crew was camped out in the main lobby. He took us through a side entrance to the building so that we could avoid being seen. At the end of a long hall, Jimmy pushed open another door and led us onto a stone path that ran behind the lagoon.

"This leads straight to the employee lot," he said, squinting against the bright sunlight. "I can walk the rest of the way there with you, if you like."

"We'll be fine from here," Rikki insisted.

Jimmy's broad forehead wrinkled. "Are you sure?"

"I think so." I offered him a smile, feeling grateful for his kindness. "Thanks again."

He gave a curt nod before retreating back down the hallway.

Rikki and I made our way silently down the path, each lost in our own thoughts. We reached the employee parking lot a few minutes later and climbed wearily onto her purple scooter. When we arrived home, my aunt trudged inside and headed straight for the stairs. "I'm going to lie down," she called over her shoulder.

"Aunt Rikki, wait." I put a hand on her arm. "I'm so sorry about Louana."

Her eyes misted, and she gave me a watery smile. "Thank you, sweetheart." Her face pinched. "I feel terrible for her *'ohana*. Lou's family lives in Salt Lake City. I wonder if the police have even been able to get hold of them yet."

I chewed my lip. "Why do you think she came back to Happy Hula? And what do you make of the bag of clothes strewn around the dumpster?"

"I don't know." Rikki shook her head, frowning. "Maybe Lou decided to take a few parting gifts when she left the store."

That was a nice way of saying she'd tried to rob my aunt. I'd been thinking the same thing. Still, it didn't explain how she'd wound up dead in that alley. Had she brought an accomplice who had killed her and then run off without the loot? Or had she stumbled upon something sinister in the alley as she exited the store? I shuddered, not sure if I really wanted to know.

Rikki rubbed her eyes. "I'm sorry, *ku'uipo*, but I really need to rest." She met my gaze again, and for the first time, I noticed the fine lines beginning to form around her eyes and mouth. I'd never seen my aunt look so tired. "There's food in the fridge if you're hungry," she said. "If you need anything else, just knock on my door."

Bless her heart, I thought, watching her trudge up the stairs. One of Rikki's employees had just been killed, and she was worried about whether or not I was comfortable. I crossed the living room and sank onto the couch. It was barely noon, but the adrenaline had seeped out of me, leaving me exhausted. I turned on the television but barely made it to the first commercial break of the daytime soap I was watching before I dozed off.

I woke up sometime later, sitting up on the couch in a cold sweat. Through the living room window, I could see the last few rays of sunlight fading from view. The soap opera had ended hours ago, and an old rerun of *Castle* was on the television.

I brushed my hair out of my face and rubbed my eyes, trying to collect my bearings. The events of the morning slammed back into focus, and my breath caught in my throat. Someone had killed Louana Watson in cold blood right outside Aunt Rikki's boutique. They'd even used merchandise from the shop to commit the crime. It seemed like a dream fueled by a night of too many mai tais—except it had really happened.

I hauled myself off the couch and climbed the stairs to the second floor. I knocked softly on the door to Rikki's bedroom. When she didn't answer, I opened it just a crack and peeked inside. My aunt was curled on her side in her bed, resting peacefully. Somehow we'd both managed to sleep the remainder of the day away. Not wanting to wake her, I quietly backed out of her room and eased the door closed behind me.

My cell phone buzzed on the coffee table as I returned to the living room. I did a double take when I saw Noa's name flash across the screen. I pressed the phone to my ear. "Noa?" I asked, unable to keep the surprise from my voice. When he'd said we should catch up soon, I'd assumed it had been an empty promise.

"I just heard about Louana," he said without preamble. His tone was tense. "Is Rikki all right?"

At least he still cared about one member of this family. "She's fine," I said. "Just a little shaken up." *And I'm all right too—thanks for asking.* A new thought lifted through me, and I frowned. "How did you find out?" I asked, reaching for the television remote and flipping through the channels. Had Lou's murder made the evening news?

"I worked a lifeguard shift at the pool today. The police were there." The worry in his voice made my gut clench. Something was wrong.

"Did they talk to you?" I asked, my voice quavering slightly.

"No, but I heard the homicide detective speaking to a few women who were shopping at Happy Hula yesterday evening. He was asking if they witnessed an argument between Rikki and Louana."

My stomach tightened even more. "What did they say?"

Noa cleared his throat. "One of the women said she'd been there when it happened. She told the detective that Louana had threatened to make Rikki regret whatever it was she'd done to her and that she'd started tearing apart the store. Did that really happen? What did Rikki do to make her so angry?"

I bit my lip. "It was more my fault than Rikki's. Louana was upset that she gave me the store manager job. She threw this huge tantrum, and she kept raving that she was going to ruin the shop. It was kind of ridiculous." My throat felt suddenly dry. "But Rikki didn't do anything wrong," I added quickly. "Hell, she didn't even fire that psycho—Louana quit on her own. Then she stomped out of the store, and that was the last we saw of her until…" My voice trailed off as the image of the dead woman flashed through my memory again. "Until I found her body this morning," I finished, my voice barely above a whisper.

Noa swore under his breath. "I'm so sorry, Kales," he said softly, using the nickname he'd called me when we were younger.

"Thanks." I swallowed. "Did you hear Detective Ray say anything else?"

"No, but I'm afraid it gets worse," he said grimly. "I stopped by the Blue Manu Coffee House on the way home and bumped into Sara Thomas. She's a cashier at your aunt's boutique."

"Yeah, I met her yesterday," I said.

"She'd just come from the police station," Noa continued. "Detective Ray called her in to ask her some questions. He wanted to know about Rikki's work relationship with Louana, and he asked if they fought often or if she'd ever heard your aunt threaten Lou before. I think he's building a case against Rikki."

Anger flared in my belly. "That's crap!" I cried. I dropped onto the couch, my free hand balling into a fist in my lap. Not wanting Rikki to hear me from upstairs, I lowered my voice. "There's no way the police could suspect her."

Even as I said it, I knew I was wrong. I recalled the way the homicide detective had looked at my aunt earlier that morning in her office. Though Ray hadn't formally accused her, there'd been no mistaking the suspicion in his dark eyes. Everyone in the store yesterday had seen Rikki's confrontation with Louana, including Harmony, Sara, and at least a half a dozen customers. *And she was murdered just a few hours later.*

There were also no witnesses that could confirm that Rikki had gone only to Coconut Cove last night when she'd left the house after dinner. In the detective's eyes, that would mean she didn't have a solid alibi. I supposed it was a reasonable assumption on his part to think that she might have had something to do with the murder. *Only reasonable if you don't know Rikki*, I thought, biting my lip.

"Are you still there?" Noa asked. He sounded concerned.

I forced out a shaky breath. "Yes," I said softly. "You and I both know Aunt Rikki isn't capable of hurting anyone, let alone killing them." I'd known my tree-hugging, happy-go-lucky aunt my whole life, and she didn't have a violent bone in her body. Sure, I hadn't seen her often over the past few years, but she was still the same kind, generous woman she'd always been. Wasn't she?

"I know," Noa replied. "Rikki's been like my second mother since I was a kid. I don't think she had anything to do with what happened to Louana." He paused, and when he spoke again, his tone was gentle. "Listen, Kaley. If there's anything I can do to help, call me. I mean it."

"Thanks," I said, feeling a rush of sincere gratitude. "I will." Despite our falling out, we both still cared about my aunt. It meant a lot to know that if things went south, he'd have her back.

I said goodbye to Noa and set the phone back on the coffee table. Frustrated, I rose from the couch and paced around the living room. It wouldn't matter whether or not Detective Ray and his team found any hard evidence that linked Rikki to Louana Watson's murder. If word got around that she was a person of interest, it would hurt her reputation and might even cause problems for her business.

I'll be damned if I'm going to sit back and let Rikki's life be ruined, I thought stubbornly. My aunt had done so much for me—taking me in and raising me like I was her own daughter. When my marriage had crumbled, she hadn't hesitated to welcome me home and give me a new start at Happy Hula. She'd never once turned her back on me, and I wouldn't turn mine on her now. If there was a way to prove that Aunt Rikki was innocent, I was going to find it.

CHAPTER FOUR

———

Jimmy Toki convinced the police to allow my aunt to open Happy Hula the next day, provided that he beef up security around the alley behind the store. It was still sectioned off by the yellow crime scene tape, and no one but Detective Ray's forensics team was allowed back there until they completed their investigation.

Rikki called an all-hands-on-deck staff meeting before the store opened for business. A few minutes before we opened, eight of us were gathered at the front of the sales floor. Sara Thomas stood between Rikki and me, her jet black hair pulled up in a sleek ponytail and her face free of makeup. The young woman's eyes were puffy, as if she'd been crying. She wasn't the only one. Two other employees were huddled close together near the cash register, a twentysomething salesgirl named Rose and an older cashier named Dorothy. Rose's dark face was also streaked with tears. She and Dorothy were whispering back and forth, casting nervous glances around the room.

A young man standing next to Rose placed a comforting hand on her shoulder. Rikki had introduced him to me earlier as Luka Hale. He looked to be around twenty or twenty-one, with bronze skin and the dark hair and eyes of the Maoli people. Despite the acne scars that marred his cheeks, he was good-looking for his age. As I watched, Luka released his grip on Rose's shoulder and dropped his arm to his side. He bowed his head, his expression unreadable under a mop of unruly hair.

Harmony Kane was leaning against the front counter, examining her manicured fingernails. I saw her cast a suspicious glance at Rikki when she thought no one was looking. After a moment, she noticed me watching her and dropped her gaze to the floor. I frowned, thinking that if Harmony wasn't giving me the stink eye then she must be upset after all.

There was one other Happy Hula staffer in the huddle that I hadn't yet met. Rikki introduced me to Tonya Friedman, a working mother in her late thirties with strawberry blonde hair and gentle blue eyes. The woman gave me a timid smile and then moved to stand next to Harmony.

"Now that we're all here," Rikki began, commanding our attention, "I want to say a few words about our dear friend and team member Louana Watson." She stepped front and center of the little group. My aunt was wearing a knee-length black tube top dress and matching sandals. Her blue-streaked hair was pulled back in a single braid, and a gold chain necklace with a lotus flower charm hung around her neck. "Lou might not have been the easiest person to get along with, but she was a member of the Happy Hula family," she said, sweeping her gaze around the group. "I know each of you cared about her. She'll be greatly missed around here."

As Aunt Rikki talked, I studied the circle of Happy Hula staffers. These were the people who had probably spent the most time with the dead woman: her coworkers. Was it possible that one of them could have killed her?

Sara and Rose sniffled and wiped at their eyes as Rikki gave her eulogy for Lou. Tonya also grew teary-eyed and hung her head, murmuring a prayer and touching her forehead, chest, and shoulders in the sign of the cross. Even Harmony had the decency to look regretful. Only Luka seemed unaffected. He blinked a few times and then stared at the floor, his expression dispassionate. I watched the stoic young man with new interest. Was he trying to hide his emotions, or was he not upset that Louana was gone?

Rikki wiped a tear from the corner of her eye. She pushed out a breath and then forced a smile onto her face. "I do have some happy news to share," she said, placing her hand on my shoulder. "I'd like to welcome my niece, Kaley, on board as our new store manager."

Everyone in the huddle clapped, albeit halfheartedly. I tried not to take the lack of enthusiasm personally. They had just lost a coworker, after all. "Thanks, Rikki." I pasted a friendly smile on my face and looked around the group. "I'm excited to be working with y'all," I said, a hint of my acquired southern accent coming through.

Tonya and Sara smiled back, and Harmony rolled her eyes. "Hick," she muttered under her breath. I ignored her, my gaze flicking back to Luka. I found him watching me with his mouth set in a hard line. When our eyes met, he looked away.

Next, Rikki announced Harmony's promotion to assistant manager. There was more polite applause. Harmony soaked up the attention, preening and cupping her hand in the regal wave she'd perfected in her beauty pageant days. It was my turn to roll my eyes.

"Does anyone else have anything they'd like to discuss before we open the shop?" Rikki asked, sending her gaze around the group.

Rose stepped forward. "People around the resort are talking," she said, giving my aunt an uncertain look. "About you and Louana." Her cheeks flushed. "Then the police came to my house yesterday."

Rikki's expression abruptly changed to one of discomfort. Her eyes pinched, and her lips pressed together in a firm line. After a moment's pause, she shook her head and cleared her throat. "I'm sure that most of you were approached by Detective Ray," she said quietly. "And I've also heard the rumors around the resort that I was involved in what happened to Lou. So I'll take this opportunity to clear the air." Rikki lifted her chin and made a point to look each person in the face as she spoke, her tone more confident now. "I was just as shocked and horrified as the rest of you to learn about her death. I can assure you all that I had nothing to do with it."

"Why should we believe you?" Dorothy, the older woman, stepped forward. She placed her hands on her hips. "How do we know for sure that you didn't kill Louana?" She looked around the room. "I don't know about the rest of you, but I don't feel safe working for a suspected murderer. My husband thinks I should quit." The woman's gaze shifted back to Rikki, her eyes narrowed in accusation. "But if I do, are you going to kill me too?"

Rikki looked as if she'd been slapped. Her face crumpled, and she took a step back. She swallowed and took a calming breath. "Dorothy, if you don't want to work here anymore, I won't make you stay," she said, her voice strained. "You can come back and pick up your last paycheck on Wednesday, or I can mail it to you."

Dorothy unpinned her name badge from her blouse and set it on the counter. She sniffed. "Mail it," she said. Everyone turned to watch her tight white curls bob out the door.

Rikki's shoulders slumped in resignation. "Anyone else?" she asked, casting a weary gaze across the cluster of remaining employees. No one so much as moved a muscle. Not even Harmony, though I personally thought that her departure would be a blessing. When it was clear that nobody else was going to come forward, Rikki straightened. "All right then," she said with a cheeriness that sounded forced. "Time to open up shop." She dismissed our little group from the huddle and walked briskly toward her office.

Tonya, who was off that day, said her goodbyes before leaving the boutique. Harmony also took off, bragging that she was going to celebrate her promotion by treating herself to a manicure before her shift started at noon. Sara held open the door for the two women and then flipped the sign in the front window from *CLOSED* to *OPEN*.

News of the murder behind the boutique brought in a crowd of curious resort guests. Business was steady throughout the day, with a throng of shoppers milling around the store. A lot of people were only interested in probing the employees for gruesome details about the killing. I began to wish we'd asked Tonya to stay and pick up an extra shift to accommodate the high traffic. I helped Rose assist customers in the dressing room and on the sales floor until Harmony returned at noon. Then I joined Rikki in her office to learn her sales reporting system.

"I'm sorry Dorothy quit," I said when we were alone in her office. I quirked my lips. "If you ask me, she seemed a bit senile. We're probably better off without her."

Rikki grimaced. "I was kind of expecting it," she replied. She shook her head, her expression downcast. "I'm surprised we didn't lose more staff. No one wants to work for an alleged murderer." She sighed. "They probably all think I'm a raving *hehena.*" She swirled her index finger next to her temple a few times.

I frowned. "They don't think you're a lunatic," I told her. "This whole thing just strikes too close to home. Someone killed Louana a few hundred yards from where you're sitting. The staff is just scared, that's all." I chewed my lip. "They have a right to be." I perched on the chair beside Rikki and let her lean her head on my shoulder, the way she'd done for me when I was upset as a child. "The police will catch the real killer, Rik," I said reassuringly. "And when people start to feel safe again, things will go back to normal."

Rikki patted my hand. "Thank you. I needed to hear that." She raised her head and met my gaze with misty eyes. "You're *laki hōkū*, Kaley. My lucky star. I don't know what I'd do if you weren't here right now."

She'd lost two employees and had been accused of murder in the two days since I'd arrived. *I wouldn't call that lucky,* I thought. "Oh, I think you'd manage," I said, offering her a wry smile.

When we were finished running sales reports, Rikki gave me a tour of the stockroom. "We just got these in from a local designer, Sage McKinnon." She gestured to an open box on one of the shelves. "Sage and I are good friends, and she designed these blouses exclusively for the boutique." Rikki beamed. "You can't even buy them on her website."

I opened the box and pulled out the blouse on the top of the stack. "These are fabulous!" I gushed, examining the teal floral pattern. I held the silky top against my chest to see how it would look with my skin tone. As I did, a button popped off and rolled across the storage room floor. The thread around the button hole began to unravel. I let out a mortified squeak. "I am *so* sorry," I cried, dropping the shirt back into the box and stooping to retrieve the loose button.

"'*A'ole pilikia,*" Rikki said, joining me on all fours in my search for the button. "It's no problem, really." She stooped next to a shelf of surplus sarongs and boxes of flip-flops, reaching underneath to retrieve it. "Sara's a whiz with a needle and thread. She keeps a sewing kit under the front counter," she explained.

"I'll take it up front and have her put the button back on." Rikki glanced up as Luka ambled toward us from across the stockroom. "Luka, can you please show Kaley where we keep the extra coat hangers and the price sticker guns? I'd like to move these shirts out to the sales floor as soon as possible."

"Yes, Miss Rikki," Luka replied in his smooth baritone voice. He motioned for me to follow him past the rows of stacked boxes as my aunt carried the blouse to the front of the store to be mended.

My mind did a little victory dance. I'd been hoping for a chance to speak to Luka alone after witnessing his peculiar stoicism during the staff meeting. Now was the perfect opportunity to see if he had an alibi for Saturday night. "So how long have you worked at Happy Hula?" I asked him casually.

"About two months." Luka sidestepped around a stack of boxes. "It's just a summer gig while I'm home from college."

"Cool. The resort is a great place to spend the summer," I said. "There's so much to do here. Have you been to one of the luaus at the Ramada Pier yet?" Though the nightly events quickly sold out, resort employees could buy discounted tickets. Rikki had taken me to the large feasts several times when I was younger. I'd filled my plate high with poi and pineapple and sneaked sips of Rikki's rum punch as we'd watched performances by local musicians and hula dancers.

"Yeah." Luka grinned, showing off the gap between his two front teeth. "My brah Kimo and I like to go to the luaus when we can get extra tickets. The Aloha Lagoon Hula Wahines are superhot, and we get to flirt with the girls from the mainland that are staying at the resort." He puffed out his chest. "Those tourist chicks just can't get enough of us."

"I'm sure the ladies love you," I agreed, humoring him. "Did you and Kimo go to the luau this past Saturday?" If he'd been at the resort after the boutique had closed for the day, he might have been nearby at the time that Louana had been killed. Even if he hadn't been involved, maybe he'd seen something.

"Kimo didn't go," Luka replied. "He had food poisoning from his sister's mahi mahi paella." He grimaced. "Brah was spewing out both ends."

I cringed, thinking I could've done without that mental image. "So you went to the luau by yourself?"

Luka nodded. He turned his back on me and began rummaging through the box of coat hangers. "I dropped by and had the buffet dinner," he said. "Didn't stay long."

"Why not?" I asked. When he lifted a questioning eyebrow, I added, "I just remember the luaus being so much fun. Steel drum bands, ukulele players, the hula dancers… Do Benny and the Wahines still perform?"

Luka nodded. "They do, but I've seen the luau shows a dozen times, so I ducked out early." He looked away, which only fueled my curiosity. "You ask a lot of questions," he said in a flat tone.

My cheeks warmed. "Just making small talk," I said brightly. It seemed if I was going to get him to open up to me, I'd have to change tactics. I picked up one of the price tag guns, noticing a small label affixed to its case. The sticker had Louana's name printed on it. *Perfect.* "Lou labeled her own work equipment?" I asked, tapping the sticker to bring it to his attention. "Doesn't this belong to the shop?"

Luka made a face. "She was really possessive," he said. "She insisted on having equipment that only she could use—but she didn't label stuff. She made me do it for her." Something flashed behind his eyes, but it was gone before I could identify it.

I scrunched my nose. "Why, though? It seems kind of silly."

"Because that's just how she was." He scowled. "Lou was a control freak. If you didn't do things her way, then she'd make your life hell."

"What do you mean by that?" I asked, studying him closely.

The young man's frown deepened. "She just had a way of making people do what she wanted them to."

I took a step closer to him, reaching out to place a hand on his shoulder. "Luka, did Louana do something to you?"

Luka pulled out of my grasp. "I don't wanna talk about her," he said, his tone gruff. He clenched his jaw, and I could see the tendons in his neck straining. A moment later the tension vanished. He picked up the box of coat hangers and smiled at me, though it didn't quite reach his eyes. "Want me to carry this out front for you?"

"Sure." I frowned when he turned his back on me. I'd struck a nerve—but why? What could Louana have done to upset Luka so badly? I couldn't let him change the subject when it seemed like I might be getting somewhere. "Luka, wait."

His body tensed. He set the box down and pivoted slowly to face me. "Yeah?" he asked, his tone impatient.

"If there's anything you know that might help prove Rikki didn't kill Louana, you'd tell me. Wouldn't you?"

His face hardened. "I don't know anything," he said. "And to tell the truth, I really don't care what happened to her. I'm just glad she's gone. She was the meanest woman on the whole island."

"Luka? Are you back here?" Harmony's voice echoed through the stockroom. Footsteps clicked across the wooden floor, and she emerged from around the corner a few moments later. "I need you to bring the ladder out front," she told him, ignoring me. "There's a woman who wants to buy the orange tankini off one of the mannequins from the display above the changing rooms. It's the only one in her size and that color that we have in stock." She rolled her eyes. "Personally, I think it's going to make that round belly of hers look like an oversized pumpkin, but whatever."

"Please tell me you didn't say that to the customer," I said, unable to keep the shock out of my voice.

Harmony waved me off. "Relax. She's pregnant. It's not like I'm calling her *fat*. And no, I didn't say it to her face." She shrugged. "But I can't help it if orange isn't her color." A mean-spirited smile crossed her lips as she glanced pointedly down at my top. "Just like yellow isn't yours."

Luka looked relieved that he had an excuse to get away from me. "Gotta go," he mumbled. He stepped around the box of coat hangers and hurried to fetch the ladder leaning against the far wall. He followed Harmony out of the stockroom without so much as another glance in my direction.

I self-consciously looked down at my daisy yellow sleeveless blouse. *Whatever*, I thought, frowning. I didn't have time for Harmony and her petty insults—though I was starting to think the wrong employee had her neck wrung.

I tried to make sense of my conversation with Luka. He'd gone to the luau on the night that Louana had been killed, which meant he'd been at the resort. He had also made it clear that he wasn't sorry the control freak assistant manager was dead. What had Lou done to Luka to make him hate her so much—and was it something worth killing over?

CHAPTER FIVE

———

Luckily for me, Sara was able to mend the blouse I'd mangled. I bumped into her as she was carrying it back to the stockroom. "Check it out," she said, holding up the flowery teal top. The loose button was expertly sewn back into place. She beamed proudly. "Good as new."

I blew out a sigh of relief as I took the expensive blouse and held it up for a closer inspection. I couldn't distinguish any difference in the new stitching and the old. I smiled at the young cashier, so happy that I could have hugged her. "I owe you big time," I said.

"It wasn't any trouble," she said with a shrug. "I love to sew. I'm actually studying fashion design and merchandising at school." She grinned. "I'm going to run my own fashion empire someday."

My smile widened. "Well, I'll be first in line to buy one of your dresses," I told her, winking. I glanced over Sara's shoulder toward the dressing rooms. Luka was climbing down the last few rungs of the ladder, the orange tankini gripped in one hand. He caught me looking at him and quickly averted his gaze.

"So what's Luka's deal?" I asked Sara in a low voice.

She knit her pencil-thin brows together. "What do you mean?"

I raised my shoulder and then let it fall. "I don't know," I said honestly. "I just get this weird vibe from him. I asked him a few questions about Louana, and he sort of clammed up on me."

"What kind of questions?" Sara eyed me with a look of uncertainty.

"I wanted to know if he knew who might have killed her."

Sara frowned. "I thought your aunt asked us not to talk about that at the shop." She darted a glance toward Rikki's closed office door. "I don't want to get fired," she said in a hushed voice, backing slowly away from me.

I gave her what I hoped was an encouraging smile. "Hey, I won't tell if you don't—but I can't sit back and let Aunt Rikki take the fall for something she didn't do." I took a step toward Sara to close the gap between us. "I didn't know Louana personally, but from what I encountered of her, she didn't seem like the most pleasant person. I'd think a woman like that probably had a lot of enemies." I wrinkled my brow. "So as far as I know, her killer could be anyone."

Sara nodded and gave me a sad little smile. "For what it's worth, I don't think Rikki did it, either. She's the kindest person I've ever met—and I'm not just saying that because she's my boss." We fell silent as Luka strode past us, the ladder hoisted over one shoulder. When he was out of earshot again, Sara leaned close to my ear. "I don't know if this will help, but you could try talking to Lou's boyfriend."

A boyfriend? I felt a seed of hope blossom in my chest. *The police would have to question him, wouldn't they?* Even if Detective Ray didn't talk to the man, I certainly would. "Do you know his name?" I asked, trying not to sound too eager.

Sara's nose scrunched up. "Hmm. Mario? Or maybe Marco." She nodded to herself. "Yeah, Marco. That sounds right. Louana was pretty hung up on him. She said he worked in the main lobby as a bellhop." The young cashier furrowed her brow. "He came in the store once last week, actually. They had an argument about something, and then he left. He seemed pretty mad." Sara looked past me toward the front counter, and her eyes widened. "Whoops! Customers. Gotta go."

I followed her gaze. A pair of teenage girls had wandered up to the counter and were browsing the jewelry racks. Sara hurried behind the register and greeted them. I crossed the sales floor after her, my insides buzzing with excitement. I was still curious about Luka, but an angry boyfriend? Surely that was a solid lead. If Marco was a bellhop at the resort, it was a good bet that he spent most of his time around the elevators and near the entrance to the main lobby, waiting to assist guests who needed help handling their luggage. I made up my mind to swing through there after work to see if I could find him.

I spent the rest of my shift helping Rose hang the new shipment of blouses and dresses that had been sitting in the stockroom. Since we'd started work when the boutique opened, Rikki and I finished up at four, leaving Harmony to close the shop at eight. I told Rikki I would meet her in the employee parking lot and then hurried over to the main building.

Dozens of resort guests moved about the lobby on their way to a late lunch at the Loco Moco Café or midafternoon drinks at The Lava Pot. I spied a tall, skinny bellhop with dirty blond hair just outside the main entrance. He was unloading luggage from the back of one of the shuttles run by Gabby's Island Adventures. Crossing the lobby, I slipped through the double doors and approached him. "Excuse me," I called, waving to get his attention.

The young man set down the duffel bag he'd been holding and looked up at me, his brow lifted in question. "Can I help you?" he asked politely.

I glanced at the name tag on the front of his Aloha Lagoon polo shirt and tried to hide my disappointment. He wasn't the man I was looking for. "Sorry to bother you, Chad," I said. "I was just wondering if Marco is working today."

Chad the bellhop shook his head. "Nope. Marco has Monday evenings off. He performs at the open mic night over at Beachcomber's."

Good to know. I grinned, an idea forming in my head. I thanked Chad and pulled my phone out of my purse as I walked through the lagoon, working up the nerve to dial Noa's number. He answered on the second ring. "Remember how you said to let you know if I needed help clearing Rikki's name?" I asked, trying not to sound as shy as I felt.

"Of course."

"Well, I'm calling in the favor. Got plans tonight?"

"Does binge watching the latest season of *House of Cards* count?" He chuckled. "I just wrapped up a big design project for one of my freelance clients, so I was hoping to unwind a little. What did you have in mind?"

"Well," I hedged, feeling my face flush. "What if I told you that my plan includes drinks and live music at Beachcomber's?"

There was a pause on the other end of the line, and I worried that he was going to say no. "I could use a drink," he finally replied.

Cool relief slipped through me. I really didn't want to go alone. "Great. Pick me up from Rikki's around eight thirty?"

"Sure. See you then."

I was pleasantly surprised at how smoothly the conversation had gone. Sure, Noa was only coming along to help Aunt Rikki, but I'd be lying if I said I wasn't a little excited at the chance to hang out with him. *Just remember it's not a date*, I told myself. While this could be the first step to repairing our friendship, part of me knew there was no use in getting my hopes up when it came to romance.

When Noa arrived at Rikki's house later that evening, I was sitting on the front porch waiting for him. Aunt Rikki was meditating in the living room, and I didn't want to disturb her. I figured she needed all the peace she could get.

Noa was dressed in khaki shorts and a black polo shirt. His dark hair was down today, spilling around his shoulders. I wondered briefly what it would be like to run my fingers through it. *Focus, Kaley. You're on a mission tonight, and it doesn't include fantasizing about your former BFF.*

Noa's eyes widened a fraction of an inch as he looked me over. "You look great," he said.

I beamed. "Thanks." I'd changed into a tight-fitting green dress and brown Steve Madden gladiator sandals that laced up my calves. I hadn't enjoyed a night out in months—and no one ever said sleuthing wear couldn't be fashionable.

Noa started to lean in for a hug and seemed to catch himself. He pulled away at the last second, leaving me standing there with my arms awkwardly half-raised. "Ready?" he asked.

I dropped my arms back down to my sides. "Yep," I said, trying to hide my embarrassment under the guise of stooping to grab my purse off the porch. "Let's go." I moved past him, silently berating myself for almost hugging him. I strode toward the Jeep, which he'd parked by the curb.

"So how will going to Beachcomber's help Rikki?" he called as he followed me.

I might have blushed a little when Noa opened the car door for me. *It's probably just an old habit,* I told myself. He had always been somewhat of a gentleman. "Louana's boyfriend is performing at their open mic night," I told him. "I want to ask him a few questions, and I figured it couldn't hurt to bring backup."

Noa climbed into the driver's seat and faced me. "You think the boyfriend killed her?" he asked, his tone skeptical. "Isn't that a little too obvious?"

"Probably." I shrugged my shoulders. "But I'd still like to feel him out. Anything to take some of the heat off Rikki." I was a "leave no stone unturned" kind of girl.

I filled Noa in on the incident with the old cashier, Dorothy, who had quit her job at Happy Hula earlier that morning. He frowned. "Poor Rik. It's already starting to affect her business, huh? How's she holding up?"

"You know Rikki." I sighed. "She's trying to stay positive, but I can tell it's tearing her up inside."

Noa gave me a sidelong look. I nearly jumped when he reached an arm across the front seat and patted my shoulder. "You're going to get through this. Both of you."

"Thanks." I relaxed a little, leaning my head back against the passenger seat headrest. I had to admit, even if things weren't back to normal between us, I was thankful that Noa was there. *Would Bryan have been this supportive?* I wondered, though I already knew the answer was a big, fat *no.* My ex had only cared about his football career and his reputation. I'd been nothing more than arm candy for the ESPY Awards and other photo ops. Noa, on the other hand, had always treated Rikki like part of his own family—and he still did even now, despite the pain I'd caused him. Guilt twisted my insides. This was just another reminder that I'd really blown it when I'd broken his heart.

We arrived at Beachcomber's ten minutes later. The dive bar was three miles from the resort in a thatch-roofed building that backed up to the water. A small neon blue sign above the door was the only indication that we'd reached the right place. The interior was dimly lit by several overhead lights and half a dozen tiki torches that boasted colored light bulbs rather than open flames. An array of surfboards, dried starfish, and other beach paraphernalia were sprawled across the dark walls, and the bar had images of mermaids and sharks carved into the wood.

Noa and I found a quiet booth near the stage and slid in. A server came over to take our drink orders, and I asked her when the open mic performances began.

"We usually run from nine thirty to eleven thirty, depending on how many performers there are," the young woman said, slipping her notepad into a pocket on her apron. "If you're thinking about signing up, we've got space for another song or two tonight." She smiled encouragingly. "Want me to add you to the roster? First prize is three hundred bucks."

I swallowed. Three weeks ago that wouldn't have seemed like much money to me, but that was before I'd lost access to the joint bank account I'd shared with Bryan. Now three hundred dollars would go a long way toward padding my quickly dwindling savings. Too bad I couldn't even carry a tune in my designer handbag. "No thanks," I smiled, suddenly feeling sheepish. "I think I'll just watch."

"You sure, Kales?" Noa teased when we were alone again. "I seem to remember you giving the performance of a lifetime at the Aloha Junior High Talent Show."

I grimaced. "It was a showstopper, all right." Only because I'd been a little too enthusiastic with my dance moves and had wound up falling off the stage and fracturing my ankle. No one had told me that you weren't *actually* supposed to break a leg in show business.

The waitress returned with our drinks just as the MC strode across the stage, microphone in hand. "Aloha and welcome to Beachcomber's Open Mic Night, where the island's best musical performers compete for glory—and a cash prize!" Cheers and bursts of applause sounded around the room. The man waited until the noise died down and then raised the microphone to his lips again. "First up tonight we have a singer-songwriter from Lihue. Let's give it up for Ariel Sanchez!"

A waifish young woman with waist-length red hair wandered onto the stage, lugging a barstool in one hand and a ukulele in the other. She perched on the stool and nervously told the audience that she'd written this song about falling in love with a boy named Eric she'd met at Shipwreck Beach.

The girl launched into her sappy acoustic ditty, and I sipped my pineapple daiquiri as I scanned the room. There were several men seated alone at various tables around the little bar. I wondered if one of them was Marco. *I'll find out soon enough*, I thought eagerly. If Chad the bellhop was right, Louana's beau would probably take the stage before long.

Returning my attention to Noa, I found that he was staring past me. I sent a glance over my shoulder, following his line of sight. He appeared to be watching the entrance to the little bar. I turned back around to face him, brow furrowed. "Are you expecting someone?"

Noa's gaze snapped back to me, and his cheeks colored. I'd known him long enough to recognize the glint of guilt in his eyes. "Yeah," he said, his tone sheepish. "I figured if we were going to be hanging out at a bar and having a few drinks, I might as well invite a couple of friends."

"Oh." I hoped he didn't hear the disappointment in my voice. Was Noa still so hurt that he couldn't even stand to be alone in the booth with me? "Cool," I said, recovering quickly. I forced a smile. "I wouldn't mind making a few new friends myself now that I'm back on the island."

As if on cue, a slender blonde woman sauntered over to our table. *I didn't realize Gwyneth Paltrow had a younger sister*, I thought, sizing her up. She was tall and supermodel gorgeous, with short sandy hair and aquamarine eyes. Her denim cutoff shorts showed off her tan, muscular legs, and she wore a black tank top with the words *Part-Time Mermaid* printed across the front. "Hi, Noa," she said cheerfully as she reached our booth.

I sucked in a breath, expecting her to lean down and plant a kiss on his lips. Of course Noa had a girlfriend. I should have been happy for him, but a certain little green monster was clawing its way out of its cage in the back of my mind.

To my surprise, the blonde didn't climb into the booth and start smooching my ex-BFF. Instead, she slid in next to me. "So you must be the infamous Kaley."

I cringed at her use of the word *infamous*. I could only imagine the horror stories she'd likely heard about me from Noa.

As far as she knew, I was probably the cold-blooded dragon lady that had stomped on his heart and flown off into the sunset with the king of douchebag jocks.

I took a sip of my daiquiri, thinking that I was going to need something stronger. "Guilty," I said, giving her a halfhearted smile.

A lopsided grin crossed the woman's narrow face. "Jamie Parker. Nice to meet ya." I stuck out my hand to shake hers, but she pulled me in for a hug instead.

I risked a glance at Noa and found him watching us, his lips curled in amusement. "Jamie's the scuba diving instructor at the resort," he said.

"Yep." Jamie released me and cocked her head. "Are you certified? You should totally come out on the water with me sometime."

I nodded. "I used to dive with my aunt at Lehua Rock every summer."

Her face lit up. "Rikki? I love her!"

I arched a brow. "You know my aunt?"

Jamie flashed me another toothy smile. "I'm probably her best customer," she said. Her cheeks colored. "Employees of the resort get a ten percent discount, and I've got a bit of a shoppin' problem. I swear if I worked there, I'd blow through my whole paycheck before I left the store."

I hadn't realized how tense I'd been until the muscles in my shoulders began to loosen. I found myself genuinely liking the woman. Her bubbly personality was infectious, and her southern drawl reminded me of my years spent in Atlanta. "Where're ya from?" I asked, slipping into my own version of a Georgia lilt.

Jamie waved her hand in the air to get our server's attention. "Born in Savannah, Georgia, but I lived in Panama City for a while," she told me. "I moved to Kauai a couple of years ago to take the scuba instructor job. I love it here."

I nodded. "Aloha Lagoon is a great place to live," I agreed. Jamie seemed like a real sweetheart. Having her around for the night wouldn't be so bad, and maybe Noa's other friend would be just as nice.

The young woman with the ukulele left the stage to a burst of applause, and she was replaced by a young man carrying a guitar and a harmonica. Noa glanced toward the entrance again as the performer began his song. He grinned. "Ah, there she is. Now we're all here."

I looked to the left, and my stomach flip-flopped as I spied the bombshell brunette strutting toward us from across the bar. It was Harmony Kane.

CHAPTER SIX

———

I felt the blood drain from my face. Noa had to be joking—he couldn't have invited Harmony to hang out with us. She hadn't shown him quite the same level of animosity as she had me when we were younger, but being my best friend hadn't exactly scored him any cool points. That, and Noa had suffered through the terrible odor in my car alongside me after the jellyfish incident. He'd hated Harmony Kane just as much as I had. The idea of Noa cozying up to the Wicked Witch of the Pacific East was absurd. There was no way he'd ever give her the time of day after she'd treated us like pariahs growing up. *Right?*

"Noa!" Harmony called, wiggling her fingers in a flirty wave.

She was wearing a low-cut purple top and a black skirt so short that it left little to the imagination. Her dark eyes locked on Noa like he was the last pair of size seven boots at a Nordstrom sale.

"Hey, gorgeous," she gushed, sliding into the booth beside him. "Sorry I'm late. I had to close the shop tonight." She lowered her eyelids to half-mast and gave him a seductive smile.

He set down his beer. "Hey, Harm," he said. "Can I buy you a drink?"

I nearly spat out the sip of daiquiri I'd just taken. *He's offering to buy her a drink? What the hell is going on here?*

"Sure," she replied. "I'll take a Blue Hawaiian. Thanks, doll." Harmony winked at him and then sent her gaze across the booth. She said hello to Jamie before glancing my way. "Oh. Hey, Kaley. Are you performing tonight?" She sneered. "I hope your dance skills have improved since junior high."

I opened my mouth to retort, but it was drowned out by applause as the latest singer finished his song and took a bow. The host returned to the microphone to announce another performer. Though I couldn't get past the fact that Noa and Harmony suddenly seemed chummy after years of burning hatred, I sat up straighter, craning my neck for a better look at the stage. I had to keep in mind the reason why I was at the bar in the first place. *Maybe Marco is next.* My hopes were dashed a moment later when the MC introduced another young female musician.

Three more performers came and went, and still there was no sign of Marco. I was starting to wonder if Louana's boyfriend would even show. As we watched the musicians, I kept sneaking glances across the table at Harmony and Noa. The way she was draping her arm over his shoulder made my stomach sour. Why hadn't he told me he was inviting her? Or that they were suddenly friends—or possibly something more? I just couldn't believe he'd stoop so low.

The latest musician strummed his last chord and took a bow. The MC returned to the stage. "*Mahalo*, Esteban." He shook the other man's hand and then turned to grin at the crowd. "We have one more performer tonight. He's one of our regulars *and* last week's Beachcomber's Open Mic Champion."

My head snapped up. *Marco?*

"Put your hands together for Marco Rossini!"

Yes! I let out a cheer, which blended with the whistles and shouts from around the bar. *Finally.* I leaned forward and propped my elbows on the table, my gaze fixed intently on the stage. A man in his mid-twenties strode onto the platform, carrying an acoustic guitar. His curly black hair fell over his eyes, and he lifted his free hand to brush the strands aside before picking up the microphone. "Aloha. How's everyone doing tonight?" he asked, flashing a dimpled grin to the crowd.

"He's cute," Jamie remarked. She'd get no argument from me. I couldn't help but wonder what a gorgeous guy like that had been doing with someone as cruel and controlling as Louana.

I studied Marco as he took a seat on the stool and strummed a few chords on the guitar, smiling to himself. If he was grief-stricken over Lou, he was good at hiding it. "Tonight I'll be covering one of my favorites," he said into the microphone. "I hope you enjoy it." He launched into a beautiful rendition of Elvis Presley's "Blue Hawaii." The crowd was instantly spellbound—including me. Marco had a beautiful voice and a captivating stage presence. It was no wonder he'd won the last open mic competition. He was an excellent performer.

"I just *love* this song." Harmony's flirtatious tone was all it took to break the spell for me.

I glanced across the booth to find her stroking Noa's arm and fluttering her too-curly-to-be-real lashes at him. The sight made me queasy. I'd wanted to give Noa the benefit of the doubt that he hadn't invited two beautiful women to join us as a way to make me jealous—but considering one of them was Harmony Kane, it certainly seemed deliberate. Dating the woman who had made my life a living hell was a surefire way for Noa to hurt me, and he knew it. But then again, Noa had never been the vengeful type. I swallowed. *What if he actually has feelings for her?* The idea was unbearable.

I tried my best to brush the thought aside. Who Noa chose to date shouldn't be any of my concern—even if she was the spawn of Satan in a miniskirt. *Focus on the real reason you're here, Kaley.* I gave myself a mental shake—and without meaning to, a physical one as well. My elbow jerked, bumping my pineapple daiquiri. Before I could catch it, the drink tipped over. A stream of yellow booze ran toward the edge of the table and spilled over the side, staining Harmony's shirt. She gave a startled cry of surprise and disentangled herself from Noa as she clambered out of the booth.

"Kaley, you idiot!" she fumed. A few heads turned toward us. Even Marco glanced our way from on stage, though he continued to sing.

"Sorry," I said, holding up my hands. A smirk threatened to tug at my lips as I struggled to keep a straight face. Though it had been an accident, the sight of Harmony drenched in the frozen cocktail was pretty satisfying. I shrugged. "Guess I'm still as clumsy as ever."

Harmony glared daggers at me before turning and stalking toward the restroom.

Marco finished his performance, and the bar patrons began to cheer and clap again. He rose from the stool and took a bow before walking off the stage. The host returned and picked up the mic. "If you want to vote for your favorite performer from this evening, your server will bring a ballot to your table. You have ten minutes to turn in your vote, and then we'll announce this week's winner. So enjoy another drink, and show tonight's contestants some love."

Now's my chance. "I'm actually gonna run to the ladies' room, myself," I told Noa and Jamie, sliding out of the booth.

"Want me to come too?" Jamie offered. "You might need a little backup after that drink fiasco." She shot a glance toward the bathroom door.

"Nah. I'll be fine. You stay here and enjoy your drink," I said, gesturing to her mai tai. "And if the server brings a ballot over, cast my vote for me." I smiled at her. "I liked that Ariel chick that played first."

Jamie bobbed her head, grinning. "Me too. She reminds me of the Little Mermaid."

Noa's forehead wrinkled, and his lips curled in a suspicious frown. His gaze darted from me to the bar, where Marco was pulling up a stool. I hadn't told him the name of Louana's boyfriend, but Noa was a smart guy. He'd likely put two and two together when I'd climbed out of the booth as soon as Marco had left the stage. That, and he probably knew me well enough to know that I wouldn't be caught dead in that tiny dive bar bathroom alone with pissed-off Harmony Kane. She'd try to stab me with one of her stilettos.

"I'll be right back," I promised, giving him what I hoped was a reassuring look. Though I'd brought him along as reinforcement, I figured it might be easier for me to chat up Marco if I approached him alone. And since Noa had invited Harmony the Horrible to join us on our little recon mission, I was less keen to include him in the action. He could hang back in the booth and keep Jamie and her company.

Winding between tables, I made my way toward Marco. He was seated at the edge of the bar, leaning over as he packed his guitar into its carrying case. "That was incredible," I said, perching on the barstool next to his. I leaned forward and lowered my voice, as if I were telling him a secret. "I voted for you," I lied, winking.

Marco looked up. "Thank you very much," he said, curling his lip in an Elvis impression. "The ladies always love it when I cover the King."

I gave an appreciative laugh. "I'm Kaley," I said, offering him my hand. "Can I buy you a drink?"

"Nice to meet you, Kaley. I'm Marco." He took my hand and grinned, showing his teeth. "And I never say no to free booze." Marco flagged one of the bartenders. I ordered a beer for him and another pineapple daiquiri to replace the one I'd spilled all over Harmony (totally worth it).

While we waited for our drinks, I turned in my seat to face him. "You look familiar," I said, tilting my head and squinting at him as if trying to place where I'd seen him. "Have we met before?"

His gaze traveled down to my legs and back up, stopping at chest level. "I'm pretty sure I'd remember meeting you."

Ugh. Seriously? I stifled a shudder. *Your girlfriend's been dead for three days, and you're already hitting on other women? What a creep.* I ignored his ogling. "Wait a minute," I said, snapping my fingers. "I think I know where I've seen you. Do you work at the Aloha Lagoon Resort across town?"

Marco nodded. "Yeah. I'm a bellhop on most weekdays, but I perform at the open mic nights here a couple nights a week." He puffed out his chest. "I won this past Saturday," he said. "They don't get a lot of real talent coming through here, so I didn't have much competition." His expression turned smug. "I was also a finalist last year in a statewide singing contest. I went up against fifty vocalists from across the islands. Maybe you saw me on TV—did you watch the latest season of *Aloha Idol*?" He looked at me expectantly.

I shook my head. "I didn't see it. Sorry," I said, trying to contain my own disappointment. If Marco had performed here on Saturday night, then there would have been dozens of witnesses. I wondered if it would have been possible for him to slip out or leave early without being missed. I only knew that Louana had been murdered sometime after eight, which was when Happy Hula had closed for the evening. I wasn't sure whether or not his open mic victory could clear him of being her killer.

"If you win, do you have to stay until the end of the competition to collect your cash prize? Or can you come back later in the week to pick it up?" I asked. When he raised a brow in question, I explained, "I'm just curious how it works. I was thinking about entering next week—if I can work up the nerve." I gave him what I hoped was a modest look. "I can't sing as well as you, of course. I doubt I'd give you a run for your money." That last part was the truth, at least.

"Oh, I'm sure you've got a nice set of pipes," he said, his gaze hovering below my collar bone again. I cleared my throat, and his eyes snapped up. "You said you recognized me from the resort," he said, cocking his head to the side. "Do you work there too?

I nodded. "Yeah. I just started this week, actually. I'm working at the Happy Hula Dress Boutique—it's one of the shops out in the courtyard."

Marco's flirty smile vanished, and his expression turned cold. "Did someone put you up to this?" he asked, his voice cold.

I kept my own face blank. "Put me up to what?"

"I don't have time for this," he said, glowering. The bartender set Marco's beer down in front of him. "Thanks for the drink," he said gruffly. "Now leave me alone." He turned his back on me.

Crap. I hadn't learned anything yet, and he was already stonewalling me. "I didn't mean to—" I put my hand on his shoulder, but he jerked out from under my grasp.

"Look," he growled, cutting me off as he whipped around to face me again. "I've already talked to the cops and one reporter. So if you're another journalist or some true-crime junkie thinking you can sweet talk your way into a scoop on Lou's murder, you can step off. I don't know anything about it," he huffed.

"No, no," I protested, holding my hands up. "You've got me all wrong. I'm not a reporter—far from it, actually." I offered him a half-smile. "In fact, I'm sick of journalists myself. I've had my fair share of bad publicity lately."

"What for?" Marco took a sip of his beer as he eyed me, his dark brows drawn together in a look of mistrust.

I sighed. As much as I hated talking about Bryan, it might help me win Marco over. "Are you a football fan?" I asked, grimacing.

He blinked. "Yeah. Why?"

"Ever heard of Bryan Colfax? He's a running back for the Atlanta Falcons."

Marco stared at me for a moment, and then his eyes widened in what I took to be recognition. "You're that Colfax guy's wife? He's the one with the sex addiction, right?"

"*Ex*-wife." I corrected him on my marital status but not the sex addiction story. If that was the angle Bryan was claiming to garner sympathy from his fans, then that was his business.

"Wow." Marco shook his head. "I read an article about that on ESPN just a few weeks ago. Three cheerleaders at once? That man is living the dream!" He balked when he caught sight of my narrow-eyed expression. "Sorry," he muttered, his tone sheepish. "That must have been brutal. For what it's worth, I saw your picture in that article, and I've gotta say that you're way hotter in person."

"Thanks," I said dryly. I took a sip of my own drink. "As I was saying, I know what it's like to be sick of everyone butting into your personal life."

"Yeah. It really sucks." He shook his head. "Hell, I don't get why everyone is grilling me, anyway. It wasn't like Lou was my girlfriend."

My brow furrowed. "She wasn't?"

Marco rubbed a hand over his face. "No," he said tersely. "Have you ever seen that movie *Wedding Crashers*?"

I blinked at him. "Uh, yeah." I wasn't sure where he was going with this.

He clenched his jaw. "Then you'll know what it means when I say that Louana Watson was a Stage Five Clinger. The chick was *nuts!*" He grunted. "We hooked up, like, three or four times, and she was practically ready to send out wedding invitations. She asked me to drop by that dress shop one day, and when I got there, she tried to introduce me to everyone as her boyfriend." Marco set down his beer and raised his hands in front of him. "I told her I wasn't looking for that kind of commitment with her, and she flipped out." His expression darkened. "That's why she ruined my big break."

"What do you mean?"

"Lou started showing up in the lobby whenever I was working, begging me to 'give our relationship a chance.'" He used his pointer and middle fingers to make quotations in the air as he said that last part. "See what I mean? Crazy."

"So she was stalking you," I observed.

"Yeah." Marco nodded. "And when I warned her to stop following me around, she was pissed. So she decided to get back at me in the worst way possible." He blew out a breath. "There was a talent agent staying at the resort, Mike Comiglio. He's a big wig in the music industry—they call him the King Maker. Mike's responsible for finding some of the biggest names in pop music." Marco met my gaze, eyes wide. "And he wanted to hear *me* sing," he said, poking his chest with his thumb.

"Wow. What an amazing opportunity." I was genuinely impressed.

"Yeah, it would have been." Marco's expression turned bitter. "I invited Mike to come hear me sing at Beachcomber's on his last night on the island. I even performed one of my own original songs. But he never showed. By the time I got to the resort for work the next day, Mike had already left. I found out that Louana had stopped him in the lobby on his way to the bar. She'd told him that I had decided to perform karaoke at the Loco Moco Café that night instead. He went there looking for me, and I guess he thought I stood him up or got stage fright or something. Not only that, but he signed this schmuck that covered some stupid Bon Jovi song." Marco cringed. "I tried reaching out to Mike through the number on the business card he gave me, but he hasn't returned my calls." He gritted his teeth, and anger flashed behind his eyes. "Louana stole my chance at a real music career."

I frowned. "That's awful. Do you know for sure that she was responsible though?"

He nodded. "Lou told me she did it. She claimed it was because she didn't want me to leave her alone on the island if I landed a recording contract, but I know she was just being vindictive." Marco raised his beer. "To Loony Louana," he said sourly before chugging the rest of the drink. He set down the empty glass and looked at me with resignation. "Lesson learned—never dip your tip in crazy." He shook his head. "Man, I'd have done just about anything to get that psycho chick off my back."

Ew. If I didn't want the information so bad, I'd have slapped him. *What a total douche canoe.* "Anything?" I asked, eying him with suspicion.

Marco flinched. "Except killing her," he added quickly. "I had nothing to do with that."

I wasn't so sure. I'd have to find out what the police considered to be the window for Lou's time of death before I wrote Marco off completely. Hearing about how she'd ruined his chance at fame—and how angry it had made him—only fueled my suspicion. "Do you have any idea who else might have wanted Louana dead?" I pressed, studying him closely for any sign of guilt.

Something that looked like regret flashed behind Marco's eyes, and he dropped his gaze to the bar counter. "Maybe my ex," he said quietly.

"Your ex?" I repeated.

He gripped his empty glass and signaled to the bartender for a refill. "Lou was sort of the reason we broke up," he mumbled, not looking at me.

Anger swelled in my chest as I read between the lines. "You cheated, didn't you?"

"Yeah." Marco had enough sense to look remorseful. He hung his head. "Louana showed up here one night and started flirting with me. I'd had a few too many drinks." His brows pinched. "Hell, I only liked her because she was easy, but she wasn't even that good of a lay. A total waste of my time."

I fought the urge to dump my daiquiri over his head. He was an arrogant, cheating scumbag, just like Bryan. "You think your ex-girlfriend was mad enough to kill?" I asked, fighting to control my anger.

Marco blew out a breath. "I don't know," he said, sounding tired. "Erin found out that I'd slept with Lou, and she dumped me. I haven't been able to get her to speak to me since. I heard she threatened to beat the snot out of Louana though. Lou actually begged me to ask Erin to leave her alone. Apparently she'd even showed up at the boutique and cussed her out."

Erin. He had an ex-girlfriend named Erin who had threatened Louana. That could be another lead. Marco turned in his seat and waved the bartender over. As he was ordering another beer, I retrieved a pen from my purse and grabbed one of the small, white cocktail napkins from the counter. "You said your girlfriend's name is Erin?" I asked, trying to sound casual. "What's her last name?"

"Malone. Why?"

I didn't answer. I was too focused on remembering the name he'd given me. *Erin Malone.* I slipped the napkin under the counter and set it on my knee, discreetly scribbling the woman's name onto the paper. Apparently I wasn't discreet enough.

Marco glanced down, his brow furrowed. "What are you doing?" Before I could stuff the napkin into my purse, Marco reached below the counter and snatched it out of my grasp. He stared at it, and his expression darkened. "If you're not working with a reporter, then why are you writing down stuff that I'm telling you?" He didn't wait for me to answer. Marco crumpled up the napkin and then stuffed it into my daiquiri.

"Hey!" I protested, watching the blue ink bleed into the yellow drink.

"I shouldn't be talking to you," Marco said gruffly. He climbed off his barstool and picked up his guitar case. He loomed over me, eyes burning with anger. "Stay the hell away from me."

CHAPTER SEVEN

———

I watched Marco go, my pulse hammering in my chest. He stomped across the bar and grabbed a seat at a table near the stage, his back turned toward me. I glanced at my second ruined pineapple daiquiri of the night and sighed. After all that, I still hadn't confirmed Marco's alibi for Saturday. What I *had* learned was that Marco Rossini had a quick temper—one that I wasn't so sure I wanted to cross again. I shuddered at the menacing way he'd hovered over me. Had those dark, burning eyes been the last thing that Louana had seen before her life was snuffed out?

"Is everything okay?" Noa had approached while I was digging around in my purse for my wallet. I looked up to find him standing next to me at the counter.

I blew out a breath. "Just effing peachy."

"What happened?" Noa's jaw clenched. "I saw that curly-haired guy get in your face. I was on my way over here to step in when he walked away." He squinted at the table where Marco was now seated, chatting up a busty blonde in a pink tube top. "Is that Louana's boyfriend?"

"According to him, no." I grimaced. "Listen, can we get out of here? I can fill you in on what he said on the ride home." The encounter with Marco had upset me more than I cared to admit.

Noa must have seen my bewilderment in my face. He bobbed his head. "Sure. I'll let the girls know we're leaving."

"I'll pay for my drink and meet you at the door," I told him. I flagged down the bartender and handed him my money before heading toward the entrance to the little dive bar.

A bald, beefy man in a black T-shirt was perched on a stool just inside the entrance. "Aloha," he said, nodding politely to me before returning his attention to his cell phone.

An idea occurred to me, and I tapped him on the shoulder. "Excuse me," I said when he looked up from the little screen, his brow lifted in question. "Did you happen to be working the door here this past Saturday night?" When he nodded, I pointed to Marco's table. "You see that guy over there?"

The bouncer's lips twisted in a smirk. "That guy," he said, shaking his head. "He's here a lot, trying to take home a different girl every time. He thinks he's Kāne's gift to the *wahines*," he'd said, referencing one of the Hawaiian deities.

God's gift to women? *Yeah, right.* I rolled my eyes. "He was here on Saturday. Do you remember when he left?" To get either in or out of the building, Marco would have had to pass the bouncer.

The man scrunched his nose. "I know he was here to collect his prize money at the end of the night," he said after a moment.

"What about before that? Any chance he left after his performance and then came back?" The resort wasn't very far from here. If Marco had been one of the first acts to take the stage, it was possible he could have sneaked away to attack Louana and had returned before the open mic competition was over. If so, the bouncer would have checked his ID on his way back in to the bar.

My new bald friend frowned. "Sorry, but I can't remember. Working the same shift night after night, it all starts to run together. Or he could've left and then come back in while I was taking my smoke break."

"Oh." I tried not to sound disappointed. That didn't really help me disprove Marco's alibi. Then again, it didn't exactly confirm it either.

Noa appeared at my side. "You ready?"

"Yeah." I glanced toward the booth. Jamie had already moved over to the bar and was flirting with one of the bartenders. Harmony was seated at our table, alone. Her arms were crossed over her chest, and she was squinting daggers at me. I noted with satisfaction that there was still a huge wet spot on the front of her shirt.

I thanked the bouncer for answering my questions and followed Noa to the parking lot. As we climbed into the Jeep, I filled him on my conversation with Marco. "I don't trust him," I said sourly. "He's a cheating piece of garbage. And just because he was at the bar at the end of the night to collect his open mic winnings, that doesn't mean he's not our guy." I recapped my conversation with Beachcomber's bouncer. "Marco apparently comes here often—so he might know when the bouncer typically takes his smoke breaks. Maybe he could have left and then slipped back in when the door was unattended."

"You're right," Noa said when I was finished. "I wouldn't count him out yet either. Just because the door guy can't remember if he saw him leave or not doesn't mean that Marco was definitely there the whole night. I've been to Beachcomber's on a Saturday night before, and it was packed. It would have been hard for someone in the bar to have their eyes on him the entire night."

"Plus he has a motive," I said. "Not only was Louana stalking him, but she also sabotaged his chance to launch his singing career—something that he was obviously still furious about." I fastened my seat belt as Noa pulled the car out of the little dive bar's parking lot. "And did I mention that he's a total creep? I was *this* close to dumping my drink over his head." I held out my hands with my two index fingers spaced barely an inch apart.

"Speaking of dumping drinks on people—you know you ruined Harmony's night, right?" Noa gave me a disapproving look, but I could see a smile trying to break through.

I ducked my head. "Believe it or not, that was an accident. Although, you did look like you needed rescuing." I crinkled my nose. "Unless you wanted her clinging to you tighter than spandex."

He lifted his shoulder and then let it fall. "What if I did?"

I shut my mouth with a click, feeling ill at the mere thought of Harmony and Noa together. *Not your business*, I reminded myself, though it didn't make me feel any better.

"So what next?" Noa asked after a moment. "Considering Marco probably won't be willing to talk to you again, what's the plan?"

"His ex-girlfriend," I suggested, thankful for a change of subject. "Erin Malone. Marco claimed she'd been threatening Louana." I nibbled my lower lip. "And then there's the kid from the stockroom at work, Luka Hale. He's harboring some major bad vibes toward Lou, though he balked when I asked him why. I do know that he was at the resort on Saturday night. He told me he'd been to the luau at the Ramada Pier but that he'd left early."

"So we have two other leads," Noa said, giving me a sidelong glance. "Which should we go after first?"

I mulled it over for a few moments. "I'll keep tabs on Luka at work and see if I can find out more about his grudge against Lou. Let's also see what we can find out about Erin Malone besides just her name. Where does she live? What does she do for a living? How crazy is she on a scale of one to bald Britney Spears?"

"I'll do a search online when I get home to see if I can find her contact information," Noa offered.

"Thanks." I reached for the radio dial, scanning through the channels. "Hey!" I smiled and turned the volume up when I stumbled across an old Kings of Leon tune. "I love this song!"

"I know." Noa's mouth twitched. "We were rocking out to it when you wrecked this very Jeep on prom night."

"Oh man. That's right." I felt a faint smile touch my lips at the memory. Noa had been my date—we'd gone as friends—and I'd driven us there in the Jeep when it had still belonged to Aunt Rikki. That same song had come on the radio, and we'd started dancing and singing along. I hadn't been paying attention to where I was going and had rolled the car right into a stop sign.

The damage hadn't been severe—just a small dent to the front fender—but I'd been too scared to tell my aunt what had really happened. Noa and I had made up a story about how I'd been forced to swerve to avoid hitting a wild chicken that had dashed into the road. It wasn't until my junior year of college that I worked up the nerve to confess to Rikki what had really caused the accident. To my relief, we'd had a good laugh about it, and she'd instantly forgiven me.

"That was quite the night," Noa said, his voice softer now. "For a number of reasons."

His words brought a rush of heat to my cheeks. One of the reasons he was referring to was our first and only kiss, shared in the Jeep as he'd tried to snap me out of my post-crash meltdown. I'd been a weepy mess, complete with a runny nose and smeared mascara. When Noa couldn't calm me down, he'd kissed me. That had stopped my hysterics *really* quick.

I felt a pang of regret. Neither Noa nor I had made a move toward pursuing a relationship in the weeks that followed that kiss. Then a month after graduation, I'd met Bryan. *What was it that held me back from just telling Noa how I felt back then?* I honestly wasn't sure.

I was ready to bolt from the car as soon as Noa parked on the curb beside Aunt Rikki's driveway. "Thanks for coming out with me tonight," I said as I slung my purse over my shoulder.

"Kaley, wait."

My hand hovered over the door handle as I turned to look at him. "What?" I asked, my throat tightening.

Noa's eyes searched mine for a few moments, his expression unreadable. Then he shook his head. "Nothing," he said. He coughed. "I have a lifeguard shift at the resort pool tomorrow evening. Call me before you go off and confront another potential psycho, okay?"

I nodded. "You got it. Good night." I shut the door to the Jeep before he could say anything else. I watched him drive away, feeling a pang of longing in my chest. Despite the fact that he'd invited Jamie and Harmony to crash our night out, I'd enjoyed spending time with Noa. When he'd stopped me from climbing out of the car just then, I'd had the strong urge to kiss him. *That would have been a mistake*, I reminded myself. I wanted to earn back Noa's friendship, not scare him off by throwing myself at him. He wasn't interested in me like that anymore. Could I turn my feelings off and just work on being his friend again? I hoped so.

* * *

It was still dark out when Aunt Rikki knocked on my bedroom door Tuesday morning. "I'm headed to sunrise yoga before work if you want to come," she said, poking her head into the room. She sounded like she was back to her old Zen self.

Even though I was finally adjusting to local time, my body wasn't having it. I mumbled something incoherent and rolled back over.

Rikki stepped fully into the room and flipped the switch on the wall. "Come on, *ku'uipo*. Get your butt out of bed. A little exercise will do you some good."

I squinted as the overhead light came on. "All right. I'm awake," I groused, sitting up and rubbing the sleep out of my eyes. "Give me ten minutes."

She nodded, seemingly satisfied. "I'll meet you downstairs."

I climbed out of bed and went to the bathroom to wash my face. After a few minutes of digging through the mound of clothing that I still hadn't unpacked, I found a pair of purple Lululemon yoga pants and a black sports bra and matching tank top. I laced up my sneakers and joined Rikki in the living room. She was dressed in teal spandex pants and a bright yellow sports bra. "Ready?" she asked.

"Yep," I replied, pulling my hair back in a ponytail. As it turned out, I was so *not* ready. The sunrise yoga class was held on the shore of Coconut Cove, a secluded beach two miles from Rikki's house. Instead of driving there, my ridiculously fit aunt insisted on jogging. I liked to think I was in decent shape, but I still huffed and puffed the entire way as I struggled to keep up with her.

When we finally reached Coconut Cove, I nearly collapsed in the sand. I unfurled the spare yoga mat I'd borrowed from Rikki and sprawled across it in corpse pose, watching the day break as the rest of the class followed the instructor through sun salutations. I managed to join in several minutes later, but by the end of the session I was exhausted and drenched in sweat, feeling anything but relaxed. I was rolling up my mat, wishing I could hail a cab home, when someone tapped me on the shoulder.

"Kaley?"

I turned around to find Jamie Parker standing on the beach, her sand-colored hair blowing in the morning breeze.

She gave me a bright smile. "I saw you and Rikki walk up just before we started. I was up front." She hiked a thumb over her shoulder to where my aunt was talking to the instructor a few yards down the shore.

"Hi, Jamie." I was surprised to see her so perky at this hour, considering she'd stayed at Beachcomber's later than I had the night before.

"I'm a total morning person," she said, as if reading my mind. She shrugged her shoulders. "It doesn't matter how late I stay out. I always like to get an early start." She leaned closer, her blue-green eyes shining. "So you and Noa left together last night, huh?" She waggled her eyebrows at me. "How'd that go?"

I grimaced. "It's not like that," I said, chewing my lip.

Jamie shook her head. "You sure? Y'all would make such a cute couple." Her lips twitched. "And the look on Harmony's face when Noa bailed with you was priceless." She snickered. "I thought the vein in her forehead was gonna explode. I hightailed it out of the booth so I wouldn't have to deal with the mess."

I couldn't help but grin. "I thought you and Harm were friends," I said, cocking my head to the side.

Jamie chuckled. "*Friends* is a strong word," she said, making a face. "I only came because Noa invited me. He's one of the first friends I made when I moved to the island."

"He's a great guy," I said truthfully.

"One of the best," she agreed. "And he has some awesome friends. I'm so glad he introduced me to you." She flashed me her brilliantly white teeth. "Your aunt talks about you all the time when I'm in her store. I feel like I know you already." Her smile widened. "Finally, someone who appreciates shopping and mani-pedis as much as I do."

I had to admit that the more I talked to Jamie, the more I liked her. My lips quirked. "I do love a good mani-pedi."

Jamie brushed her hair out of her eyes as the breeze picked up. She glanced at her watch. "I should head out. I've got clients for a diving lesson in a couple of hours."

I looked at my aunt, who was jogging in place in the sand. As I watched, she dropped to the ground and began doing pushups. I cringed. The thought of having to jog back home made me want to curl up in child's pose and hide my head in the sand. I gave Jamie a hopeful look. "Any chance you would give me a lift home? It's only a couple of miles from here, and it's on the way to the resort."

Jamie nodded. "Rikki made you run here, didn't she?" she asked with a knowing grin. "I've passed her jogging on her way to class before."

I grimaced. "I don't know how she has so much energy." I told Rikki I'd meet her at home and then followed Jamie across the sand. A seafoam green Chevy Malibu was parked beside the road. I knew before we even came to a stop beside the vehicle that it had to belong to Jamie. A pair of scuba foot fins could be seen through the back window, and the license plate read *MERMAID*.

A blue Honda Accord was parked across the street from Jamie's Mer-mobile. A woman climbed out of the driver's seat and started walking toward us. "Mrs. Colfax?" she called.

I bristled at the mention of my former last name, and my heart gave a hard thump. I watched the slender woman as she approached. Her wavy chestnut hair streamed behind her as she strode toward us, her eyes hidden behind a pair of dark sunglasses. Despite the summer heat, she was dressed in a fitted black pant suit and heels.

"Who are you?" I asked warily when she reached us.

The woman flashed me a triumphant grin, evidently pleased that she'd managed to track me down. "My name is Felicity Chase. I write for the *Aloha Sun*."

Perfect, I thought bitterly. *Another vulture reporter.* "My name isn't Mrs. Colfax," I told the brazen woman. "It's Kalua. Kaley Kalua."

"Right, of course." Felicity made a show of smacking her forehead. "Kalua—kind of like the liqueur, right?" When I didn't answer, she shook her head. "Sorry about that. I did read that your divorce had already been processed. That was fast, huh?" Felicity ignored my icy glare and pulled out her cell phone. She pressed a button on the device and then held it out in front of her. "So, *Ms. Kalua*," she tried again. "Mind if I ask you a few questions?" She didn't even wait for a response. "Is it true you were the one who found Louana Watson's body on Sunday morning?"

Anger flared in my chest. I held my hands in front of my face to shield myself from her camera. "I'm not going to talk to you," I said stiffly.

"You don't have to answer her questions." Jamie shot Felicity a dirty look as she stepped protectively in front of me. "Kaley's been through enough without having to deal with nosy newshounds like you," she said angrily. "Get out of her face."

"I'm just trying to find out the truth." Felicity sidestepped around Jamie. She pushed her sunglasses atop her head and met my gaze with calculating green eyes. "Come on. Don't you want to set the story straight?" she pressed. The reporter's lips curled. "The word all over town is that your aunt killed the poor woman "

I bit the inside of my cheek to keep from yelling at her. She was trying to goad me into saying something she could print, and I knew it. I'd dealt with a hundred others like her over the past five years. I wasn't going to let her get to me. "No comment," I said frostily.

My answer didn't deter the reporter in the slightest. "What about *you*?" she asked. Her eyes narrowed. "The ex-wife of a hotshot NFL star moves back to the island in the wake of a whirlwind divorce, and one of her new coworkers is murdered just a few hours later." She smirked. "Sounds a bit like an episode of *Snapped*." Felicity licked her lips. "You can understand why my readers will want to know if there's a connection."

Her accusation made me see red. I wanted to rip the woman's fake pearl earrings right out of her lobes. Instead, I took a calming breath. Now that I was home, I'd been hoping to fly under the media radar until some other scandal replaced my divorce as the flavor of the month. Maybe another steroid bust or a quarterback with a DUI. If I blew up at her, she'd probably print some scathing article about how I'd gone off the deep end after my split from Bryan. "No comment," I said again, this time through teeth clenched so hard that I nearly cracked a molar.

"There's gonna be a connection between my fist and your face if you don't leave right now," Jamie warned. She glared at Felicity. "Why don't you find someone else to torment for your stupid gossip column?"

The other woman's grin faded. "It's not gossip," she said defensively. "I only report real news." Felicity flashed me a friendly smile, apparently changing tactics. "You know, if you want to give your side of the story, my readers would *love* to hear it. Remember Tiger Woods' sex scandal several years ago?" Her green eyes shone with excitement. "The whole world sided with his ex-wife. Now it's your turn. You can trash your cheating hubby as much as you want, and the public will adore you. I might even be able to talk my editor into bumping it up to the front page." Her mouth twitched. "Plus, it'll be therapeutic. Get all those feelings out in the open, and you'll feel better."

My patience hit its limit. I scowled at her. "Wow, you're really desperate for a headline, aren't you? I moved here to get away from people like you." I grabbed Jamie's arm. "Let's go."

"Call me if you change your mind," Felicity yelled after me. "My number's listed on the *Aloha Sun* website."

"Not gonna happen," I muttered. There wasn't a chance in hell that I'd be calling her. I'd already had to change my own phone number to stop reporters like her from harassing me at all hours. I held my breath as I watched Felicity return to her car, and I didn't exhale until she'd driven away. "That was close," I said, feeling the tension drain out of me. "I was worried she'd spot Aunt Rikki and go after her next."

Jamie made a not-so-ladylike gesture in the direction of the reporter's disappearing taillights. "Don't let her get to you," she said, rolling her eyes. "I've seen that woman around the island. Felicity Chase is nothin' but a piece of tabloid trash posing as a serious journalist. She's always skulking around the resort, trying to dig up something she can report. I heard that when Jennifer Lawrence stayed here last month, Felicity went into full stalker mode. Resort security told her that if they caught her on the property again, she'd be arrested."

"Thanks for having my back," I said, giving her a grateful smile.

Jamie shrugged. "Sure. What are friends for?" Her forehead wrinkled. "I'm sorry she said all that stuff about you and your aunt." Her eyes shone with sympathy. "Rikki's a really sweet woman. If there's anything I can do to help..." Her voice trailed off.

"I appreciate you saying that," I said softly. A thought pushed its way to the forefront of my mind. Maybe she really could help me. "You wouldn't happen to know a woman by the name of Erin Malone, would you?" I arched a brow at Jamie.

She frowned. "Doesn't ring a bell."

My head drooped. "That's too bad. I really need to talk to her. She might know something that could help clear Rikki's name." I decided to leave out the fact that she might be Lou's real killer.

Thankfully, Jamie didn't ask questions—but she did whip out her cell phone. After tapping at the screen for a few moments, she looked up at me, her lips spread in a wide grin. "She lives in an apartment complex about three miles from here," she said.

"You found her address?"

"I'm about ninety-nine percent sure," she admitted. "I just searched the web for an Erin Malone in Aloha Lagoon, and only one result popped up." She opened the driver's-side door and climbed into the car. "Hop in." Jamie motioned to the passenger seat.

I chewed my lip. "You're not thinking of driving over there?" I asked as I fastened my seat belt. I'd promised Noa that I'd call him before I went after another potential murderer. If he was still the late sleeper that he'd been when we were younger, I doubted he was awake yet.

Jamie shrugged. "Why not? It's only a mile past your aunt's place, and I've got plenty of time for a quick drive by. Couldn't hurt, right?"

"I guess not." Though Noa wasn't around, it wasn't like I would be approaching Erin alone. Plus, for all I knew, we might not even have the right person. "All right." I grinned at Jamie. "Just a quick trip past her apartment, and then you can drop me at home." After all, I had to get ready for work, myself.

"Deal." She pulled onto the road, heading in the direction of Erin Malone's apartment. Within a few minutes, we'd reached Sunset Tower, a cream-colored high-rise building on a gated beachfront lot. Jamie pulled up to the little security shack at the parking lot entrance, and a uniformed officer stepped out.

"Who are you here to see?" he asked when Jamie rolled down the driver's-side window.

"Erin Malone," she replied breezily.

The man checked the clipboard in his hand. "What apartment number?"

"12-B."

"Your name?"

"Kaley Kalua," I piped up, leaning across Jamie toward the window. There was no harm in giving him my name. After all, I just wanted to talk to Erin. That wasn't a crime.

The security guard scribbled on his clipboard and then returned to his little thatch-roof shack. Jamie and I watched as he picked up a phone and mashed several buttons. After a few moments, he hung up and returned to Jamie's car. "Sorry. She's not answering, and we can't let guests onto the property without obtaining permission from the resident."

"Oh." I slumped back against my seat, feeling disappointed.

"Thanks anyway," Jamie told the man before putting her car in reverse, forcing the Mercedes waiting behind us to back up and let her out of the lane.

"Well, that was a bust," I said glumly as Jamie navigated the Chevy Malibu back onto the road.

"Cheer up, buttercup," she said, giving me a sidelong glance. "We can always come back later." She grinned. "Hey, what are you doing tonight after work?"

I shrugged. "No plans to speak of." I was sure that whatever I wound up doing would revolve around trying to track down Erin Malone.

She winked. "Why don't we grab drinks at the pool bar? My buddy Timo is working there tonight," she added, giving me a sly look. "And I think you'll want to meet him. He knows practically everyone on the island, and he's always got the scoop on the latest resort gossip."

I felt a genuine smile tug at my lips. Timo might be able to help me get in touch with Erin. Or maybe he'd have some information about Marco or Luka. If he was the best source for resort gossip, then he was someone I needed to talk to. The fact that Noa was lifeguarding at the pool that evening might have also factored into my decision—but only by a little.

"I like the way you think," I said, grinning at Jamie. "Let's have a girls' night."

CHAPTER EIGHT

———

When we reached Rikki's house, I thanked Jamie for the ride and hauled my sweaty self inside, making a beeline for the shower. My aunt was already dressed when I emerged with my damp hair wrapped in a towel. I finished getting ready for work while she made breakfast, and after scarfing down two pieces each of avocado toast, we sped toward the resort on her eggplant-colored scooter.

I spent the morning on the sales floor, assisting a handful of customers, checking our inventory, and making notes on garments we needed to restock. In the afternoon, I returned to Rikki's office, where we reviewed clothing catalogs from the vendors that she worked with. It was by far the most fun part of my new job, browsing the swimsuit and dress collections and the upcoming fall lines from some of my favorite designers. Rikki showed me where to access the store's merchandise budget and allowed me to order a shipment each of two new pieces to stock the following month. I chose a cute pink A-line dress and a short-sleeved floral shift dress, both from Liz Claiborne's new island-themed collection.

"Those are gorgeous," gushed a cheery voice at the door. I turned to look over my shoulder and found Sara standing in the entrance to Rikki's office. She gestured to the screen of the laptop in front of me. "*Please* tell me you're ordering that flowery dress. Is that Liz Claiborne?"

Rikki beamed proudly. "Kaley picked that out. The new shipment should arrive in about two weeks."

"I love it!" Sara pumped her fist in the air. "I'll definitely be snagging one when they come in." She shifted her gaze to

Rikki. "Anyway, I just wanted to let you know Tonya just got here to relieve me, so I'm headed out for the day."

"Thanks." Rikki smiled at her. "Enjoy your afternoon."

Sara gave us a little wave before turning and fluttering back down the hallway toward the front of the shop.

I glanced at the clock on the wall. It was nearly four, and my shift was ending too. "I think I'm going to hang around the resort until I meet up for drinks with Jamie later," I told Rikki. "She's going to give me a ride home. I should be back before dinner."

My aunt stretched her arms over her head, yawning. "What do you think of having takeout tonight? I'm not really in the mood to cook," she said. She rubbed her flat tummy. "I've been craving some pineapple fried rice from Sir Spamalot's. If Jamie doesn't mind taking you by there to pick up some food, I'll buy you both dinner and she can join us." She reached for her wallet, but I waved her off.

"My treat this time," I said. "You've done more than enough for me in the past few days—or, rather, the past fifteen years."

"And I would do it all again in a heartbeat." She planted a kiss on my cheek. "You go ahead and get out of here." She shooed me toward the door. "Have fun."

I removed my name tag and shoved it in my purse. I was heading toward the restroom when Harmony stepped in front of me, blocking my path. I'd managed to avoid her since she'd arrived for her shift, but now there was no escape.

She leaned toward me, red-faced and furious. "The little stunt you pulled last night at Beachcomber's was *not* cool," she growled. "That top was Versace. You could have ruined it."

I took a step back from her. "Accidents happen." I shrugged. "And it looked to me like it washed out just fine."

"You're lucky it did." She clenched her jaw and stepped forward, invading my personal space again. "And another thing," she said, poking my chest with her index finger. "I don't care about whatever unrequited-love crap that happened between you and Noa Kahele when we were in school. He's off limits to you now."

"Um, excuse me?" I felt my face grow hot. "Noa's his own person. He can talk to whomever he wants." I'd had to tell myself the same thing when he'd been friendly with her the night before. I squinted at Harmony. "It's not like you're dating him." There might have been a hint of a question in my voice.

Harmony stuck out her chin. "Not *yet*," she said, staring down her nose at me. "But it's only a matter of time. This is a small island—all the single men are being snatched up faster than your ex during the NFL draft. But just because he dropped you like a bad pass doesn't mean you can show up on the island thinking you've got a shot with Noa—because he's mine." She fluffed her hair, her expression smug. "His taste in women sure has improved a lot since you two were friends."

"Whatever you say." I rolled my eyes. I brushed past Harmony and made my way to the restroom to throw on the new designer bathing suit I'd bought on my lunch break. *She's delusional*, I thought. Harmony couldn't keep me from being friends with Noa any more than I could keep her from throwing herself at him. The fact that she was suddenly so into him irked me. In my opinion, Noa was a total catch, but Harmony had always been cruel to him in high school. Now that he'd grown up to have the body of a surfer god and the face of a Hollywood A-lister, she was starting to show interest. That just went to show that Harmony was only after him for his looks. Noa deserved someone who saw him as more than just a new piece of arm candy.

I slipped into the black and white striped bikini and tied my new scarlet sarong around my waist. *Thank goodness for the employee discount*, I thought, removing the price tags from my new outfit. I stashed my work clothes in my oversized purse and hurried out the front door, excited for the chance to relax by the pool for a couple of hours and work on my tan.

Unfortunately, several dozen guests had the same idea for how to spend their afternoon. The pool area was so crowded that I couldn't find a place to settle in. The hot afternoon sun beat down on my back as I edged my way through a crowd of sunscreen-lathered tourists and their screaming kids.

So much for working on my tan, I thought moodily. I considered grabbing a towel and hitting the beach, but I didn't want to be covered in sand when I met up with Jamie for happy hour. Instead, I continued to scan the pool area for an empty seat. Spying a free chair in a shaded corner of the patio, I wedged my way through the crowd. I set down my purse on the little seat and removed the sarong from around my waist, retying it around my neck so that the garment was draped over me like a halter dress. I pulled my bag into my lap as I sank down into the lounger.

Noa was perched on the lifeguard chair across the patio, elevated high enough to oversee the entire pool area. His bronze skin glistened with moisture, and his hair was wet, as if he'd just climbed out of the water. He moved his head from side to side as he surveyed the patio. I tried to contain my drooling as I lifted my hand to wave. Noa's gaze settled on me, and he waved back. Then he pressed his thumb to his ear and his pinky to his lips.

I squinted at him in confusion. *Call me?* It certainly looked like the hand gesture for a cell phone, though I was pretty sure he couldn't take calls during his shift. Plus, if Noa had something to say to me, he could just climb down from that oversized chair and walk over to tell me in person.

When I shrugged, he made the hand gesture again and pointed to my purse. Frowning, I rifled around inside the bag until I found my phone. *Oh. Duh.* I had a text from him. He must have sent it while I was still at work. I clicked on the blinking icon and read his message: *Found Erin Malone's info as promised. Here are her address and phone number.*

The address in Noa's text was the same one that Jamie and I had already visited that morning. I read the phone number he'd typed below it. If I couldn't get past security at Erin's gated apartment complex, at least I could try calling her.

I gave Noa a thumbs-up and then dialed the number from his text message. After three rings, the call went to voicemail. "You've reached Erin's phone," said a youthful, feminine voice. "I can't take your call right now, but if you leave a message, I'll get back to you." The recorded clip ended with a high-pitched beep.

"Er, hi, Erin," I stammered, realizing I should have worked out a plan before placing the call. I looked at Noa as I fumbled for what to say to the woman's machine. He'd turned his attention to a pair of kids who were running near the edge of the pool. *I can't hang up now*, I thought. But I couldn't exactly tell her that I was calling to question her about a murder either. What could I say that would make her want to call me back? I flicked a glance across the courtyard, and my gaze settled on the Happy Hula sign above the shop's awning. It gave me an idea.

"Hi, Erin. This is Kaley calling from the Happy Hula Dress Boutique," I said, using my cheeriest customer service voice. "I have some good news. We recently partnered with Sunset Tower to give away a free charm bracelet to one lucky resident, and your name was drawn as our lucky winner. Congratulations!" It was a terrible lie, but it was the first thing that popped into my head, so I rolled with it. The high-rise apartment building had hundreds of residents, which I imagined kept their staff quite busy. Everyone loved winning something for free, and I hoped that Erin would be so excited that she wouldn't think to ask the front office at Sunset Tower if they'd actually hosted the contest.

"Please drop by the Happy Hula Dress Boutique any day this week between the hours of eight and four to pick up your bracelet," I continued. "We're located in the merchant village in the main courtyard of the Aloha Lagoon Resort. Be sure to ask for Kaley." I quickly ended the call and exhaled a long breath, sagging against the little patio chair.

Not my finest work, I thought, wiping a bead of sweat off my brow. *But quick thinking, at least.* I'd have to wait and see if Erin actually called me back or showed up to the boutique. And in the meantime, I'd meet up with Jamie for happy hour drinks, as planned. Maybe her friend, Timo, the all-knowing bartender, would be able to give me the scoop on Miss Malone.

With an hour and a half to kill until Jamie arrived, I pulled up the e-reader app on my phone and skimmed a James Patterson novel, resisting the urge to sneak the occasional peek in Noa's direction.

Evening settled over the resort, signaling the end of the family-friendly pool atmosphere. Parents and their children began to trickle out of the patio area, making their way to dinner or heading back to their rooms. Someone turned up the volume on the pool speakers, and an island pop song blared around me as happy hour began at the little tiki bar.

I stowed my phone away in my purse and rose from my chair when I saw Jamie sidle through the pool area's gated entrance. Waving, I made my way around the patio to meet her. A cluster of bikini-clad twentysomething girls were gathered together near the water, sipping cocktails and swaying to the music. They squealed when a young man in the pool tried to flirt with them by splashing water in their direction. I gave the splash zone a wide birth, not wanting to get my black leather Tory Burch flip-flops wet.

Jamie had taken a seat on one of the barstools. The straps of her yellow bikini peeked out from beneath her pink maxi dress as she patted the empty seat next to her. "Perfect timing," she exclaimed when I joined her. She lifted a slender hand to flag down the bartender, who hurried over to our corner. "We'll each take a Tequila Sunrise and one of the Hawaiian shooters that are on special." She winked at me. "Trust me. You'll love these."

"What's in the shooter?" I asked.

"Nothin' too strong," she replied. "It's like the fruit salad of booze. It's got peach liqueur, melon liqueur, orange liqueur…" She scrunched her nose as she tried to tick off each ingredient from memory.

I turned my attention to the bartender, who was filling a glass with my cocktail. He was of average height, with a slim build and dark curly hair. He met my gaze with friendly brown eyes as he slid the drink and a straw across the counter toward me. I flicked a glance at the name tag pinned to his polo shirt and felt a wide grin spread across my face. *Just the man I wanted to see.*

Jamie stopped counting fruity liqueurs on her fingers and glanced up. As if reading my mind, she smiled at the bartender and said, "Timo, this is Kaley."

The young man nodded at me. "You're the new girl at Happy Hula," he said in a matter-of-fact tone.

"Not entirely new," I replied, shrugging. "I'm originally from Aloha Lagoon." I leaned across the counter toward him and lowered my voice. "So I hear you're the source for all the best resort gossip."

"I guess." Timo's lips turned up at the corners. "You hear a lot of interesting things working behind a bar." He set down two double shot glasses in front of Jamie and me. "Hawaiian shooters for the ladies."

Jamie grabbed one and then handed me the other. She grinned and clinked her glass against mine. "Bottoms up!"

I lifted the colorful shot to my lips and tilted my head back, letting the mixture of booze and tropical juice slide down my throat. The alcohol instantly warmed my insides. "That was delicious," I said, licking my lips.

Jamie set her empty glass on the counter. Her face puckered from the tart drink. "A little on the sour side though." She chased it with a sip of her cocktail before turning her attention to Timo. "Kaley has a few questions for you, if you don't mind."

He lifted one shoulder and then let it fall. "Ask away."

I leaned forward. "Do you know a bellhop at the resort named Marco?"

Timo nodded. "Yeah, Marco Rossini. Talented guy— I've heard him sing a few times. A bit of a dog with the ladies though."

"So I've noticed," I said dryly. "What do you know about his ex-girlfriend, Erin Malone? I'm trying to find her."

"You won't have to look very far." Timo nodded toward the main resort building. "She works on the housekeeping staff."

Jamie and I traded an excited look. "Good to know," I said, beaming.

A young woman slinked over to the bar and leaned on the counter. I recognized her as the redhead that had been seated in front of me on my flight to Kauai. "Aloha. Can I have a Sex on the Beach?" she asked, fluttering her lashes at Timo.

"Excuse me a sec," he said to Jamie and me. He shifted his attention to the girl, who continued to flirt with him as he mixed her drink.

I scooted my barstool closer to Jamie's. "Noa did some digging on Erin this morning too. He sent me her phone number," I told her in a low voice. I swirled the straw in my drink. "I actually tried calling her a little while ago."

Jamie cocked her head. "What did she say?"

"Nothing. I got her voicemail." I ducked my head, feeling sheepish. "I sort of panicked and left a message saying that she'd won a free charm bracelet from the boutique. I was hoping that might entice her to call me back or drop by the shop so I can talk to her in person."

"Nice." Jamie smirked. "Maybe I should ignore your phone calls so you'll offer me fancy jewelry," she added with a snort.

I rolled my eyes. "Yeah, yeah. If this works, I'll buy her one of the little gold pineapple charm bracelets on the display at the front of the store. They aren't expensive. The thirty bucks would be worth it if I can find out where she was on Saturday night." I inclined my head in Timo's direction. "But if she works here at the resort like he says, I may be able to track her down even if she doesn't come into the boutique."

"True." Jamie took a sip of her drink. "Ya know, I'm actually not surprised, now that I think about it. Most locals work for the resort in some capacity."

"Good point." I glanced in the direction of the main building as I sipped my cocktail, wondering if Erin Malone was in there at that very moment.

The flirty redhead took her drink from Timo and slipped him a twenty-dollar bill along with her number, telling him with a wink that he could keep the change as long as he called her before she flew back to Milwaukee in a few days. Then she turned and strutted back across the patio to rejoin her brunette friend. Timo made change and deposited the extra bills into the tip jar before coming back to our end of the bar. "Can I get you ladies anything else?"

"More information," Jamie replied. She hiccuped, and her cheeks colored. "And another Tequila Sunrise."

Timo set to work mixing Jamie's cocktail.

"I heard a rumor that Erin threatened Louana Watson before she was killed," I said, watching him pour the mixture of tequila, grenadine, and orange juice from his shaker into a fresh glass. Since it had come from that sleazebag Marco's lips, I couldn't be one hundred percent certain it was the truth. I was hoping that Timo could confirm it.

He handed Jamie her drink and then stooped beneath the counter to retrieve a bowl of fresh limes. "You're trying to prove your aunt didn't kill Louana," he said in that same assured tone. When I blinked at him, he said, "I hear about pretty much everything that goes on around here. People have been talking about Rikki, just as they've been talking about your divorce from that football star."

Heat spread throughout my whole body. It hadn't even occurred to me that the bartender would know about that. I glanced at Jamie, feeling embarrassed.

She gave me a reassuring smile and reached over to give my hand a squeeze. She narrowed her eyes, shooting Timo what seemed like a warning look. "Just tell us what you know about the rumor that Erin threatened Lou, okay?"

Timo looked neither embarrassed nor remorseful. He just shrugged. "That's actually not a rumor," he said as he cut the little citrus fruits into garnishes. "I heard about it from Erin herself."

If I leaned any farther forward, I would have been on the same side of the bar as him. "What happened?" I asked, my pulse quickening with excitement. This was what I'd come here to find out from the skinny bartender. I fished around in the depths of my purse and found a crumpled five-dollar bill, which I slid across the counter to encourage him to keep talking.

Timo thanked me with a curt nod and pocketed the cash. He went back to work slicing limes. "Erin dropped by here a couple of weeks ago after her shift ended. She and one of the other housekeepers, Anaida, had a few drinks right where you two are sitting. The bar was pretty busy, so I only caught part of their conversation." Timo finished cutting up the fruit and set the bowl and knife back under the counter. He looked from Jamie to me. "Erin was talking about her breakup with Marco. She'd dropped by his house without calling first one night after work, and Louana was there. Erin dumped him on the spot."

"How did Erin seem when you saw her?" I studied him carefully.

"Was she sad?" Jamie chimed in, placing her elbows on the bar. "Hurt? Or just really pissed off? If I'd walked in on my boyfriend with another woman, I'd have been royally pissed."

I felt a twinge of hurt, recalling my own personal experience with Bryan and his home-wrecking pom-pom girls. Forcing the memory down, I returned my attention to Timo. "Well?" I asked, my tone perhaps a little too eager.

He shrugged. "She was understandably angry."

"What about the threat?" Jamie asked. "What did she say she was gonna do to Lou for stealing her man?"

"She didn't spell it out, exactly." Timo set down the dishrag he'd been using to wipe the counter clean. "But the way her voice sounded made it seem like a threat to me."

"What did she say?" I pressed, the tiny hairs on my arms and neck prickling.

Timo placed both hands on the bar and leaned toward us, the fire from the tiki torches dancing in his eyes. "Erin said that she blamed Louana for destroying her relationship. When her friend asked what she was going to do about it, Erin just smiled and said that sooner or later, Lou was going to get exactly what she deserved."

CHAPTER NINE

———

I stared at Timo, trying to process what he'd just told us. What had Erin meant when she'd said Louana would get exactly what she deserved? I agreed with the bartender; it *did* sound an awful lot like a threat. *But did Erin really think Lou deserved to die?* I mean, I was the first to admit I'd wished ill on the trio of cheerleaders who had ended my marriage—but I'd only hoped that maybe their hair would fall out or they'd get fat. I hadn't wanted to *murder* them.

I wanted to ask Timo if he'd heard Erin say anything else about Lou or her unfaithful ex, but a cluster of guests staggered up to the bar then, crowding around the small counter and waving hands full of cash. The bartender bowed his head to Jamie and me and excused himself to attend to the newcomers.

"Wow," Jamie breathed. "That story totally gave me the chills!" She held up her tan arms to show me the pimply gooseflesh. "Do you think that maybe Erin is Louana's killer?"

"It's possible." I sipped my drink, nearly spilling it as an overweight man in a red aloha shirt bumped into my stool. I wobbled on the seat before regaining my balance.

Instead of apologizing, the man eyed my chair and then gave me a pointed look. "You ladies about through here?" he asked. He inclined his head to an enormous woman in a rainbow muumuu waddling toward the bar from across the patio. "Mind if my wife and I take those seats?"

Jamie opened her mouth, looking as if she were about to protest, but I held up a hand. "They're all yours," I said, sliding off my stool. I turned to Jamie, grabbing her arm. "Come on. Let's take a dip in the pool."

Jamie glanced back at the large couple. "Some people are so rude," she said, rolling her eyes.

"It's no big deal, really," I told her, shrugging. My mind was still focused on Timo's story about Erin. The bartender didn't have anything to gain by lying to me. I believed him—and that meant I had found a clear motive for Erin Malone. *But what about her alibi?* I'd still need to try to talk to her myself to find out where she was on the night that Louana had been murdered.

I spotted a couple of empty lounge chairs near the edge of the pool and steered Jamie in their direction. "I'll grab some towels," I said, setting my purse down on the edge of one. I walked over to the shelves of folded beach towels near the pool area's gated entrance and grabbed two off the top of the stack.

Jamie had already removed her maxi dress and jumped in the pool by the time I returned. Dropping the towels on our loungers, I slipped out of my own cover-up and shoes. I glanced up to find Noa looking my way from his perch in the lifeguard chair. I could practically feel his eyes on me as I stepped toward the edge of the water, and I suddenly felt naked in my skimpy swimwear.

Despite the fact that it was a warm evening, I still dipped a toe below the water's surface to test the temperature. Satisfied, I descended the stairs leading into the shallow end. The underwater orbs of light that lined the pool walls illuminated its floor as I waded in up to my waist. The balmy night air felt good on my bare shoulders, and I sighed with contentment.

"Isn't this great?" Jamie asked, treading water beside me. She floated on her back for a few moments and dipped her hair below the surface before touching her feet to the pool floor.

We relaxed on the submerged stairs, and another server dropped by to offer us more frozen cocktails. I sneaked a glance toward the bar, where Timo was busy mixing drinks for a gaggle of middle-aged women in bright pink shirts that read *I got lei'd on Harriet's Over the Hill Hawaiian Vacation.*

"Thanks for sticking up for me back there," I said to Jamie. "I knew people had been talking around the resort about Aunt Rikki being accused of Lou's murder. I guess I shouldn't be surprised that people have been talking to Timo about my divorce too."

Jamie took a sip of her drink and fixed me with an apologetic expression. "I should have warned you that Timo doesn't have much of a filter. People say whatever's on their minds around him, so he does the same. I don't think he meant to offend you." She clinked her glass against mine, her lips turning up at the corners. "But it's all good. Sounds to me like you found a solid motive for Erin, and you deserve better than some philandering jock, anyway. There are plenty of hot men on this island that would worship the sand you walk in, if given a chance." She looked over my shoulder, and her grin spread even wider. "In fact, I see one right now."

I followed her gaze, blushing when I realized she was talking about Noa. I watched as he climbed down from his lifeguard chair and retrieved a drawstring backpack from a hook on the back of the seat. He rifled around in it, retrieving an Aloha Lagoon Resort polo. After putting the shirt on, he slung the backpack over his shoulder and approached our corner of the pool. "I hope you ladies don't need rescuing," he teased. "Because I'm off duty."

Jamie's lips quirked. "Nah. I'm practically part fish." She handed me her drink and dove under the surface before swimming a lap around the pool.

"I'm guessing you read my text?" Noa asked.

"Yeah, and I've got a lot to catch you up on."

Jamie splashed her way back over to us and took her frozen daiquiri from my outstretched hand. She tilted her head, and her brow wrinkled. "Are those drums?"

I listened for a moment. A faint beating rhythm could be heard in the distance. "Yeah, I think so," I said, nodding.

"The luau must be starting over at the Ramada Pier," Noa said.

"Yum." Jamie licked her lips. "The roast pork with pineapple is to die for." She patted her stomach. "All this talk about food is making me hungry."

I snapped my fingers. I'd nearly forgotten about my aunt's request for takeout. "I sort of promised Rikki I'd bring home dinner from Sir Spamalot's." I met Jamie's gaze. "If you don't mind stopping by there before you drop me off," I added.

"Oh. Driving...yikes." Jamie grimaced. "I'm sorry, Kaley. I think I'm too tipsy to get behind the wheel right now." She glanced at the drink in her hand. "Timo's cocktails are really strong."

I could attest to that. For the past several minutes, my limbs had felt like Jell-O.

"I think I'm gonna head over to the Loco Moco Café and grab a bite while I sober up." Jamie's cheeks turned pink as she set her drink glass down by the pool's edge. She looked up at Noa and fluttered her lashes. "Any chance you'd do Kaley and me both a solid and give her a lift home. Please?" She laid her accent thick on that last word, stretching it into two syllables.

Noa nodded. "Sure." He smirked at Jamie. "But you owe me, Parker."

She bobbed her head. "Totally. Next time we go to The Lava Pot, the first round of Shark Bites are on me." Jamie flung her arms around my neck. "You're welcome," she whispered in my ear, though it was so loud that I was pretty sure everyone at the pool could hear. She pulled back and gave me an exaggerated wink. Jamie placed her hands on the patio and hoisted herself out of the pool before grabbing one of the towels I'd draped across our loungers. When she'd dried herself off, she shimmied back into her dress. "See y'all later," she said, giving us a little wave before flouncing toward the courtyard.

"Should we make sure *she* gets home okay?" I frowned after Jamie's retreating figure.

Noa shook his head. "Nah. She'll be fine. Jamie's pretty responsible."

"And inhumanly perky after a night of drinking," I remarked, shaking my head. "I ran into her at sunrise yoga this morning. She's like a clone of Rikki but with a southern accent and fewer wrinkles."

Noa chuckled. "I knew you two would get along."

"Yeah, she's great. And I could use a friend right about now." I climbed out of the pool and reached for my towel. To my surprise, Noa had already grabbed it and was holding it open for me. I stepped forward and let him wrap it around my shoulders.

"That's kind of why I introduced you two," he replied. When I blinked at him, his cheeks colored. "I just figure you're going through a rough patch right now. I thought maybe having someone to confide in might not be a bad thing. You know, because of..." His words trailed off, and he dropped his gaze to the ground. "Because of everything going on with Rikki," he finished.

"Or with my life in general," I blurted. I hadn't meant to say that out loud, and I immediately regretted it. Embarrassed, I turned away from Noa, making a startled squeak as I teetered on my feet. Noa's hands shot forward, and he gripped my arms to steady me. He gently turned me around so that I was facing him. "Thanks," I mumbled, feeling a blush creep into my cheeks. "I might be a little drunk."

Noa smirked. "A word of advice. Lay off of Timo's cocktails. They'll make you spill your secrets. Rumor has it he swaps out the tequila for truth serum."

"It would explain how he knows so much about everything that goes on at the resort," I muttered. I pulled the towel more tightly around my shoulders, shivering. "Can we get out of here?"

Noa nodded. "Sure. Let's go."

"Do you mind if we swing by Sir Spamalot's? I'll buy your dinner if you're hungry," I offered.

"Deal." Noa grinned. "I've actually been craving their Spam Musubi for days." He waited as I deposited the dirty beach towel in the appropriate hamper and tied my sarong around my waist. Then we worked our way toward the gate that led from the pool area back into the courtyard. "So what's the update on Erin Malone?" he asked as we walked toward his car.

"Well, for starters, she works at the resort. She's on the housekeeping staff."

He raised his eyebrows. "So she should be easy to track down, right?"

I nodded. "I hope so." I told him about visiting her apartment complex that morning with Jamie, as well as the voicemail I'd left, luring her to visit me in the boutique so I could get a read on her.

"And there's more," I said as we stepped into the dimly lit employee parking lot. "Timo said he overheard Erin talking to one of her friends about Louana a couple of weeks ago.

According to him, Erin said that Louana was going to get exactly what she deserved."

We reached Noa's Jeep, and he leaned against the passenger side. He furrowed his brow. "What's that supposed to mean?"

I shrugged. "Sounds ominous, doesn't it?"

"I suppose jealousy is a solid motive," he said, his tone thoughtful. "The scorned ex-girlfriend wants her man back, so she gets rid of the other woman. It's worth checking out."

"I think so too," I agreed.

A rustling noise to the right pulled my attention to a red Acura a few slots over. My shoulders stiffened. *Speaking of jealousy...* Harmony was bent forward, shoving several plastic garment bags into the trunk of the little car. She straightened and slammed the lid down before marching around to the driver's-side of the car. Harmony passed under one of the parking lot security lights, and I saw her overly glossed lips drawn down in a scowl. I watched her put the Acura in reverse and then speed out of the parking lot, a peppy Taylor Swift song blasting from her car speakers. "That was close," I muttered, relieved she hadn't seen us. The last thing I wanted to deal with right then was Harmony threatening me or throwing herself at Noa again.

"What was close?" Noa looked to the trail of exhaust left by Harmony's car and then back at me, his expression curious. I wasn't sure if he'd seen her or not.

My face flushed. "Nothing," I said quickly, opening the Jeep's passenger-side door. "Let's get out of here. I'm starving."

Noa followed suit, climbing behind the wheel. He backed out of the parking spot and pointed the Jeep in the direction of Sir Spamalot's. The little open air eatery was a short drive from the resort. It was located directly on the beach, nestled beneath a cluster of palm trees. Noa parked in a small nearby lot, and we removed our shoes to make the trek across the dunes. The sun had set by now, and the sand felt cool under my bare feet as I followed him toward the café's walk-up counter. A petite woman with black hair rang up our orders and then retrieved the food from under a heat lamp.

I couldn't resist opening the to-go bag and breathing in the tangy aroma of my grilled Spam and pineapple kabobs. The scent reminded me of my childhood. Both Rikki and my mother had whipped up recipes featuring the canned meat that would have rivaled those of a Michelin-star chef—in my opinion, at least. I'd always loved Spam, though Bryan's friends in Atlanta had given me funny looks whenever I'd suggested eating it. Now I was free to enjoy it anytime I pleased.

"Do you want to stay for dinner?" I asked as Noa pulled onto Kalapaki Drive. Rikki had told me to invite Jamie to join us, but since Noa had given me a ride home instead, I figured I might as well extend the same invitation to him.

"Looks like Rikki already has company," he replied, rolling the Jeep to a stop in front of my aunt's house.

I glanced up, following his gaze to the driveway. A dark blue sedan was parked next to Rikki's Vespa. A feeling of dread crawled down my spine, and my chest tightened. *Something's wrong.*

Noa must have seen my worry in my expression. "Is everything okay?" he asked, frowning at the blue car. He removed the keys from Jeep's ignition and placed his hand on the door handle. "Want me to go in with you?"

"No." I swallowed the lump forming in my throat. "I'm sure everything's fine. Maybe it's just one of Rikki's friends dropping by for a visit." The visceral tug in my middle section told me that probably wasn't the case, but I didn't want Noa to see how anxious I was. "Thanks again for the lift," I said, climbing out of the car.

When he was gone, I steeled my nerves and walked quickly across the front porch, suddenly feeling very sober. I hesitated at the front door, taking a deep breath and then pushing it out again. Then I let myself into the house to face Rikki's mystery visitor.

My gut feeling had been right on the money. Detective Ray was seated in the living room, his plump belly spilling over the waistband of his khakis. He'd traded his floral collared shirt for one with a palm tree pattern. Rikki had pulled one of the wicker chairs from her dining set into the living room. Judging by the tense look on her face, I didn't think the detective had dropped in for a social call.

"Kaley." The man's dark eyes fixed on me as I stepped into the house, and he rose from the couch. "Good evening." His tone was polite as he shook my hand. "I was just wrapping up asking your aunt a few questions." He looked at Rikki. "Thank you for your cooperation, and I apologize again for dropping by so late."

"I told you, Detective. It's really no trouble," she said, flashing him a smile that didn't quite reach her eyes. "After all, I have nothing to hide."

My aunt and the detective stared at one another for several moments, the air thick with tension as a silent conversation seemed to pass between them. Finally, Detective Ray's gaze broke away from Rikki. "I should go. I'd hate for your dinner to get cold," he said, flicking a glance at the bag of Sir Spamalot's takeout still in my hand. He rubbed his belly. "I love their grilled Spam kabobs." The detective looked over at my aunt again. "It'd be wise for you to stick around town the next few days, Rikki. I'll be in touch."

My gut clenched at the subtle threat behind his words.

The detective walked to the door, bowing his head to us both before disappearing into the night. I dropped the bag of food on the coffee table and dashed after him. "Wait," I called as I bounded onto the porch.

Ray turned to look at me, arching one bushy eyebrow. "What is it, Kaley?"

"Why did you come here?" I demanded breathlessly. "Rikki hasn't done anything wrong."

The detective sighed. "Another witness came forward this afternoon claiming to have seen your aunt assault Louana Watson in the employee parking lot of the resort five days before she was killed."

His words sent a shock through my middle. "Assault?" I shook my head vehemently. "No way. Whoever told you that must have been mistaken. Aunt Rikki would never attack someone."

His mouth twitched. "It's my duty to follow up on this type of information. That incident and Rikki's tiff with the deceased at the shop could have been dismissed as coincidence, but when you pair them with the fact that she doesn't have an alibi for the night of Miss Watson's death, it makes them worth investigating. I'm only doing my job, Ms. Kalua. It's nothing personal." He started toward his car.

I followed him, my jaw clenched. It was personal to me. "Are you following up on any other leads? From what I understand, there are plenty of people on the island who wouldn't lose sleep over killing Louana Watson. Maybe you're looking in the wrong place." I stood next to his car, my hands on my hips. "For starters, have you talked to Marco Rossini, the man that Lou was seeing? She squashed his chance at launching his singing career. Or what about Marco's ex-girlfriend, Erin Malone? Louana is the reason they broke up. The word around the resort is that she had been harassing Lou for a few weeks before she was killed."

Detective Ray gave me a patient smile. "Yes, I have been following several other leads," he said gently. "But I'm sure you can understand that I'm not at liberty to discuss them." He opened the car door and settled into the driver's seat. "Now, if you'll excuse me, I don't want to be late for my own dinner. My wife is making paella tonight." Ray closed the door before I could protest and pulled his car out of the driveway.

Frustrated, I kicked at the gravel. I'd had the feeling the detective wasn't taking me seriously. Shoulders slumped, I trudged back toward the house. Rikki had moved to the couch and had her legs curled beneath her. She looked up when I walked in, her dark eyes pinched with concern.

"Why does Detective Ray think you assaulted Louana in the resort parking lot?" I asked, thinking that there was no way it could be true.

Rikki's cheeks turned red. "Because I did," she replied, holding up a hand to stop me from speaking. "Sort of." She sighed wearily. "As you might have noticed, the employee parking lot isn't very well lit. There are only a couple of security lights. It would be easy for an assailant to sneak up on an unsuspecting woman as she walked to her car at night." She frowned. "I don't like the idea of any of the girls walking out there alone in the dark after closing the shop."

My forehead wrinkled. This was Aloha Lagoon, not New York City. The island wasn't a dangerous place. *Then again, Louana probably thought that too—before she was murdered on the resort property.* "So how does that explain why you attacked Lou?" I asked.

Rikki lifted her chin. "I was trying to teach her self-defense. I took a martial arts class last summer, and I've been offering to show the staff some moves. Last week I brought it up again while walking with Harmony and Louana to the parking lot. I simply demonstrated a palm heel strike and a knee strike with Lou—but I didn't hurt her. I only went through the motions. Would you like to see?"

Before I could respond, my aunt rose from the couch. She uttered a high-pitched screech and rushed at me. I let out a startled cry as she hurtled forward, thrusting the palm of her hand at my face. I ducked and skittered backward and wound up slamming into the front door. "Ow," I muttered, gingerly rubbing the back of my head.

Rikki dropped back, a horrified expression pulling her features tight. "*Ku'uipo*, are you all right?"

"I'll live," I said dryly. "Just remind me to never get on your bad side."

My aunt ducked her head. "You know, Louana had pretty much the same reaction to that move as you did. I suppose I can see why someone watching us from a distance might have thought I was attacking her."

I clenched my jaw. I wasn't so sure it had been someone watching her from a distance. Rikki had said that Harmony was there too. I couldn't help but wonder if she had called in the tip as a way to get back at me for humiliating her in front of Noa the night before. Harmony had a vindictive streak, and I wouldn't put it past her to hurt Rikki as a way to get at me. I was going to really let her have it the next time I saw her.

Still rubbing the sore spot on my head, I moved to the couch. "Did you explain all of that to Detective Ray?"

My aunt settled onto the cushions beside me. "Of course. I offered to demonstrate for him too, but he asked me not to."

I said a silent thank-you that the detective had refused Rikki's invitation. I didn't even want to think about the horrible situation I might have come home to if she'd rushed an armed police officer, screeching like a banshee.

"Anyway, I don't think he believed me." Rikki glared out the window. "That man is *pilikia*. Trouble. All he brings with him is trouble." She blew out a breath and then shifted her gaze to the coffee table, staring forlornly down at the bag of takeout. "Thank you for picking up dinner, but I'm afraid I'm just not hungry anymore," she said quietly.

I couldn't blame her—after the encounter with the homicide detective, I'd lost my appetite too. I grabbed the Sir Spamalot's bag and carried it to the kitchen, sticking it in the fridge. When I returned to the living room, Rikki was watching an episode of *Hawaii Five-O*. I rejoined her on the couch, and we sat in silence. I tried to focus on the procedural drama in paradise, but it reminded me too much of my poor aunt's current situation. Apparently, the parallels weren't lost on her either. A few minutes into the episode, she stood up and walked toward the stairs.

"I think I'm just going to go to bed," she said. "Good night, Kaley."

"Good night." I turned off the television and trudged up to my own room. Feeling helpless, I climbed into bed. I knew of three people who might have wanted Louana Watson dead, but so far I couldn't prove that any of them had committed the crime. It seemed that with each day that passed, Detective Ray was becoming more convinced of Rikki's guilt. If one of my leads didn't pan out soon, the next time he showed up on our doorstep, my aunt could end up behind bars.

CHAPTER TEN

———

Rikki decided to take the next day off from work, claiming she wasn't feeling well. Though she didn't say as much, I suspected the real reason she'd opted to stay home was to protect her business. She'd already lost two employees in less than a week. Now that the police had made it clear she was the lead suspect in Louana's murder investigation, she was probably worried that her presence might rattle the rest of the staff or even scare off the customers.

Unable to get hold of Jamie, I chanced driving Rikki's Vespa to work. It was either that or call and beg Noa for another ride, and I was beginning to worry that I'd been overstepping my bounds with him over the past few days. As much as I wanted to be around him, I couldn't just expect him to drop everything to chauffeur me around the island. He wasn't my boyfriend, after all.

And whose fault is that? my pesky conscience taunted as I begrudgingly pulled on my helmet. I started the scooter and revved the engine before rocketing out of the driveway much faster than intended. As it turned out, the trip to work wasn't so bad. In fact, as much as I hated to admit it, zipping along on the little purple Vespa was actually kind of fun.

Despite Rikki's personal woes, business at Happy Hula was booming. A large party arrived at the resort for a wedding that weekend, and nearly two dozen guests crowded into the tiny shop in search of dresses to wear to the rehearsal dinner and reception. Rose and I divided the party into two groups and spent the morning scurrying around the sales floor, helping the women find garments in the right size and making dress style and color recommendations. By the time each customer had visited Tonya at the register to complete their purchase, it was almost eleven.

Without my aunt or Harmony there, I was in charge of running the boutique on my own, and the rush put me behind on my managerial duties. When there was finally a lull in customer traffic, I headed to Rikki's office to run the previous day's sales reports. Next, I moved on to building the staff schedule for the next two weeks. I put Luka down for the early shift, which was when I would be working. So far this morning, he'd kept busy in the stockroom, and I suspected he was avoiding me—but he couldn't hide from me forever. One way or another, I'd find out where he'd been after the luau on Saturday night.

I also made a few adjustments to Harmony's schedule. I'll admit that I felt a teensy bit of wicked satisfaction when I assigned her with closing shifts every night for the rest of the week and over the Fourth of July holiday weekend. As it turns out, being the store manager does have its perks.

Once I'd finalized the schedule, I pulled out my cell phone, intending to text Jamie and make sure she'd made it home all right after she'd sobered up the night before. To my surprise, I had a message from Noa asking me to meet him at the Loco Moco Café on my break. I dropped by the bathroom to do a quick makeup check and then let Tonya and Rose know I was stepping out for lunch.

When I arrived, he was already waiting for me at the front counter, dressed in gray and black plaid shorts and a fitted black T-shirt. "I ordered you a pineapple iced tea," he said, handing me the drink when I took a seat next to him. "I know it's not the same as that sugar water they try to pass for tea in Georgia, but I remembered that you used to order it all the time." He nudged a ramekin of fresh pineapple chunks toward me. "And here's your side of extra fruit."

Aww. I stared down at the bowl of fruit, feeling touched by his thoughtfulness. Whenever we'd gone out for lunch in the past, I'd always ordered extra pineapple to add to my tea. Though it seemed like such an insignificant detail, that fact that he'd remembered meant a lot to me. "Thanks," I said, smiling at him.

"Don't mention it." He leaned closer, his dark eyebrows knit together in a look of concern. "So what happened last night?" he asked, keeping his voice low. "Who was Rikki's mystery visitor?"

"It was Ray Kahoalani," I said grimly. "The detective." The server behind the counter approached and took our lunch orders. When he was gone again, I filled Noa in on the details of Detective Ray's late-night house call. "Someone told him they witnessed Rikki attacking Louana in the parking lot last week, but it was a misunderstanding. She told me she'd been demonstrating some self-defense moves. I don't think he believed her." My shoulders slumped. "And when I tried to tell him everything we'd found out, he gave me the brush off."

"It's all right," Noa said, giving me a comforting smile. "All we really have right now are a couple of theories. Once we've got some hard evidence, we can take that to the detective. Then he'll have to listen." He took a sip of his drink. "For now, let's focus on Erin Malone. Has she returned your call yet?"

I shook my head. "As far as I know, she hasn't come by the shop either. Maybe she doesn't want to be found."

"Well, if she won't come to us, then we need to go to her. She might be working today." Noa's expression turned thoughtful. "I know who we can ask."

The food arrived, and I polished off my tropical Cobb salad while Noa wolfed down half a pulled-pork sandwich. When we'd finished eating, he led me across the main lobby toward the front desk. A skinny young blonde sat behind the counter, her blue doe eyes glued to a computer screen. She looked up as we approached and greeted us with a bright smile.

"Hey, Noa," she said cheerily. "How's it going?"

Noa flashed her a *shaka* sign with his right hand. "Can't complain," he replied in an equally warm tone. He placed a hand on the small of my back to nudge me forward, and I wasn't sure if the tingling I felt from his touch was real or imaginary. "Summer, this is Kaley Kalua. She's the new store manager at the Happy Hula Dress Boutique."

The young woman grinned and bobbed her head. "Cool! I love that shop." She looked from Noa to me. "So how can I help you two today?"

I let Noa do the talking. He offered her a charming smile, one that showed off his killer dimples. "We're looking for someone on the housekeeping staff. Do you know if Erin Malone is working today?"

Summer removed the pencil that was holding her hair atop her head. The blonde strands fell, cascading freely about her shoulders. She bit her lip, and her thin eyebrows drew together. "I'm not sure," she said, an apology in her tone.

"Is there someone else we could ask?" I met her gaze, feeling hopeful. "I need to talk to her as soon as possible, but she didn't answer her phone. It's really important."

Summer nibbled her lower lip. She cast a look around, as if making sure no one else was within earshot. Then she leaned over the counter, beckoning for us to move closer. "There's a cleaning supply closet at the end of that hall." Summer raised a slender arm and gestured to a hallway at the opposite end of the lobby. "Only the housekeeping staff is allowed back there, but their schedule is posted to the wall, if you want to pop in there really quick and take a peek. Just try not to let anyone see you." She rolled her eyes. "If guests find out where all the extra mini shampoo bottles are stored, we'd probably run out by the end of the week."

I did a mental fist pump. "Thanks, Summer." I smiled gratefully at her.

"You're welcome." She waved as we hurried away from the counter.

I recognized the hall Summer had pointed out as the one Jimmy Toki had escorted Rikki and me through on the morning I'd found Louana's body. The housekeeping supply closet was at the far end, right next to the exit that led to the path behind the lagoon. I knocked softly, and we stood silent for several moments, waiting. When no one responded, I gripped the handle. It was unlocked, so I carefully pushed open the door and peeked inside. Noa and I traded a look. "There's no one in there," I whispered.

Noa glanced back down the deserted hallway and then gave me a thumbs-up. "We're clear. Let's make this quick."

I slipped into the room, and he followed, pulling the door closed behind us. The supply room was about five times the size of a normal walk-in closet. The far wall was lined with shelves full of fresh folded towels, tiny bottles of shampoo and conditioner, and other toiletries that were provided for guests of the resort when their rooms were freshened. The other side of the closet contained various cleaning supplies.

I spotted a clipboard hanging on the wall next to the door. The words *WEEKLY SCHEDULE* were printed across the top of the first page. "Found it!" I exclaimed in a hushed voice.

Noa smirked. "Why are you still whispering?" He looked pointedly around the room. "We're alone."

"Oh." My cheeks warmed. "Right." I returned my attention to the clipboard in my hands. Noa moved closer, and we peered down at the pages together, scanning the print for Erin's name. I found her on the second page. According to the schedule, she was off that day, but she had worked from three in the afternoon to ten at night on Saturday.

"So she *was* here on the night that Louana was murdered," I breathed. When I considered that she'd also threatened Lou and had a strong motive, my theory that Erin could be the killer was beginning to seem even more plausible. I pumped my fist.
The celebration over our discovery was short-lived. The doorknob began to turn as I was placing the clipboard back on the wall. *Crap!* Summer had told us not to get caught. I flashed Noa a panicked look and then sent my gaze around the room, searching frantically for another way out. There was none. I spied a large bin marked *Lost and Found* a few steps away and, thinking fast, moved over to it just as the door to the supply closet pushed open.

A plump Polynesian woman in an Aloha Lagoon staff uniform appeared in the doorway, pulling a cart of toiletries and cleaning supplies beside her. She stared at us, her expression blank. "Can I help you?" she asked in a thick accent.

"Here it is, honey!" I exclaimed, stooping to reach my hand into the bin full of lost items. Without looking, I scooped up the first item that brushed against my fingers. "I found your—" I glanced down at my hand and nearly choked. I was holding a Speedo. A neon orange Speedo. "—bathing suit," I finished, my cheeks flushing.

To his credit, Noa didn't even flinch. "All right! Thanks, babe," he said, taking the DayGlo banana hammock from my outstretched hand. "Now we can hit the beach." He gently gripped my arm and tugged me toward the door.

I spotted a bin full of little hand sanitizer bottles on the nearest shelf, and I snagged one as he pulled me past. The cleaning lady arched an eyebrow at me. A nervous laugh bubbled out of my throat. "I'm, er, a real stickler for hygiene."

The woman must have bought our story, because she stepped aside to let us out into the hall without protest. She shook her head and muttered something to herself in her native tongue before pushing the cart into the supply closet and closing the door behind her.

"That was close," Noa whispered when we were alone in the hall. His dark eyes shone with excitement. "And fun. Way to go on the quick thinking with the lost and found bin." Noa's lips quirked, and his eyes crinkled at the corners. "But maybe next time you can grab something other than a used weenie bikini."

If my face burned any hotter, it might actually catch fire. I opened the bottle of hand sanitizer and dumped half the container into my hands, gagging as the strong scent of disinfectant permeated the air around us. "Yuck," I muttered. I offered the bottle to Noa, and he stuffed the Speedo into his back pocket before slathering the gel on his palms.

The door on the opposite side of the hall opened, and I nearly jumped out of my skin. "Kaley? Noa?" Jimmy Toki poked his head through the open doorway. "I thought I heard someone out here." His nose twitched as he sniffed the air, and his face puckered. "Did someone spill a whole bottle of Purell?"

"Hi, Jimmy," I said, giving him a little wave. "It's kind of a long story." The adrenaline from our little mission began to wear off, and I realized that the tall, handsome head of security might be able to help us. I grinned at him. "Mind if we come in and explain?"

He gave me a curious look. "No, of course not," he said after a moment. "Come on in."

Noa shot me a questioning glance but followed as Jimmy stepped back to allow us to enter the room. Every inch of the far wall was covered with television monitors, each displaying a live camera feed from a different area of the resort.

In the opposite corner, an old oak desk was set up to face the screens.

"Okay." Jimmy closed the door and then came to stand in front of us, his arms crossed over his broad shoulders. "What's going on?" His gaze flicked to the bright orange mankini sticking out of Noa's pocket, and he flinched. "That yours, brah?"

Before Noa could answer, I cleared my throat, bringing Jimmy's attention back to me. It was best to be honest with him about what Noa and I had been up to. Jimmy was the head of security, after all. It would help to have him on our side if Detective Ray came after Rikki again. I took a deep breath and then squared my shoulders. "I'm sure you've heard the rumors around the resort," I began, meeting his gaze. "People are saying that my aunt was the one who killed Louana Watson. Now the police seem to think so too. Noa and I are trying to prove Rikki's innocence, and we could really use your help."

Jimmy's jaw clenched. He glanced from Noa as to me as he considered my plea. My heart began to pound in my chest as I waited for him to break the silence. "It's my duty to keep everyone on this resort safe," he said finally. "That includes both the guests and the employees. Part of my job is to read people and assess whether or not they could pose a threat." He uncrossed his arms. "Your Aunt Rikki is a kind and generous woman." His mouth twitched. "A bit eccentric but certainly no threat. What can I do to help?"

Relief flooded through me. I glanced past Jimmy to the wall of monitors, an idea taking root. "Where are the security cameras set up around the resort?" I asked, gesturing to the screens.

Jimmy sent a look over his shoulder, following my gaze. "Right now we have cameras set up in all the high-traffic areas— the lagoon, the main lobby and hallways, the courtyard. Places like that."

"What about the shops?"

The beefy head of security shook his head. "There aren't currently cameras set up in Happy Hula, if that's what you're after. The police wanted to know the same thing." He held up a finger. "And before you ask, there's not one in the back alley where Louana was killed either," he added. "I'm sorry, Kaley. I wish I had better news."

"You mentioned there were cameras in the lobbies and some of the hallways?" When he nodded, I grinned. "Then you might still be able to help us." I glanced at a laptop computer on Jimmy's desk. "Could you pull up the footage from the courtyard and this hallway on Saturday night?" Detective Ray seemed to be focusing on Rikki, so he might not have been looking for Erin in any of the security feeds that he reviewed. If that were the case, he might have overlooked something important.

Jimmy sat down behind the desk and began scrolling through a folder of video files on the laptop. "Can you narrow down the timeline?" he asked, glancing over his shoulder at me. "What exactly are you hoping to find?"

Noa stepped up beside me. "We've been checking out a few different people who may have wanted Lou dead. I think what Kaley's getting at is that maybe one of them will show up in the feed out in the courtyard sometime after Happy Hula closed on Saturday. If we could place any of our three suspects near the shop around the time that Louana was killed, it could help convince the police to shift their attention toward them instead of Rikki." He flicked a glance at me, raising his eyebrows. "Right?"

I beamed at him, glad that we were on the same wavelength. "Yes," I agreed, turning my gaze toward Jimmy. "And one of our people of interest is a housekeeper named Erin Malone. We were in the hallway because we'd just visited the supply closet to check Erin's work schedule." My cheeks warmed when Jimmy gave me a stern look. "She worked until ten on Saturday night, so she was definitely at the resort. If the cameras picked her up anywhere after that, we can prove that she stuck around after work. That might be enough to get Detective Ray to vet her alibi, if he hasn't already."

A frown wrinkled Jimmy's handsome face. "So you want review the footage from both the hallway and the courtyard cameras beginning around the time that the boutique closed on Saturday?"

"Starting around eight in the evening," I said, nodding. "And Rikki and I arrived to open up on Sunday at around a quarter till eight in the morning—so maybe we should look at the footage running until an hour or two before then." I wasn't an expert, but, having seen Lou's pale corpse up close, it had seemed to me that she'd been dead for a while before I'd found her. "I realize it's a tall order," I said, my tone pleading. "But I wouldn't ask if it weren't important. If you can just locate that window of time in the footage, I'll come by after work and watch it all myself."

Jimmy shook his head. "No, that's all right. I'll do it. Who are the other two people you want me to keep an eye out for?"

"Marco Rossini and Luka Hale," Noa answered. "Are you familiar with them? Marco is a bellhop, and Luka works for Happy Hula."

Jimmy's brow furrowed. "I know Luka, and I'm sure I'd know Marco if I saw him. I'll pull up their pictures from their employment files to be sure."

"Thanks, Jimmy," I said, feeling my smile stretch from ear to ear. "If I can ever do anything to repay you, just name it."

The brawny man smiled modestly. "Just doing my job. I'll call Noa if I see Erin, Luka, or Marco in any of the security footage." He escorted us back into the hall.

"Thanks, brah." Noa bumped his fist.

I checked my watch as Jimmy disappeared back into the security office. "My lunch break is up," I said, glancing at Noa. "I need to get back to work."

Noa walked me down the hall toward the main lobby. "Think Jimmy will find anything?"

"I hope so." A sigh slipped from me as we crossed through the double doors leading out into the courtyard. "I'd feel better if we could find something concrete. Or if we could at least get hold of Erin Malone." I'd already gone to her apartment complex, called her, and looked for her at work. I was running out of ideas. "If the universe were to drop her in my lap right about now, that would be super." I raised my eyes toward the sky, as if daring the clouds to grant my wish.

Noa walked me to the shop entrance. "I'm going to grab my laptop from the car and post up somewhere in the sun," he said. "I've got a big client project to work on, but it's too nice out to stay indoors all afternoon." He met my gaze. "Why don't you head back to Loco Moco after work and meet me on the patio? Maybe Jimmy will have some news for us by then."

"Are you sure?" I wrinkled my brow. "If you have work to do, I don't want to distract you." As much as I wanted to spend time with him, I didn't want to keep him from running his business.

"It's fine," Noa insisted. "You get off at four, right? Three and a half hours is plenty of time for me to finish the website mockup that I'm working on. I'm almost done with it."

"All right. I'll see you there." I watched him retrace his steps across the courtyard, smirking when he paused to deposit the orange Speedo in the nearest trash can. When he'd disappeared back through the main building's double doors, I turned to enter the shop.

"There she is right now." Tonya's cheery voice pulled my attention to the front counter as soon as I stepped through the front door. "Kaley, you have a visitor."

I plastered what I hoped was a polite expression on my face and made my way toward the cash register. A young woman with curly brown hair and a heart-shaped face stood there, watching me through narrowed eyes. My smile faded at the sight of her scowl.

"You're Kaley?" she asked, her tone impatient.

I nodded uncertainly, wondering why a woman I'd never met seemed so irritated with me. "Can I help you?"

"I sure hope so," she said, stepping forward and placing her hands on her hips. "My name is Erin Malone. I want to know why you've been looking for me."

CHAPTER ELEVEN

———

I blinked at Erin, feeling the blood rush to my face. Judging by her angry expression, I assumed she hadn't bought the voicemail ploy about winning the free charm bracelet. Not wanting things to escalate in front of Tonya or the handful of customers milling about the store, I forced myself to stay calm. "It's nice to finally meet you, Erin," I said, which wasn't entirely a lie. After all, I had spent most of the past day trying to track her down. "Why don't you come with me? Please," I added, giving her what was meant to be a reassuring look. "I'll only take a few minutes of your time."

Erin placed her hands on her hips, her green eyes narrowed in mistrust. Despite her ugly expression, she was a lovely girl, with soft brown curls, a creamy complexion, and the type of curves I'd only ever dreamed of having. She also had good fashion sense, playing up her figure with a green shirt dress that was cinched at her narrow waist by a brown belt. She completed the look with ballet flats that matched the belt and a pair of heart-shaped sunglasses, which were currently holding the hair back from her face. It occurred to me that if I'd met her under different circumstances, perhaps we could have been friends.

After a few moments of staring at me with that suspicious scowl, she finally relented. "I'll give you five minutes," she said in a clipped tone.

"Harmony and Sara are here now," Tonya told me. "Harm's in the office, and Sara's helping Luka unpack a new dress shipment in the stockroom."

Crap. The two most private places in the shop were occupied. "Thanks, Tonya," I said, ignoring the cashier's curious look. I glanced around the store, relieved for once that there were only a few customers browsing the racks. I smiled at Erin. "Right this way," I said, leading her across the sales floor to an empty corner. The little nook was obscured from the view of the front counter by a display of mannequins in sundresses.

"Why are you stalking me?" Erin demanded as soon as we reached the corner.

I took a breath to speak but caught it when she steamrolled forward.

"First, I got a notification from security at my apartment complex that you came to the front gate looking for me. Then, I stopped by the pool to relax with a drink on my day off and found out from Timo that you were asking about me there too." Her green eyes flashed. "Oh, and *then* there was that weird voicemail about winning a charm bracelet. I called the office at my apartment complex, and they didn't know anything about your giveaway. And neither did your cashier." Her lip curled. "I am totally still taking the bracelet, by the way."

I gave myself a mental kick. I should have known that phony contest ploy wasn't going to work. "Of course," I said, nodding.

Erin harrumphed, as if my permission didn't matter. "I've never even met you," she said stiffly. "So why are you harassing me?"

I lifted my chin. It wasn't as if I'd been trying to hide the fact that I'd been looking for her, but I could understand her anger. "I'm sorry if I freaked you out. You're just a hard woman to get hold of," I said, meeting her gaze. "I want to ask you a few questions about Louana Watson."

The young housekeeper let out a low groan. "Of course," she groused. "The woman is dead, and she's still making my life hell. I should have known this was about her when you asked me to come into this shop, of all places."

"So you admit that you knew her?"

Erin nodded, her glossy lips pressed tight.

"And that you threatened her?"

She rolled her eyes. "I'm guessing you heard that from Timo," she said, cutting me a dark look. "I never actually threatened her." She blew out a frustrated breath. "So I had a few drinks and mouthed off at the bar—who hasn't done that? I was just blowing off steam."

I squinted at her. "You said that Lou would get exactly what she deserved, and then she died."

Erin shrugged her shoulders. "Coincidence," she said, but her voice quavered slightly. She dropped her gaze to the ground and was silent for a few seconds, as if she was considering the gravity of that so-called coincidence. Then her eyes snapped to me, and the scowl slipped back into place. "I came in here and cussed her out—and she deserved it."

I frowned. Was that really all she'd meant? "What about Marco?" I asked, switching tactics. "Why would you only give Lou grief? He's not exactly blameless in all this." I leaned forward slightly in anticipation.

At the mention of her ex, the color drained from Erin's face. All the anger seemed to seep out of the woman, and her eyes pinched. "I don't want to talk about him," she said quietly.

"But he's the whole reason you were angry with Louana in the first place," I pressed.

Erin winced, as if the mere thought of her sleazy ex hurt her. "Have you ever been cheated on?" she asked.

I swallowed, forcing down my own wave of pain. "I have," I answered honestly.

"Then you know the anguish that comes with being betrayed like that," she said, tugging nervously at the sleeve of her dress. "How it feels to lose your own sense of confidence and self-worth because of some arrogant jerk."

I blinked at her. She'd hit the nail on the head. "Yeah. I do."

Erin stared at the ground, her expression hardening. "Then you should understand why I never want to hear that spineless douchebag's name ever again." Her back stiffened, and she moved away from me. "There. Your five minutes are up." Erin turned and stalked toward the jewelry displays. She snatched a gold bangle bracelet from the stand. "I'm not paying for this," she called out when Tonya made a squeak of protest. She slipped it on her wrist and disappeared through the shop door.

"Let her go," I said when Rose left her post near the changing rooms, hurrying toward the shop entrance. "I'll pay for it." Both Tonya and Rose gave me skeptical looks "It was a present," I lied.

I quickly handed Tonya my credit card and silently prayed she wouldn't press the issue. Thankfully, she didn't. I felt a pang of buyer's remorse as I scribbled my signature on the credit slip. Erin had grabbed one of our pricier bracelets. Trying to clear Aunt Rikki's name was getting expensive. I shoved my card back into my wallet, vowing that *this* time, I really was going to cut it in half as soon as I got home.

I made my way to the rear hallway to deposit my purse in one of the storage cubbies. As I went, my thoughts shifted back to my conversation with Erin. I wasn't sure what to make of the fiery young housekeeper. She claimed to want nothing to do with her ex, which would squash my theory that she'd killed Louana to get her out of the way so she could have Marco back. She'd also claimed her threats toward Lou had been empty—nothing more than drunk ranting.

But that look. I pictured the emotion that had passed behind Erin's eyes and the telltale tremor of guilt in her voice. *Maybe the timing of her threat in relation to Louana's murder wasn't the coincidence she claimed.* She'd certainly given me a lot to think about. Though I regretted that Erin had stormed out before I could coax her to give me her alibi for the rest of Saturday night, I hoped that the security footage that Jimmy Toki was reviewing would shed some light on the scorned housekeeper's whereabouts.

The next hour dragged on. Harmony had set up shop in Rikki's office to practice reconciling sales reports using notes that Rikki had provided for her. When I asked her if she'd been the one to tell the police about my aunt "assaulting" Louana in the employee parking lot, she gave me a wide-eyed look of mock innocence and claimed she didn't know what I was talking about. "You shouldn't go around accusing people of stuff, Kaley," she said with thinly veiled disdain. A sneer curled her lips. "Although, judging by the cellulite on those thighs of yours, it looks like jumping to conclusions is the only type of workout you've been getting lately."

I stalked out of the office before Harmony became the second Happy Hula assistant manager to be murdered in less than a week. I certainly didn't head straight for one of the changing rooms to evaluate my thighs in the full-length mirror. *Nope.* And the fact that I pulled my skirt down a little lower on my hips so that the hem line touched my knees was completely unrelated. *That's my story, and I'm sticking to it.*

Jamie dropped in the store around two fifteen. She spotted me rearranging a rack of peasant tops by size and bounded toward me, a wide grin on her pretty face. I noted that she'd donned different clothes and fresh makeup since I'd last seen her. Today she was wearing a pair of green shorts with a white tank top that had two purple clams printed across the chest to resemble the seashell bra that Ariel had worn in *The Little Mermaid.* "Glad to see you made it home in one piece last night," I said dryly.

She winked. "Who says I made it to *my* home?" When I raised a curious eyebrow, she gestured to her outfit. "I always keep spare clothes in my car just in case. You never know when you'll need them." Jamie leaned closer and lowered her voice. "I met a hot surfer at the café last night after I left the pool. Let's just say the ocean isn't the only place where he hangs ten." She waggled her eyebrows.

"So we've already worked our way up to oversharing, I see." I smirked. "This friendship of ours seems to be moving awfully fast."

Jamie giggled. "Okay, fine. I'll dial back the kissing and telling—or the *telling* part, at least." She gently nudged me with her elbow. "But first you have to tell me how things went with Noa last night. Am I a great wing woman or what?"

I rolled my eyes. "You might want to work on your skills. You were about as subtle as a foghorn." As sigh slipped from me, and I shook my head. "Nothing happened though—and nothing is going to happen."

Jamie poked out her bottom lip. "Aww, why not?" she pouted. "It's obvious that you've got the hots for him. And the chemistry between you two is off the charts."

"Is it?" I frowned. While I still felt a strong attraction to Noa, I didn't get the impression that he felt the same way.

"Are you blind?" Jamie blinked at me. "Didn't you see the way he looked at you last night at the pool? Or at Beachcomber's? He ditched two hot chicks to take you home," she said, giving me a wry smile.

I wrinkled my nose. "I still don't get why he invited Harmony in the first place."

"Me neither." Jamie shrugged. "But who cares? Noa is into you. You're into him. Why are y'all making it so complicated?"

I hung another peasant top on the rack and then turned back to face her. "Because it *is* complicated." I sighed again, guilt settling heavily in my gut. "Has he told you that until this week, we hadn't even spoken in five and a half years?"

Jamie grimaced. "Yeah. But I only got the cliff notes version. Noa doesn't have the same oversharing issue that I do."

I glanced up as a petite woman with short gray hair ambled over and began browsing the rack to our right. "Do you have this in a four?" she asked me, holding up a lacy green Vera Wang dress.

I helped the woman find the size she'd requested. When she'd thanked me and headed toward the checkout, I turned back to Jamie. "I broke Noa's heart," I told her. "I loved him, but by the time he wanted to be with me, I was already engaged to Bryan—and then I left. I felt too guilty for hurting him to try to keep in touch." I felt my throat tighten. "The only reason he's even speaking to me now is because he's always had a soft spot for Aunt Rikki, and she needs our help. I'm not sure we'll ever repair our friendship, let alone start a relationship." I looked away so she couldn't see the tears pricking the corners of my eyes. "Maybe that's what I deserve after the way I treated him."

"Oh, Kaley. Bless your heart." Jamie reached out and patted my shoulder. "You've been holding on to that for years, huh?"

I forced a smile, though I was pretty sure she could see the pain in my eyes. "Yep."

An odd little smile played across her lips. "I really think you should talk to him about it. His side of the story is a bit different."

"What do you mean?" I blinked at her.

Jamie held up her hands. "Not for me to tell. Just promise me you'll talk to him, okay?"

I stared at her, my guilt dissolving into confusion. "Okay," I said after a moment.

"Good." She nodded, seemingly satisfied. "Well, I've gotta run. Hot Surfer Guy dropped me off here so I could get my car, and I figured I'd pop in to say hello before I head home. It's my day off." Her gaze shifted to the display of new bathing suit cover-ups I'd helped Tonya hang along the far wall earlier that morning. Her smile widened. "But first, I'm going to buy that *adorable* new coral crocheted tunic." She sighed. "I'm telling you, Kaley. I would go broke if I spent as much time in here as you do."

"It helps to have the extra discount." I quirked my lips. "Resort employees get ten percent, but Happy Hula staffers get twenty."

"Jealous," Jamie sang, and she stuck her tongue out at me. "I'll catch ya later." She gave a little wave and then walked over to grab her new cover-up.

When she was gone, I finished reorganizing the rack of peasant tops, my thoughts still focused on our conversation. What had Noa told her about our falling out? How would it change anything? Even if he was over me, the fact that I'd completely thrown away our eighteen years of friendship by not keeping in touch was unacceptable. Just because Jamie thought that he and I should air our grievances, it didn't mean that anything I could say to him would make him forget how horrible I'd been. *So, what did he tell her to make her think we could work things out?*

I had to file it away for later thought when a door slammed, bringing my attention to the back hallway. Luka appeared on the sales floor, red-faced and features tight with anger. Sara was on his heels. The young cashier met my gaze as she followed after him. Though she kept her expression composed, I could see the alarm flash behind her eyes. A little red flag rose up in the back of my mind.

I hurried across the shop to intercept them before they reached the front door. "Luka, is everything all right?" I asked, keeping my tone even.

He halted, narrowing his dark eyes at me. "Everything is fine," he said, though the coldness in his voice suggested otherwise. "It's two thirty. I was only supposed to work from nine to two. I'm going home." He brushed past me and walked stiffly out the door.

I frowned. "What's wrong with him?" I asked Sara.

She shot a glance toward the cash register, where Tonya was busy wiping down the counter. "Can I talk to you for a moment in private?"

"Sure." I motioned for her to follow me to the back of the store. I leaned against the wall just outside Rikki's office and crossed my arms over my chest. "What's up?"

Sara placed her hands on her hips. "Luka just snapped," she said, her expression bewildered. "We were almost done unpacking the skirt delivery that came in today. I grabbed one of the tag guns off the shelf so we could put the price stickers on them, and I realized it was the one that Louana had labeled with her name." She shrugged. "I figured there was no point in keeping it on there, so I peeled it off. But Luka saw me do it, and he totally flipped out."

I squinted. "Why would he be upset about you removing the label?"

"It wasn't really about the label." Sara cast a glance over her shoulder, as if making sure we were really alone. When she met my gaze, her face pinched. "He started muttering to himself about how things were better now that Lou didn't have control over him anymore." Sara chewed her lip. "When I asked him what he meant, he wouldn't answer me at first. I probably shouldn't have pressed him, but I was curious."

"What did he tell you?" I asked, keeping my voice low.

Sara sucked in a breath. "Don't tell him I told you this, okay?"

"I won't."

"Luka said the reason he used to do all of Lou's chores for her was because she was blackmailing him. She said that if he didn't do whatever she told him to, then she would claim he'd sexually assaulted her." Sara grimaced. "Isn't that crazy?"

I stared at her, feeling the blood drain from my face. That was a very serious accusation. "Why didn't he tell Rikki?"

Sara shrugged. "No clue. This was the first I'd heard of it. I asked him how long it had been going on, and he said almost a month. At first she was only making him do mundane chores around work, but he said that over the past few weeks, she'd started harassing him on his off time—asking him to run errands for her and stuff." Sara puffed her cheeks, letting her breath out in a steady stream. "That's pretty heavy, right?"

I nodded. "Why did he seem so angry at you when he left?"

"Because I told him that he should report it." Sara stuck out her chin. "It doesn't matter that Louana's dead. Luka needs to tell the police. That way, they don't think he was trying to hide it from them, since that would seem suspicious. That's the right thing to do, isn't it? Tell the police?" Sara blinked at me, her narrow face twisted in a look of uncertainty.

"I think so," I said, smiling to reassure her.

"Thanks." Sara's shoulders sagged. "It was just kind of scary. He said he wished he hadn't told me—and then he said that if I told anyone else, he'd make sure I regretted it." She sighed. "I'm sorry I even asked in the first place."

"Well, I'm glad you told me," I said, squeezing her shoulder. I sent Sara up to the front counter to take over for Tonya, since it was time for both Rose and her to go home. I remained in the hallway, a dozen thoughts pinging through my mind. I felt bad that poor Sara had borne the brunt of Luka's anger, but she might have uncovered his motive for murder—which was more than I'd gotten out of the secretive stockroom worker.

Blackmail. That's what Luka's been hiding. If Louana had convinced Rikki or the police that he had assaulted her, it would have cost him a lot more than his job. He might have been arrested, and that would have followed him around for the rest of his life. Being charged as a sex offender could have potentially affected everything from college scholarships to job prospects. Could Luka have killed Louana to protect his freedom and future?

CHAPTER TWELVE

———

I sent Harmony out to the sales floor to begin preparing the mannequins for our Fourth of July weekend display, and I shut myself in Rikki's office. I spent the rest of my shift there, my legs curled beneath me on the desk chair as I worked on my aunt's laptop. I searched the vendor catalogs she'd bookmarked and ordered a shipment of Michael Kors peep-toe wedge sandals in three different colors. Rikki preferred to save electronic receipt copies in their own folder, so I saved a PDF file with the purchase and delivery information and dragged it toward a folder on the desktop labeled *Orders*.

As I saving the file, another little icon near the bottom of the screen caught my attention. It was the same little folder image, but it had Louana's name on it. My curiosity stirred. Though the folder probably only contained work-related documents, it couldn't hurt to take a peek. I double-clicked the little image, and a window popped up, revealing the folder's contents.

To my disappointment, there was nothing suspicious inside—no subfolders full of incriminating photos or documents labeled *List of People Who Want Me Dead*. All the folder contained were a couple of inventory spreadsheets and a list of other clothing vendors. I recognized the names of some. Louana had placed an asterisk next to the ones she'd browsed most often, including the online catalog I'd just visited to order the Michael Kors shoes.

One vendor was even highlighted in yellow. I copied the website URL from the list and pasted it into the internet browser, making a little squeal of delight when I spied an adorable yellow bikini with pink palm trees on it from Olivia Jake's new Island

Punk collection. I was pretty sure we already had the same bathing suit in stock at the boutique. Louana must have ordered it from this vendor. *The woman may have been nasty, but she had great taste in fashion*, I thought, bookmarking the site so I could browse it when I placed our next product order.

The office door opened without warning, and Harmony stepped inside. "There's a woman at the front counter asking for you," she said in a bored tone.

I lifted an eyebrow. "She asked for me by name?" I wasn't expecting anyone. Had Erin come back to give me another tongue lashing?

"Yes." Harmony heaved an exasperated sigh. "For some reason, someone at this store actually *wants* to talk to you." She rolled her eyes and then flounced out of the office.

I (just barely) resisted the urge to make faces behind Harmony's back as I followed her to the front of the store. A woman in a pale blue skirt and white blouse stood with her back to us, waiting at the counter. Her reddish brown hair was rolled into a low bun at the nape of her neck. She turned around as I approached, and my stomach did a barrel roll. "What are you doing here?" I practically hissed at Felicity Chase.

The *Aloha Sun* reporter's lips stretched in a wide grin. "Just the woman I wanted to see," she said, unaffected by my reaction.

I glared at her. "Aren't you banned from the resort? I'll call security."

Felicity laughed. "I'm not bothering anyone," she said. "I'm a paying customer." She held up a wide-brimmed beach hat and a brown short-sleeved Donna Karan dress that had been lying on the counter in front of her. She pushed them toward Sara and handed the young cashier her credit card. "Ring these up, please." Turning back to me, she added, "And as a customer, I asked to speak with the manager on duty." Her eyes gleamed. "So you have to talk to me."

I glanced at my watched and smirked. It was two minutes after four. "Sorry, but I'm off the clock." I unpinned my name tag from my blouse and pointed to Harmony, who was watching our exchange with her brows knit in confusion. "She's the manager on duty," I said, thinking this was the only time since I'd known Harm that I was actually glad to see her.

Felicity's lips parted. "But—"

"Sorry," I interrupted. I met Harmony's gaze, grinning. "Miss Chase is all yours."

"Okay," the brunette assistant manager said slowly. She looked from me to Felicity, squinting. "Hold up. You're Felicity Chase!" Her expression brightened. "I've seen your picture on the *Aloha Sun* website. I love your entertainment column."

"Thanks," Felicity said, looking pleased with herself. I spun on my heel, intent on retrieving my purse, when she reached out and placed a hand on my arm. "Kaley, wait," she pleaded. "Just give me a few minutes of your time, and then I'll leave. I promise." She gave me a sincere look. "I want to interview you about your attempts to clear your aunt's name in Louana Watson's murder investigation."

Both Sara and Harmony were staring at us now, their eyes narrowed in twin looks of curiosity. I felt my blood rush to my face. "Fine," I said through clenched teeth. "Follow me." I wrenched my arm out of the reporter's grasp and walked briskly back toward Rikki's office. As soon as the door closed behind us, I rounded on her. "How do you know about that?" I demanded, my anger bubbling over.

Felicity's lips quirked. "I have my sources," she said, her tone smug. When I glowered at her, she sighed and threw up her hands. "Okay, fine. I sneaked into the pool area and spoke to that know-it-all bartender, Tim, and he said you were asking questions about a woman that had threatened Louana."

"His name is Timo. I thought reporters paid better attention to detail." I felt a sense of satisfaction when her cheeks turned pink. Though I was annoyed that Timo had spilled the beans to the nosy reporter, I couldn't exactly fault him for it. Felicity was right—he had told me everything he'd overheard Erin Malone say about Lou. "Why should I talk to you about any of this?" I asked the reporter.

"Because I want to help."

I eyed her skeptically. "What's in it for you?"

Felicity grinned. "A story," she answered matter-of-factly. A strand of hair had come loose from her bun, and she brushed it out of her face. "Just hear me out, okay? Think about it—a down-on-her-luck ex-wife of a megastar athlete breezes into town and solves a murder case in order to save her beloved aunt from going to prison." Her lips twitched. "I don't know about you, but in my opinion, that has major blockbuster potential."

I gave her a blank look. "Blockbuster potential?"

Felicity took a breath. "What I'm saying is that I'm rooting for you. It makes for an excellent human interest piece—especially if you actually find evidence that helps prove your aunt's innocence." Her eyes shone with excitement. "That kind of story could land me a syndicated column, or something even better. Plus true-crime books are flying off the shelves these days. I could land a book deal with movie rights." She grinned. "Who would you want to play you on the big screen? Megan Fox? Emma Watson?" She tilted her head to the side as she gave me an appraising look. "Maybe Shailene Woodley?"

I stared at her for a few moments, feeling bewildered. "You're delusional. I'm trying to protect an innocent person, and all you care about is glory and a book deal?" I pointed to the door. "Get out."

Felicity's expression deflated. "But—"

"Out," I repeated. I opened the office door.

The reporter pursed her lips. "You're making a mistake," she said sulkily.

"No, I'm not." I placed my hands on my hips. "I moved home to get away from the spotlight. I've already had my divorce dragged through every news outlet from here to Hong Kong, thanks to Bryan's celeb status. I'm not going through that again, and I'm not putting Rikki through it either."

Felicity's shoulders slumped. "I'm sorry," she said quietly. To her credit, she sounded sincere. "For what it's worth, I do hope you clear your aunt's name." She lifted her chin. "But I'd be lying if I said I wasn't planning to report it, no matter what the outcome. A good story sells papers." She walked through the open door and then turned back to face me. "Good luck, Kaley."

I gave the reporter a three-minute head start before coming out of the office. I retrieved my purse and breezed across the sales floor, making a beeline for the shop entrance. "Everything okay?" Sara asked as I passed the front counter.

"Yep. Just fine," I said without looking at her. "I'm running late to meet Noa. I'll see you tomorrow." Out of the corner of my eye, I caught Harmony scowling at me.

"Hold up a sec," Sara called. She followed me to the door. "Miss Chase forgot her credit card," she said, showing me a red VISA. "What should I do with it?"

I frowned at the card. I was about ninety-nine percent sure Felicity had left it behind on purpose. Either she thought I'd track her down to return it, or she figured it would give her an excuse to come back to the store and harass me again—or worse, to harass Rikki. "Give it to me," I said, sighing in resignation. I took the card from the cashier's outstretched hand. "I'll return it to her." *Though I ought to charge a round or three of drinks to it first*, I thought as I left the store. *It would serve her right.*

* * *

The wide back patio at the Loco Moco Café had a perfect view of the ocean. A makeshift stage was set up on one end, and a steel drum band was performing instrumental covers of pop music hits as I stepped outside. I spotted Noa seated at one of the wicker tables near the back of the patio, munching on a bowl of chips with pineapple salsa. His laptop was open in front of him, and he was bobbing his head to the music as he worked. I couldn't help but smile. It was kind of adorable.

My promise to Jamie echoed through my thoughts, but I forced it aside. For now, all I cared about was catching him up to speed on the afternoon's events. So much had happened in the few hours since we'd parted ways. "What a day," I said, grabbing a seat across the table from him. "I have so much to tell you. Have you heard from Jimmy yet?"

Noa glanced up from his laptop. "Not yet," he said, his eyes sparkling in the afternoon sun. "But I've got other news." He offered me the bowl of chips. "You go first."

"Where should I start?" I grinned. "We've got a motive for Luka Hale: blackmail." I recounted what I'd learned about Louana's threats to have Luka fired. "She could have ruined his life," I said, grabbing a chip and dipping it into the salsa. "And that's not all." I licked my lips. "You'll never guess who came into Happy Hula this afternoon."

Noa's mouth turned up at the corners. "Elvis?" he teased. "I knew the King was still alive. How's he looking these days?"

I rolled my eyes. "Come on, Noa. I'm not playing around." I leaned forward and lowered my voice. "Erin Malone."

His eyebrows reached for the sky. "What did she say?"

"Aside from reaming me out for essentially stalking her?" I grabbed another chip. "Well, I'll start by telling you what she *didn't* tell me, which was her alibi for Saturday." I felt my face warm. "She sort of stormed out of the store before I could coax it out of her. I did get her to talk about Louana though. Erin claims she was just being a loud drunk the night Timo heard her talking about Lou getting what was coming to her. Then she nearly shut down when I brought up Marco, saying that she never wants to hear that cheating jerk's name again."

Noa grinned. "I'm glad you brought him up." He closed his laptop and set it aside. "Guess who I saw in the lobby on my way into the café? Our favorite slimeball bellhop."

My pulse picked up speed. "Did you talk to him?" I asked, barely able to contain my excitement.

"No." he shook his head. "But I did overhear Marco talking to one of the other bellhops. He was leaving work so he could head to the gym and then grab a shower before his date tonight."

"Marco is already dating again? That was fast." I crinkled my nose. "I guess I shouldn't be surprised, considering he hit on me while I was interrogating him," I added with a shudder.

Noa's lips twitched. "Well, get ready to be surprised after all. This girl must be something special, because he's taking her to dinner at Starlight on the Lagoon."

Both my eyebrows shot up. "You're kidding." Starlight on the Lagoon was the swankiest restaurant in town. With Lou dead less than a week and Erin not speaking to him, who could Marco be taking on such a fancy date?

Noa's expression was deadpan. "I never joke about fine dining." He cracked a smile. "That's not even the best part."

"Okay," I said slowly, not sure what to expect. "Then what is?"

"We have a reservation there tonight at eight o'clock—the same time as Marco and his mystery date. We'll be able to see who he's taking to dinner, and maybe we'll get another chance to talk to him about his alibi."

"How did you manage to get us in?" I asked, unable to hide my surprise. The upscale eatery was popular among the resort guests. Their tables usually filled up quickly, making it difficult to get a reservation.

He shrugged. "I gave them a good price on a website redesign a few months ago, so they owed me a favor."

"Wow." I was genuinely impressed. "You must be really great at your job."

Noa smiled proudly. "I am." He flagged down his waitress, a cute brunette in a Loco Moco T-shirt. "Hey, Carrie. Can I get my check, please?"

The brunette smiled brightly. "Sure thing. You can pay whenever you're ready." She handed it to him and then made her way to another table to take drink orders from a middle-aged couple.

Noa took out his wallet and set a couple of bills down on the table. "I should head home and take a shower myself." He stowed his computer in a canvas bag and slung the strap over his shoulder. "Do you need a ride home to get ready?"

"Not today. I've got Rikki's Vespa."

He smirked. "I can't picture you scooting around town on that thing." Noa rose from the table. "I'll pick you up at seven forty-five."

I hung back for a moment as he left the table, watching him stride across the café patio. My heart raced as the reality of what had just happened began to sink in. I'd just agreed to go to dinner with Noa at the resort's most romantic restaurant. Just the two of us. Under any other circumstances, that would have *date* written all over it.

But it's not one, I reminded myself. *It's a chance to spy on Marco.* Who would his mystery dinner guest be? An accomplice, maybe? I couldn't wait to find out. I jumped up from my chair and hurried home to get ready.

CHAPTER THIRTEEN

Rikki was in the backyard when I arrived home twenty minutes later. I walked outside to find her doing yoga in the grass next to the flower garden we'd planted when I was in college.

She peered up at me from between her legs as she moved into the downward dog position. "How were things at the shop today?"

"We had a busy morning," I said, hoping the boost in revenue would also lift her spirits. "Are you feeling better?"

She stood up and languidly lifted one ankle, pulling it behind her as she stretched. "I am," she said, smiling at me. "Exercise goes a long way to bringing me out of a funk. That, and there have been no surprise visits from the police today." Rikki gave me a wry smile. "What are your plans for the evening?"

I felt a blush begin to creep up my neck. "Noa is taking me to Starlight on the Lagoon. He'll be here in a few hours to pick me up."

"A date?" An amused smile played across my aunt's lips. "Well, it's about time. I always knew you two would work out." Her mouth twitched. "I didn't even give up hope when you married that football player."

I grimaced. "Rikki, Noa and I aren't…" My voice trailed off as I searched for the right words to say. "I mean, I care about him, but after the way I—"

"Stop making excuses," she interrupted me. "I've watched you two dance around your feelings for one another since you were *keiki*, just a couple of kids." Rikki straightened and walked across the grass to me, placing her hands on my shoulders. "Kaley, my *ku'uipo*, let go of your past mistakes. You may have temporarily wandered down a different path, but it led you back here. The same goes for Noa. If you want things to change between the two of you, then you should tell him how you feel."

I swallowed the lump forming in my throat and shook my head. "What if he doesn't feel the same way?" I asked, my voice hoarse.

Aunt Rikki squeezed my shoulder. "Then at least you'll know for certain where you stand." Her eyes twinkled. "But I have a feeling that things will work out. You two deserve each other." She took my hand and walked with me back into the house. "I'm going to rinse off and then fix myself a snack. Let me know if you want help getting ready for your dinner date."

I spent the rest of afternoon trying not to read too much into the dinner reservation Noa had made, but I couldn't help it. I blamed Jamie and Rikki for planting the idea in my head that perhaps he wasn't just spending so much time with me because he wanted to help my aunt. After all, we could easily find out the identity of Marco's date by hanging around the resort lobby to watch them arrive for dinner. Yet Noa had called in a favor to get us a reservation at the same restaurant—a place where many couples went to get engaged or celebrate anniversaries. With the incredible food and wine, the soft music, and the gorgeous view of the island, it was undoubtedly the perfect setting for a romantic evening. Would I be able to make it through dinner without confessing my feelings? Did I even want to try?

Not quite ready to answer that question, I shifted my thoughts back to Marco Rossini and his dinner date as I styled my hair. What if Erin had been lying to me when she'd claimed she wanted nothing to do with him? If she'd seen Louana as the only person standing in the way of getting Marco back, perhaps he had played that to his advantage and convinced her to kill the other woman while he had remained at Beachcomber's the whole time, establishing his own alibi. Or what if he'd moved on from her and had invited some other woman out for a fancy dinner? The night could lead me to a dead end. At the very least, I'd enjoy a nice meal. *And the company.*

Rikki came up to my room at seven to help me get pick out an outfit. We dug through my closet and assessed my wardrobe, deciding on a tight black halter dress and matching sling-back heels. I had curled my long hair, and Rikki loaned me a gold hibiscus flower clip to pin it back from my face. "Are you sure this isn't too formal?" I asked, nervously checking my lipstick in the mirror for the third time.

"It's perfect," Rikki replied, standing back to admire my completed look. "You're beautiful."

Noa arrived just as I was spritzing a little of my favorite perfume on my wrists. I heard Rikki greet him and let him in the front door. I took a deep breath and squared my shoulders. Then I lifted my chin and pasted what I hoped was a carefree smile on my face before heading downstairs to join them.

Noa was dressed in a pair of nice dark slacks and a blue button-down shirt. He'd tied his own long hair back in a low ponytail at the nape of his neck. His gaze fixed on me, never wavering as I descended the steps and walked across the living room toward him. His lips parted. "Kaley…wow."

"*Mahalo*." I grinned at him.

Rikki chuckled. "Close your mouth, boy," she said, patting him on the back. "I don't want you getting drool all over my coffee table."

Noa shut his mouth with a click, and his cheeks turned an adorable shade of pink. "We should go," he said. "Our reservation is in fifteen minutes."

"I'll be home in a few hours," I told Rikki.

"Take your time." My aunt's eyes twinkled. "I think I may go for a run later tonight. It'll help clear my head." She gave me a hug and placed her lips close to my ear. "Then maybe you two can enjoy a little private time," she whispered. She winked and gently nudged my side with her elbow as she pulled away.

My face flushed. I hoped Noa hadn't heard her. "Have a good run," I said, turning to follow Noa to his Jeep.

Starlight on the Lagoon was located in the main building of the resort. Noa ushered me through the front lobby and toward the elevators. Once upstairs, we traveled down the wide hallway that led to the upscale eatery's main entrance. Classical music

Anne Marie Stoddard | 134

filtered out of the open doorway, mingling with the sounds of muted conversations and the soft clink of silverware on plates.

A young woman with waist-length brown hair stood behind the hostess stand. Her hazel eyes lit up as we approached. "Aloha, Noa," she said warmly. I thought I detected a faint German accent in her voice. "You're right on time."

"Aloha, Stella." Noa grinned at the girl. "Thanks again for fitting us in on such short notice."

Stella nodded. "I was happy to help." She grabbed two menus off the stack on the hostess stand and motioned for us to follow her. "Right this way."

I discreetly scanned the restaurant for any sign of Erin as we made our way to our table. The light coral and turquoise color scheme was a sophisticated tribute to the ocean that surrounded the island. Guests seated around the main dining room were dressed in their most elegant attire, an array of brightly colored dresses, slacks, suits, and even a few tuxedos. My gaze roved over the section near the window that overlooked the beautiful lagoon, and I swooned inwardly. It really was quite the romantic setting.

"Here we are," Stella said brightly, pulling my attention back to her. The hostess had stopped in front of a table next to one of the large windows. She pulled out my chair for me and then placed a napkin in my lap. "Your server will be by shortly," she said, smiling from me to Noa. "Enjoy yourselves. Your dinner is on the house tonight, compliments of the owner." She bowed and then turned to make her way back to the hostess station.

"Wow." I raised a surprised brow at Noa.

He grinned. "I told you they owed me a favor."

"You must have done an excellent job on their website."

"Well, I don't like to brag." He dipped his head, looking embarrassed.

"Don't be so modest." I smiled at him from across the table. "It sounds to me like you're great at what you do," I said. "I'm proud of you." I suddenly felt shy. I took a slow breath, trying to summon the courage for what I wanted to say next. *It's easy, Kaley. Just tell him how you feel. What's the worst that could happen?* More heartbreak. That was what.

"Noa, listen," I began, but he held up a hand to stop me.

His gaze was fixated on something to my left. "There he is," he whispered.

I swiveled my head to follow his line of vision. Sure enough, Marco Rossini was seated just a few tables over. His dark hair was slicked back, and he was dressed in a nice pair of slacks and a tan sport coat. Marco had a flute of champagne lifted in his hand. As I watched, he sipped it and then leaned forward to grip the hand of the woman seated across from him.

"That liar," I murmured, watching Erin Malone raise her own glass. Since leaving the boutique, she'd changed into a silky red dress and pinned back her dark curls. The gold bracelet she'd taken from the store that afternoon slid down her wrist as she took a sip of her champagne. I turned back around to face Noa. "That's Erin," I said in a low voice.

Noa's brow furrowed. "I thought she told you she never wanted to see him again."

"She did." I leaned forward in my chair. "But she may have just been saying that to throw us off her trail. If we thought Erin didn't want Marco back, then we'd have no reason to suspect her of killing Louana."

"What does this mean?" Noa looked over at their table and then back at me.

I filled my glass with ice water from a carafe in the center of the table. Then I cast a furtive glance toward the couple to make sure they hadn't noticed us. "Marco told me that he tried to call it quits with Louana when she started calling him her boyfriend," I said. "Apparently, he wasn't that committed to her. His attempt backfired, and she wound up stalking him. Then she ruined his chance at a big break with that talent agent." I sipped my water. "So, my first theory is that Marco knocked off Lou to get revenge. Maybe he also realized that he still loved Erin, and he brought her here tonight to grovel and beg for a second chance."

Noa fixed me with an intent stare. "What's your second theory?"

"That Erin wanted to get Marco back and decided to eliminate her competition."

Noa considered that for a few moments and then nodded. "Both seem plausible." His forehead wrinkled. "And then there's Luka."

I frowned. "Right." After my conversation with Sara, I was surer than ever that the young stockroom worker could have been involved in the crime. "I'm having trouble deciding who had the strongest motive. They're all pretty solid."

Our server arrived to make wine recommendations and tell us about the evening's specials. The nervous excitement coursing through me had killed my appetite, but I wasn't about to turn down a free meal at the fanciest restaurant on the island. Noa and I decided to split an appetizer of fruit kabobs, and I ordered the chicken teriyaki with fried rice, served in a fresh pineapple boat. Noa had the grilled shrimp skewers with basmati rice. For dessert, we shared the Big Kahuna sampler, which featured miniature versions of the restaurant's three most popular desserts: pineapple crème brûlée, macadamia biscotti, and chocolate coconut éclair cake.

Throughout our meal, I couldn't help but steal glances at the table where Erin and Marco were seated. As the night wore on, it became apparent that things weren't as peachy between the pair as they'd first seemed. Erin's posture was stiff, and she spent most of the meal with her arms wrapped across her middle. She kept nervously licking her lips and squirming in her seat. I got the impression that the young woman didn't want to be there. Perhaps she hadn't been so quick to forgive Marco for his infidelity after all. Or was Erin only drawing out Marco's groveling to punish him for cheating? I wasn't sure what to think.

"I wish I could hear what they're saying," I said, leaning in the direction of the couple's table and straining to hear.

Noa's lips curled up at the corners. "I'm pretty sure the ladies' room is that way," he said, giving me a pointed look.

"Ah." I beamed at him, nodding in understanding. "I think you're right." I pushed my chair away from the table as our server swooped by to drop off our boxed-up leftovers. Not wanting to be recognized, I kept my head down as I walked toward their table, pretending to rifle through my purse.

"Coming here was a mistake," Erin was saying as I approached. "I should have known you would overreact."

I risked a peek at Marco and found him gripping the edge of the table, his shoulders shaking with barely controlled anger. "I just can't believe you'd do something like this," he said, a hard edge to his words. "Did you really think I wouldn't be upset?"

What are they talking about? I edged a little closer, my gaze fixed intently on the arguing couple. So intently, in fact, that I didn't see the server walking toward me.

"Miss, look out!" The cry jerked my attention away from the table, but it was too late. I collided with the young man, and the tray he'd been carrying flipped forward. A bowl of gelato dumped onto the front of my dress. I let out a startled squeal as the cold dessert dripped down my skin. "I'm so sorry," the server gushed, scrambling to grab a napkin from the nearest empty table and handing it to me.

The dull chattering around the room abruptly ceased. Mortified, I glanced around to find that all eyes had turned my way. I flicked my gaze back to Marco and Erin. The pair stared up at me from their table, and I saw the recognition dawn on both their faces. *Uh-oh.*

"You again?" Marco clenched his jaw.

Anger flashed in Erin's green eyes. "Are you kidding me?" she demanded. "You really *are* stalking me, aren't you?" She snatched the napkin from her lap and dropped it on the table, rising from her seat. "That's it. I'm out of here." She stormed away from the table.

Marco stood too. "I told you to stay away from me," he said, his tone gruff. He turned and started after Erin.

I tossed aside the napkin that the waiter had given me, no longer caring about the cold, sticky dessert that coated my dress. Darting a glance at our table, I saw Noa had already risen from his chair and was heading straight toward me. I didn't wait for him to catch up but instead took off in the direction that Marco and Erin had headed.

I caught up to Marco as he made his way out of the restaurant, but Erin was nowhere to be seen. "Wait!" I called, closing the gap between us. I shrank back when Marco rounded on me, his chest puffed out and a menacing look on his face.

"What do you want now?" he growled.

Noa appeared at my side. "Do we have a problem here, brah?" he asked Marco. Though his expression was calm, his voice carried a dangerous tone. Noa handed me the box containing our leftovers and then moved to stand protectively in front of me.

"Yeah," Marco said, scowling. "We do." He glared past Noa at me. "This nosy chick needs to butt out of things that don't concern her."

Noa took a step toward him. "That's just it. This *does* concern her." His shoulders tensed, and though I couldn't see his face, I could sense his anger. "Kaley's just trying to prove that her aunt didn't kill Louana Watson. If you want us to leave you alone, then tell us where you were on Saturday night."

Marco rolled his eyes. "I was at the open mic contest at Beachcomber's. She already knows that from when she freakin' interrogated me the other night."

"You didn't leave the bar and then come back?"

He shook his head. "No. If you don't believe me, talk to the MC for the competition, Jeff. When he wasn't onstage, he sat at my table. We were hitting on a couple of chicks who were visiting the island while on vacation from Idaho."

I frowned. "What about after you left the bar?"

A greasy smile spread across Marco's lips. "I took one of the girls home with me," he said smugly.

My nose crinkled in disgust. I stepped up beside Noa. "Then why were you here with Erin tonight?" I asked the bellhop.

Marco's smile vanished. "I'm done talking," he said in an irritated tone. "And I'm done with Erin. If you want to know what *she* was doing on Saturday, you can ask her yourself." He turned and stomped toward the open elevator, glaring at us from inside until the double doors closed.

Noa placed a hand on my arm when I started to follow. "Let him go," he said. "He's not going to tell us anything else."

"I know." I glanced up and down the hallway leading to the restaurant entrance and sighed in disappointment. "And we lost Erin." I looked up at Noa, frowning. "Did you see how angry Marco got when I asked him about her? When I was walking up to their table, I heard them arguing. He was upset with her about something that she did." I blew out a breath. "I wish I knew what."

Noa's phone beeped from his pocket. "Hold that thought," he said, pulling it out and pressing it to his ear. "Hey, Jimmy. What's up, brah? Got any good news for us?"

My chest swelled with hope. Jimmy Toki must have found something on one of the security tapes. Why else would he be calling? I held my breath as Noa listened to Jimmy's response.

"Really? Where are you now?" Noa's lips curled at the ends. "Great. We'll be right there." He pocketed his cell and met my gaze, his eyes shining with excitement. "Jimmy found something he thinks we'll want to see. He's downstairs right now in the security office." He motioned for me to follow him to the elevator.

The main lobby was packed for a Wednesday night. A shuttle from a nighttime excursion to Shipwreck Beach had just arrived back at the resort, and nearly two dozen guests in *Miller Family Reunion* T-shirts hustled past us on their way to their rooms.

Noa and I stepped off the elevator and waded through the crowd. I practically broke into a run when we reached the hallway and made our way toward Jimmy's office. My mind was racing. *What did he find?* Which of our suspects would show up in the security footage?

The beefy head of security pulled open the door before Noa had even raised his hand to knock. "Come in," he said in a low voice.

Noa and I stepped into the room for the second time that day and followed Jimmy over to the desk. "I would have called you sooner, but I was hung up with a domestic disturbance upstairs," Jimmy said as he sat down in front of the computer. He shook his head. "A woman had a few too many Shark Bites at The Lava Pot and then got into an argument with her husband when they returned to their room. When I got there, she was pelting him with items from the minibar. There were tiny liquor bottles and macadamia nuts everywhere."

"Yikes." Noa grimaced. "That's one expensive fight."

Jimmy snickered. "No kidding. It's been a busy day. I haven't even had a chance to grab dinner yet."

I held out the box of leftovers. "How does some teriyaki chicken and pineapple fried rice from Starlight on the Lagoon sound?"

He gave me a grateful smile and took the box. "You're a lifesaver, Kaley. I'm starving." Jimmy arched an eyebrow as his gaze moved over the front of my dress. "What happened to you?"

I glanced down at the sticky mess left behind by the gelato, and my cheeks flushed. "It's a long story," I mumbled.

Jimmy shook his head again, chuckling to himself as he turned his attention to the computer. He set the food aside and pulled up the video recording on the monitor. "We'll start with the courtyard footage," he said. "The police have already watched this, so it's nothing new to them—but I thought you'd still want to see."

My heart thumped loudly in my chest. I huddled close to Noa as we both peered at the monitor. The time stamp on the bottom of the screen read five minutes before ten. The merchant shops had all been closed for nearly two hours, and the dark courtyard was mostly deserted. As we watched, a curvy woman appeared on the screen, walking purposefully toward the cluster of small buildings. I didn't recognize her right away, but as she approached Happy Hula, her identity became clear. "That's Louana," I breathed.

"Wow. That's ballsy," Noa remarked when Lou strolled up to the shop entrance and unlocked the door without a moment's hesitation.

"She either didn't know there were security cameras around, or she just didn't care," I agreed. A chill zipped down my spine as she disappeared inside the shop. We'd just caught the last glimpse of Louana Watson while she was still alive. I glanced at Jimmy, who had begun chowing down on the leftover food I'd given him. "She doesn't ever come back out, does she?"

He shook his head. "Not through the entrance, anyway. Based on this video, the police are estimating that her time of death is likely sometime shortly after ten on Saturday night." He set the food down again and reached for the laptop, locating the second video feed. "Here's where it gets really interesting."

Noa gently nudged me with his elbow. "Wasn't Erin scheduled to get off work at ten that night?"

I nodded, excitement mounting in my chest. I leaned closer as the recording filled the screen. Judging by the angle of the video, the security camera must have been placed in the ceiling above the housekeeper's supply closet. Though the door to the little room couldn't be seen in the footage, the camera captured anyone who walked up to it. The exit at the end of the hallway was also clearly visible in the background.

Jimmy fast-forwarded through a section of the video. "Once I knew what time Louana entered the shop, it was easier to narrow down what time window to watch in this feed." He pressed play again when Erin appeared on the screen. She wheeled her cleaning cart up to the supply closet and opened the door, apparently oblivious to the camera above her head. The young woman disappeared from view as she stowed the cart inside the room, and she emerged a few moments later without it.

As we watched, Erin's head suddenly jerked toward the exit. Though there was no sound on the video feed, it seemed as if she'd heard a noise by the door. She cast a quick glance down the other end of the hallway and then walked over to the exit.

I checked the time stamp in the corner of the video: three minutes after ten. Erin opened the exit door a crack and then stepped aside. She turned her head, and I could clearly make out the smile curving her lips. She was happy to see whoever was on the other side of the door.

Who's there? Before I realized what I was doing, I reached for Noa's hand. He didn't pull away. I squeezed his fingers as we watched the young housekeeper pull the door open to reveal the person waiting outside. Her visitor's face appeared on the screen, and I inhaled sharply.

It was Luka Hale.

CHAPTER FOURTEEN

———

"Luka?" I exclaimed, gawking at computer screen. The man's face was partially obscured by the door, but there was no mistaking his dark brows and acne-scarred complexion. Lou had threatened to ruin Luka's life, and she had ruined Erin's relationship with Marco. *They both had a reason to kill her.* Had the pair worked together to take down the tyrant assistant manager?

I filed the thought away for later and returned my attention to the video, not wanting to miss anything. On the screen, Erin shot another look down the hallway. Then she slipped through the exit, and she and Luka disappeared from view as the door closed behind her.

"Is there more?" I asked when Jimmy paused the video. "Footage from outside the building maybe?" I let go of Noa's hand and stepped toward the security guard, unable to contain my excitement. "We have to find out where they were going."

Jimmy's regret showed on his face. "Sorry, Kaley." He shook his head. "Unfortunately, the security camera outside that door was down on Saturday. I had someone come by to fix it on Monday, but I'm afraid we can't recover any of the video feed from the weekend."

My hope deflated. "Does that area lead anywhere besides the employee parking lot?"

Jimmy grinned. "As a matter of fact, it does. There's a path to the left that cuts through the brush behind the lagoon. The trail ends on one of the utility access roads." His lips twitched. "And that road leads to the alley behind the merchant section of the courtyard. That's how the garbage and delivery trucks get back there."

I was so happy I could have kissed him—not that I would have, of course. "This is the best news I've heard all week!" I exclaimed, beaming at Jimmy. "Thank you."

"Don't mention it. Thanks again for the grub." He picked up the box of food and ate another forkful of rice.

Noa and I left Jimmy to enjoy his dinner. "Come on." I motioned for him to follow me as soon as we were out in the hall.

"Where are we going?"

"To check out that trail." I reached the exit first and pushed it open. "If Luka and Erin knew about it, they might have used it to sneak toward the alley behind Happy Hula." I turned around in the doorway to face Noa. "The housekeeping supply closet is right across the hall from the security office. What if Erin overheard Jimmy or one of the other guards mentioning that the camera on this side of the building was broken? Then she would have known that she and Luka could sneak down the trail and reach the alley undetected."

"It's possible," Noa agreed.

We stepped out into the balmy night, and the door closed heavily behind us. My gaze traveled first down the path that led behind the lagoon. "That's the shortcut to the employee parking lot," I said, pointing. I shifted my attention to the second trailhead. Unlike the well-lit, concrete walkway that led toward our car, the path was dark and unpaved. "This must be it." I dug my phone out of my purse and turned on the flashlight app. "Let's check it out."

Noa moved closer to me, and I held out my phone in front of us to light our way. We pushed aside the frangipani leaves that hung low over the trail and pressed onward. After five minutes of stumbling through the soft dirt and underbrush, we reached the end of the path. It opened onto a wide paved road, just as Jimmy had said it would.

"Why didn't I think of this before?" Noa stepped in front of me. "I knew about the utility roads—I've just never actually seen them. They run behind the shops and other parts of the resort so that electricians, garbage truck drivers, and other workers can travel around the resort without shattering the whole 'island paradise' illusion for the guests."

"I'm pretty sure Happy Hula is this way," I said, heading to the right. Sure enough, less than a minute later, Noa and I were staring at the entrance to the alley. A police car was parked in the way of the opening, and yellow crime scene tape still served as a barrier to prevent entry into the dark roadway.

"Here we are," I whispered, not wanting to attract the attention of the cop. "And that took us less than ten minutes." I grabbed Noa's arm excitedly. "On the tape, Erin and Luka walked outside at four minutes past ten. That totally fits the timeline Jimmy told us."

"Uh-oh," Noa whispered. He grabbed my arm and pulled me back just as a beam of light passed over the ground where I'd been standing.

I whipped my head around in time to see the officer walking toward us from his car, panning his flashlight across the road. *Crap.* I really didn't want to explain to the cop on duty why we were sneaking around the alley at night. As quietly as possible, Noa and I hurried back down the road to the little trailhead.

When we emerged near the resort's main building again a few minutes later, we turned onto the concrete path that led to the employee parking lot. "So you think Luka and Erin were accomplices?" Noa asked as he pulled the Jeep onto the main road that ran in front of the resort.

"I do." Luka and Erin both had motives, and now we knew they'd both been at the resort at the time Louana had been killed. "Do you think that could be why Marco was so upset with Erin tonight at dinner? What if she confessed to him what she and Luka had done?"

Noa shot me a sidelong glance. "Why would Marco be upset that Lou was dead? He hated her."

My forehead wrinkled. "You've got a point." Another question wormed its way to the forefront of my brain. "How do you suppose Erin and Luka know each other?"

"Your guess is as good as mine," he said. "It's a small island, and they look to be around the same age. Maybe they went to school together."

"Yeah, maybe." I sat back, frowning out the window. Something wasn't adding up. Marco had finally provided us with an alibi, and while I knew I shouldn't just take his word for truth, I was beginning to suspect him less. The video evidence against Luka and Erin was too compelling. It placed them at the resort at the same time that Lou was inside Happy Hula. Still, Louana had been strangled, and her body hadn't been moved. So why would either Erin or Luka need an accomplice? Couldn't one of them have easily killed her without having the other around as a witness? The more I thought about it, the more it bothered me. *What am I missing?*

Noa parked in the driveway next to Aunt Rikki's Vespa, and I fished around in my purse for my keys. Rikki had left a piece of paper taped to the door handle. I pulled the note off the front door and skimmed it. "She went out for a jog. Looks like we just missed her," I told Noa, reading the time that she'd recorded in the bottom corner: fifteen minutes until ten.

"How long do you think she'll be gone?" he asked.

I pushed open the door and flipped on the living room lights. "Rikki usually runs about six or seven miles, so she'll probably be gone awhile." *Probably even longer than usual since she's trying to give us some privacy*, I thought, feeling my cheeks warm.

"Want me to stay and keep you company?" Noa offered.

"You don't have to," I told him. "I need to shower and get out of these sticky clothes." I frowned down at my dress, hoping that dry cleaning it would remove all the residue.

"I don't mind." Noa stepped further into the house. His brow furrowed. "Unless you want me to leave."

"No," I said, perhaps a little too quickly. "What I meant to say is, make yourself at home. I'll be back down in a few." I hurried upstairs to clean up. I spent a little longer than I'd like to admit agonizing over what to wear when I returned to the living room. *Noa has seen you in sweats and a T-shirt before*, I reminded myself. I finally threw on a pair of comfy black yoga pants and a pink camisole before padding back downstairs.

Noa had raided Rikki's wine cabinet and selected a bottle of merlot. He'd filled two glasses and had set them on the coffee table. "Here," he said, offering me one when I joined him in the couch.

"Thanks." I took a sip of my drink. "Now what?" I asked.

Noa's brow pinched. "I don't know about you, but I could use a break from formulating any more theories tonight. Why don't we just try to relax until Rikki gets home? We could watch some TV," he suggested.

He was right. As badly as I wanted to figure this out, I was driving myself mad, puzzling over who had killed Louana and how. Maybe if I slept on it, the whole "Luka and Erin" connection would make more sense in the morning.

"All right," I agreed, settling back against the couch cushions. Noa flipped off the overhead lights and queued up an old rerun of *How I Met Your Mother* on Netflix. We were about halfway through a second episode—and more than halfway through the bottle of wine—when Noa's phone dinged with a new text message.

My gut clenched. "Who is it?" I asked, trying to sound casual, though I was pretty sure I failed. A text this late was usually either one of two things: an emergency or a booty call—or, in some cases, both.

Noa glanced at the screen. "It's Harmony." He slipped the phone back into his pocket without replying. His expression was unreadable in the faint glow from the television.

"Why do you like her?" I blurted. I couldn't stay silent anymore. The wine had given me the liquid courage I needed to speak my mind. I set down my glass and pulled my legs onto the couch, turning so that I sat facing Noa. "She's horrible."

He quirked his lips. "Are you jealous?"

"Don't do that," I said, feeling heat churning in my middle. "Don't dangle her in front of me like this is some kind of game." I blew out a breath. "I just don't get what you see in her is all. She made our lives hell for so long." I forced down the lump in my throat. "I know I don't have the right to tell you who you should or shouldn't be with," I said, my voice quavering slightly. "But I think you deserve better than Harmony Kane."

Noa stared at me for a few moments. "Kaley, I don't want to date Harmony," he said finally, his voice carrying a trace of guilt. "She's just a client. She approached me a couple of weeks ago and asked me to help her build a website. Harm wants to open her own online clothing store."

I blinked at him, feeling simultaneously relieved and confused. "Really? Then why did you invite her out with us to Beachcomber's the other night?"

He rolled his eyes. "She actually invited herself. I asked Jamie to join us because I knew the two of you would become fast friends. Then Harmony called and asked if we could discuss the layout for her website. When I told her I already had plans with you, she insisted on tagging along." He leaned forward, his brows pinched. "I know Harmony's been kind of flirty with me lately, but I don't date my clients. I'll admit I might have let her carry on for a little longer than I should have, but I'm not interested in her like that."

"Noa, I..." My throat suddenly felt dry, and I drained the last few sips of wine from my glass. *Just let it rip. Quick—like taking off a Band-Aid.* The words bubbled out of my mouth before I could change my mind. "I've missed you—and I've regretted the way things ended between us every day for the past five and a half years." I stared at him, feeling tears prick my eyes. "I knew I made a mistake marrying Bryan, and I'm sorry that I hurt you. I hate that I was too ashamed to reach out when I moved away. I should have called, but I was scared that if I heard your voice, I'd be on the next plane to Los Angeles." I swallowed. "I know you've only been spending time with me these past few days for Aunt Rikki's sake, but having you back in my life has meant more to me than you know. I can accept that I blew my chance and that nothing is ever going to happen between us—but when this is all over, I hope you'll let me at least try to earn back your friendship."

There. After all that time, I'd finally let Noa know how I felt. Now it was up to him to decide if he could ever forgive me. I let my words hang between us, feeling every second that passed in excruciating slow motion as I waited for him to respond.

Noa opened his mouth as if he were going to speak. Then he closed it again. He stared at me, and an emotion flashed behind his eyes. It was gone before I could identify it. His brow pinched, and his expression became strained. "Kaley, I don't—"

Whatever he'd been about to say died on his lips as an explosion of sound erupted behind us. I shrieked. Noa instinctively lunged toward me and pulled me off the couch, his body shielding mine as we rolled onto the floor. Shards of broken glass rained down where we'd just been sitting. Something sailed overhead, landing hard on the center of the coffee table. The wood splintered, and Noa's wine glass crashed to the floor, splattering the dark liquid all over us both. I heard an engine start outside, and then a vehicle sped away. Noa and I were left lying in a heap on the living room floor, panting.

"Are you okay?" he asked breathlessly after a few moments. He gently untangled his limbs from mine and rolled onto his back, hissing in pain as glass crunched underneath him.

"I'm all right," I said shakily. "I think." I sat up slowly and looked at him, my heartfelt confession temporarily forgotten. Fear resonated through me all over again at the sight of the red streaks on Noa's face. "Are *you* okay?" I asked, unsure if it was wine or blood.

"Yeah." He grunted as he hauled himself off the ground. "Just a few scrapes." He crouched down, holding a finger to his lips and signaling for me to be quiet. "Don't move," he mouthed.

Noa crawled as soundlessly as possible toward the edge of the sofa and looked around it. Rising to his full height, he armed himself with Rikki's stained-glass palm tree lamp and pressed his back against the living room wall. Noa edged his way toward the broken window. With the lamp held high above his head, he slowly peeked around the corner. He stayed that way for what felt like an eternity, not moving a muscle. Finally, his posture relaxed, and he lowered the lamp.

"All clear," he said. Noa set the glass palm tree back on Rikki's desk and then helped me off the floor. We huddled together, peering down at the object lying in a nest of splintered wood on the coffee table. It was a rock nearly half the size of my head. A sheet of white printer paper was wrapped loosely around it.

"I think there's something written on there," I said, squinting. I reached out to retrieve the paper from the rock, but Noa stopped me.

"Don't touch it with your bare hands," he warned. "Not until after we've called the police. They'll probably want to dust it for fingerprints."

"Good point." I dashed into the kitchen to grab a sheet of napkin. I used it to shield my skin as I carefully nudged the rock to the side and freed the paper. Still using the napkin, I flipped the crumpled sheet over and smoothed it out. My blood chilled in my veins as I scanned the message written there. Someone had scrawled a two-word warning across the paper with a black marker.

BACK OFF.

CHAPTER FIFTEEN

———

It didn't take the police long to arrive once Noa called. Detective Ray led the charge as he and two uniformed officers entered Rikki's home. After they'd swept the whole house and had determined that there was no immediate danger, the homicide detective ushered Noa and me into the kitchen. He stayed with us while the other two cops investigated the scene in the living room.

"Are you two all right?" Ray looked genuinely concerned.

"We weren't badly hurt, if that's what you're asking." I moved closer to Noa. "Mostly shaken up."

Detective Ray's dark eyes roamed over us, taking in the shards of glass stuck to Noa's pants and the wine splattered across my shirt. "Where is your aunt?" he asked me.

I bit the inside of my cheek to keep from erupting at him. *He has to ask that. It doesn't mean he thinks she had anything to do with vandalizing her own house.* "She went for a jog," I said, my voice stiff. "She should be back anytime now."

Detective Ray jotted something down on his little notepad and then chewed the top of his pen as he scanned his notes. He met my gaze. "You said you had dinner at the resort tonight. Did you see any cars following you too closely on the way home? Or maybe someone parked near the house when you arrived?"

Noa shook his head. "Not that I noticed."

"I have a few guesses about who might have done this." I took a step toward Ray, feeling determined. "Noa and I learned some new information tonight that might help you with your investigation into Louana Watson's murder."

The detective's dark brows reached for his hairline. "You did?" He sounded skeptical.

I nodded emphatically. "Jimmy Toki, the head of Aloha Lagoon Resort security, showed us some security footage that you need to see." I told him about the recording of Erin Malone and Luka Hale from the night of the murder, as well as the trail that provided a shortcut to the alley behind the courtyard shops. "I think Erin and Luka could have been involved in what happened to Louana," I said. "From what I've heard, Luka was being blackmailed by Lou, and Erin wanted—"

"Hold on," Detective Ray said, cutting me off. "Let me get this straight." He took a step back and folded his large arms across his barrel of a chest. "You've been playing detective behind my back?"

I gulped. "Sort of. I tried to tell you the other night…" My words died in my throat when I saw the angry look on his face. I snapped my mouth shut.

"Do you have any idea how dangerous that is?" Detective Ray hiked his thumb over his shoulder toward the living room, where the two beat cops were placing the rock and the note into evidence bags. He glared at me. "What if someone had shown up here tonight with a gun instead of that rock? Or something even worse?"

I hated to think what he considered worse than a gun-toting lunatic on my doorstep. *An axe murderer? A maniac with a machete? One of those door-to-door kitchen knife salesmen?* "At least this proves Aunt Rikki is innocent," I insisted. *Doesn't it?* "Why would she throw a rock through her own window?" I placed my hands on my hips. "If I had to guess, I'd say it was mostly likely Erin Malone. She was really upset when she found out I'd been asking about her around the resort, and she stormed off before we could learn her alibi when we saw her tonight at Starlight on the Lagoon."

Detective Ray's face turned the same shade of eggplant as Rikki's scooter. "Please tell me you're not stalking people."

Whoops. Me and my big mouth. I had to stop incriminating myself. "Not exactly," I said in a squeaky voice.

"Erin happened to be at the same restaurant where we had dinner," Noa said, coming to my aid. "We saw her with her ex-boyfriend when we were leaving," he explained, which wasn't entirely untrue.

"I assume you've viewed the security footage that shows Louana entering the boutique," I said, meeting the detective's gaze. Of course, I knew he already had because Jimmy had told me, but I didn't want Ray to think the head of security had been sharing information about the investigation. "I just think it might be worth your time to review the recording from the main hallway from around that same time. If you haven't already, that is," I added, not wanting to give him the impression that I thought he wasn't doing a thorough job.

"We did review the film from the courtyard," Detective Ray said, his complexion returning to its normal color. "But I haven't yet obtained the video from the hallway. I'll give Mr. Toki a call tomorrow. Perhaps I'll also pay Miss Malone a visit." The detective gave me a pointed look. "But you should stop following people around and hounding them with questions, before you wind up with a restraining order. Is that clear?"

I nodded. If he was going to take me seriously and check out our leads, then I had no reason to interfere any further. "Though you may also want to consider talking to Luka Hale," I added, shrinking back when he cut me another disapproving look.

Detective Ray joined his men in the living room, and I sagged against the kitchen counter, feeling as if a weight had been lifted from my shoulders. The detective offered to have one of the beat cops posted outside the house for the rest of the night, but Noa insisted that he would stay with Rikki and me to make sure we were safe.

When we were alone again, Noa sat down at the kitchen table. He flinched as he plucked a small piece of glass out of his arm. "Does Rikki have a first aid kit?" he asked. His voice was tight with pain.

"I think there's one in the upstairs bathroom." I hurried to the second floor and retrieved the kit from Rikki's medicine cabinet. I set it down on the kitchen table and examined the cuts on Noa's arm. Some of them were still bleeding. "Maybe I should have called an ambulance," I said, unable to keep the worry from my voice.

"Nah. I'll be fine," he insisted. "They're all superficial wounds. A washcloth and a few Band-Aids will do the trick." He glanced down at his clothes, which were stained with wine. "And some laundry detergent." He chuckled. Then his smile faded. He looked up at me. "Listen, Kaley, about what you said before," he began, his face pulled tight in a grimace.

"Don't worry about it." I focused intently on the bandages so I wouldn't have to look him in the eye. "I shouldn't have unloaded on you like that. It was selfish."

Noa gently pushed my hands away and straightened in his seat. "No," he said firmly. "I need to say this." He met my gaze with the same pained expression. "I had no idea you'd been blaming yourself all this time for what happened that night before you left for Atlanta." He blew out a breath. "The truth is, it was really my fault. I knew you were with Bryan, but I couldn't help myself. I had to let you know how I felt before I lost you for good. Then you were gone, and all I could do was beat myself up for scaring you away. I thought by not keeping in touch after that, I was respecting your decision to be with Bryan instead of me." Noa's dark eyes searched mine. "I've missed you like crazy, Kales. When you came back, I didn't want to come on too strong and risk losing you all over again. I want to clear Rikki's name as badly as you do, but being so close to you these past few days has been torture. All I can think about is how badly I want to kiss you."

Noa rose from his chair, reaching out a hand to cup my face. Before I realized what was happening, his lips crushed mine with such force that I staggered back toward the kitchen counter. Noa moved with me, his strong arms lifting me onto the counter.

I kissed him back, hardly able to believe this was really happening. I closed my eyes and lost myself in him. Kissing Bryan had never felt like this. Being with Noa just felt so...*right*. An electric current zinged through my body, setting every nerve ending on fire, and I wrapped my legs around Noa's middle. He wound one hand through my hair, and the other wrapped tightly around the back of my neck. For several moments, the room around us fell away as we melted together in a blur of lust and adrenaline. All that mattered was the heat radiating between us.

The kiss ended as abruptly as it had begun. One of the glass shards stuck to Noa's slacks grazed my calf, and I jerked back, swearing.

"Are you okay?" he released me, his face pinched with worry. "I didn't mean to hurt you."

"You didn't," I rasped, still breathless from the kiss. I sucked in a mouthful of air as my pulse slowly returned to normal. I felt a smile spread wide across my face. "I've wanted to do that for a long time."

He grinned. "Me too." He reached for my hand, but I pulled back at the sight of fresh blood on his arm.

"We should finish cleaning up your cuts." I glanced down at his pants. "And you should probably take those off."

Noa waggled his eyebrows at me. "Kalani Evalina Kalua," he said, giving me a look of mock astonishment. He'd only ever evoked my full name when teasing me. "Are you trying to get me naked?"

I blushed. "I just meant so we could clean the wine and glass off of them." *Although I wouldn't mind seeing him in the buff,* I thought, feeling my cheeks burn even hotter. I pushed away from Noa and returned to the kitchen table. It wasn't until I glanced toward the disaster area in the living room that I felt the harsh reality of the situation crash over me again. "Noa," I said, fear tamping my adrenaline-fueled libido. "I'm glad you were here." If someone had wanted to scare me, they'd done a damned good job of it.

Noa's own expression turned serious. "Me too," he said, quietly. "I can't even imagine what could have happened if you'd been alone." He clenched his jaw.

I closed my eyes and exhaled a shaky breath. I didn't want to think about that. I was grateful that Rikki hadn't been home. I couldn't stand the idea that my aunt could have been hurt, especially after all she'd already been through this week.

I helped Noa clean the scrapes on his arms and face. He waited downstairs while I went up to my room to change out of my wine-stained top. When I returned, he was in the living room, using Rikki's handheld vacuum to clean up the smaller debris from the couch and floor. He'd stripped out of his dirty clothes and was wearing nothing but a pair of pineapple-patterned boxers.

Though I'd admired him from a distance at the pool the day before, I hadn't seen Noa Kahele up close without his shirt since he was a scrawny twenty-two-year-old. He had filled out a *lot*. I tried not to stare at his rippling abs (*holy mother...is that an* eight *pack??)* as I offered him a fresh towel and my pink silk bathrobe. "It's the only thing I have that will fit you," I said sheepishly. "If you'll leave your boxers outside the bathroom door, I'll put them in the laundry with your other clothes." I turned and hurried into the kitchen, not wanting Noa to see that the idea of seeing him naked had me blushing all over.

While Noa showered, I washed his clothes and then busied myself with cleaning up the remaining glass. As I worked, I couldn't stop thinking about him. *I still can't believe that he's wanted to be with me all this time,* I thought, feeling giddy as I recalled our steamy kiss in the kitchen. Noa had offered to sleep on the couch that night. Part of me wanted to invite him to share my bed, but I didn't want to rush things. We'd only confessed our feelings for one another less than an hour ago. I didn't want to jeopardize whatever was happening between us by moving too fast.

Then again, I was worried about him being alone downstairs the whole night. What if whoever had threatened me decided to come back? I pictured Luka Hale bursting through the door and attacking Noa as he slept on the couch. With any luck, Detective Ray had already tracked Luka down and was questioning Erin and him at that very moment. If either confessed, the whole case could be wrapped up by morning. *So why does it feel like it's not over?*

I had the living room looking almost back to normal by the time Noa emerged from the shower. I couldn't help but laugh as he descended the stairs with my robe stretched tightly around him. His hair was wrapped in a towel, and he smelled like my white tea and ginger body wash. "Lookin' sharp, Kahele," I teased.

"Go ahead," he said. "Get a good look." He twirled around in a slow circle and then moved toward me, smiling warmly. "I'm just happy to hear your laugh again."

We settled onto the couch to wait for his clothes to dry and for Rikki to return home. "She's going to be so upset," I said, frowning at the splintered furniture in front of us. "She loved that coffee table."

"Maybe we can find her another one just like it," Noa suggested. "I'm pretty sure I saw that same table at the Home Goods in Lihue a few weeks ago. I'll have to make a trip over there anyway to visit Lowes for the supplies I need to repair your window."

"You don't have to do that."

Noa waved his hand. "I know I don't *have* to," he said. "I want to. You and Rikki both mean a lot to me, and I want you to feel safe." He wrapped his arm around my waist and pulled me closer. "So first thing tomorrow, I'm fixing that window."

"Thank you." I smiled up at him and then leaned my head against his shoulder.

I didn't remember falling asleep, but the next thing I knew, I was waking up to a gentle breeze on my face. Opening my eyes, I found myself lying on the couch with Noa curled around me, snoring softly in my ear. I smiled to myself and pulled his arms more tightly around my middle. Lying there with him, I felt more content than I had in years. The happy feeling was short-lived, however. The events of the previous night flashed through my memory, and I eased out of his grasp and sat up.

Noa grunted and rolled onto his back. He squinted up at me. "Good morning, beautiful," he said, his voice still thick with sleep. He closed his eyes again.

I shook his shoulder. "Noa, get up," I said, my concern mounting. "We fell asleep before Rikki came home." I swept my gaze around the room, searching for any sign that my aunt had returned. If Rikki had come back, surely she would have woken us up—especially after she'd seen the shattered living room window. I left Noa on the couch and climbed the stairs, peeking into Rikki's room. Her bed was made, and when I checked her closet, I saw that her running shoes were gone. Had my aunt ever returned from her night jog?

Panic swelling in my chest, I hurried back to the living room. "Noa, I don't think Rikki ever came home last night," I said, feeling my throat go dry.

Noa opened his eyes and quickly sat up. "She didn't?" He hoisted himself off the couch and moved over to window, peering out at the driveway. When he turned around, the worry had vanished from his face. "Her Vespa's gone," he said. "She must have come in after we fell asleep. Then she left again this morning without waking us." Noa crossed the living room and wrapped his arms around my shoulders. "Maybe she went out to grab some breakfast. Or she could have gone to that sunrise yoga class over at Coconut Cove."

The tension in my chest didn't let up. "What time is it?" I dashed into the kitchen and checked the digital clock on the microwave. It was almost eight thirty. "I'm late for work," I said, whipping around to face Noa. "There's no way Rikki would have let me sleep past the beginning of my shift. Something's wrong." I went back to the living room and dumped the contents of my purse onto the splintered coffee table. Snatching my phone from the pile of makeup and receipts, I checked the screen. I had a voicemail from a number I didn't recognize.

Heart pounding, I punched in my pin number and turned up the volume so that we could both hear the message. Noa and I listened as my aunt's frightened voice shattered the silence. "Kaley, it's Rikki. I need you to come down to the Aloha Lagoon Police Department. I've been arrested. They think I—"

The message ended abruptly as my phone cut off. Frantic, I pressed the power button several times to no avail. The battery was dead. "Damnit!" I swore. I threw the phone on the couch. "Detective Ray arrested her. Buy why?" I took several deep breaths, but it was no use. I couldn't calm down. The alarm in Rikki's voice had sent me into a spiral of fear and guilt. I'd spent the night cuddled on the couch with Noa while my poor aunt was being thrown into a jail cell. *How could I let this happen?*

The room started to spin, and I gripped Noa's arms. He eased out of my grasp and retrieved his own phone. "Here," he said, pressing it into my palm. "Call Detective Ray. We'll get her out of there."

I quickly dialed the police station's number, insisting that the receptionist connect me with Detective Ray immediately. A few moments later, I was patched through to his direct line. "Why did you arrest my aunt?" I demanded as soon as he answered.

"Ms. Kalua." The homicide detective sounded tired. "I wondered when I'd be hearing from you." He sighed. "I got the call shortly after I left your house. Rikki mowed someone down with her Vespa last night in a hit-and-run. I'm sorry, Kaley, but there was just no way around it. The boy's own mother saw her strike him and just keep driving. She ditched the bike somewhere, but my men picked her up about a mile from your house."

My heart dropped to my stomach. How could a witness have seen Rikki commit such a heinous crime? My aunt would never do something that horrible. She wasn't capable of that kind of violence. *Was she?* A thin line of doubt traced its way through my thoughts. *If someone actually saw her do it...* "No way. I don't believe you," I said, shaking my head stubbornly even though he couldn't see me. "Who was the witness?" Maybe I'd go talk to the woman myself. She had to have been mistaken. *Or maybe even lying.*

There was a long pause on the other end of the line. "Nancy Hale," Detective Ray said finally.

"Hale?" I gripped the kitchen counter so tightly that my knuckles turned white. *I just heard him wrong. That's all.*

"Yes," he replied. "Last night your aunt tried to kill a man that you claimed was attempting to frame her. She attacked Luka Hale."

CHAPTER SIXTEEN

―――

Wilcox Memorial Hospital in Lihue was already a short drive from Aloha Lagoon, but Noa and I made it there in record time. As desperate as I was to get Rikki out of jail, there was little I could do until her bail was set. *She would want you to keep the boutique open*, I reminded myself. I plugged my phone into Noa's car charger on the drive so I could call Harmony, instructing her to head over to Happy Hula and open the shop. She grudgingly agreed after I promised to come in at noon and cover her closing shift. News of Rikki's arrest hadn't reached Harm yet, so I claimed we had a family emergency and left it at that. There was no need to drag my aunt's name through the mud if there was a chance that she wasn't really responsible for what had happened to Luka.

The lobby of the hospital's trauma center was packed when we arrived. After scanning the crowd of people, I spotted a woman with dark hair and a narrow nose and chin like Luka's. She was seated in the far corner of the room, wringing her hands and uttering prayers under her breath.

"Mrs. Hale?" I asked hesitantly, approaching the tearful woman.

She looked up at me with wide brown eyes. "Yes?" She asked, her voice hopeful. Her face fell as she realized I wasn't one of her son's doctors.

Noa stood behind me, his hand on my shoulder. He gave me a gentle nudge forward.

"My name is Jamie," I lied. I wasn't sure if Mrs. Hale knew Rikki had a niece, but I wasn't going to take any chances. I needed her to open up to me. "And this is Noa. We're friends of Luka's. We came as soon as we heard about what had happened to him." I chewed my lip and held out a bouquet of tropical blossoms that we'd picked up in the gift shop on the way into the lobby. "Here. We brought you these."

"Oh. Thank you," Nancy Hale said absently. She took the flowers from my outstretched hands and clutched them in her lap. "He's in bad shape," she said, her voice strained. "He has several broken bones, and he's still unconscious." A sob worked its way out of her throat, and she held her head in her hands, her shoulders shaking. "I can't believe that monster ran over my baby."

I bit my tongue, fighting the urge to defend my aunt. "I heard that you saw it happen," I said, reaching out to give her shoulder a comforting squeeze. I felt like the scum of the earth for what I was about to do, but if Luka wasn't awake to tell me his side of the story, then I had no choice. "What happened?" I asked gently.

Mrs. Hale took a ragged breath. "Luka still lives at home," she said, giving me a sad little smile. "He's saving up for an apartment in Honolulu." Her lips trembled. "Luka went out to pick up some fast food last night. He said he was craving French fries. I was getting ready for bed when I realized that I'd left my phone charger in the car when I'd come home from work. I walked outside just as Luka was parking his car on the curb—we don't have a very large driveway." Her eyes grew misty, and her shoulders began to shake. I felt sick with guilt over asking the poor woman to relive the moment. "I saw him get out of his car," she said, closing her eyes. "And that's when that psycho on her purple scooter ran him down in the middle of the street." She began to sob.

I grabbed Noa's hand and squeezed it. *Lord, forgive me*, I thought, taking a deep breath and forcing it back out. "Are you sure it was a purple scooter?" I asked softly. "It must have been hard to tell since it was dark outside."

Mrs. Hale's head snapped up. "How could you ask me that?" she cried, and several other people around the waiting room gave us curious looks. "Of course I'm sure."

My face went hot. "I'm sorry, Mrs. Hale," I backpedaled. "I guess I'm just shocked that someone could hurt poor Luka like that and just drive away. He's such a sweet guy." I swallowed and glanced nervously at Noa. "We just want to be on the lookout so that maybe we can help the police catch whoever did this. Was the driver wearing a helmet? Did you see his face?"

"*Her* face," Nancy Hale corrected me. "And I didn't have to see it," she said coldly. "I recognized that scooter. It belonged to Luka's crazy boss, Rikki Kalua."

My hands involuntarily balled into fists at my sides. "Are you sure?" I asked again, fighting to keep my voice calm.

"Definitely." She wiped away a tear, her features tight with anger. "I couldn't see her face because she was wearing a helmet, but I just *know* it was her. They say she killed that poor Watson girl that worked for her, too." She scowled. "That maniac was going to take out her employees one by one. Good thing the police caught her." Mrs. Hale wiped her hand over her face and then blinked up at me. "I'm sorry—what did you say your name was? Jamie?" She sighed. "It's been a long night, and I just need to be alone right now while I wait for Luka to wake up. But thank you for stopping by. It means a lot."

"Sure. We understand." I backed away from the woman, tugging Noa along with me. We turned and left the poor woman to stew in her misery. Shoulders slumped, I trudged back to the parking lot and climbed into Noa's Jeep. "What now?" I asked him, fighting back tears. "Rikki's Vespa was parked at the house when we came back from dinner last night. Does Detective Ray really think she returned from her jog, hopped on the scooter, and took off again to go run over Luka? It just doesn't add up."

Noa's face hardened. "Do you think someone stole it?" He met my gaze. "The rock coming through the window last night could have been a diversion. What if the person who threw it took the Vespa and then attacked Luka?"

My breath caught in my throat. "Yes! That *has* to be what happened, right? Someone tried to scare us off their trail and then made sure that Luka couldn't talk to the police—and they found a way to frame Rikki again in the process." My heart sank. "So once again my aunt has no alibi, and now one of our suspects is in the hospital."

Noa reached for my hand and gently stroked my fingers. "We'll get through this," he said softly. "Mrs. Hale said whoever was driving Rikki's Vespa was wearing a helmet, but she seemed certain it was your aunt. Could that be because the driver had a similar build? That would mean it must have been a woman, right?"

I felt my face go slack as the realization sunk in. "It was Erin! It's the only explanation that makes sense." I sat up straight in the passenger seat as I strung together the thoughts pinging through my brain. "What if Erin figured out we were onto her after she spotted me at Starlight on the Lagoon last night? If she and Luka really did work together to get rid of Louana, she could have decided to shut him up so he couldn't take her down with him if he decided to confess." *And just in time, too*, I thought. We'd just pointed Detective Ray in Luka's direction mere hours before the attack. Unfortunately for us, it seemed as if Erin had managed to reach him first.

"She could have stolen your aunt's Vespa so that she could pin Luka's attack on her too," Noa observed. "Rikki was already suspected of killing Lou." His jaw clenched. "With a case already built against her, it probably didn't take much to convince the police that Rik was behind both incidents."

I swore under my breath, feeling helpless and angry. "There has to be something we can do," I said, knitting my brows. "We should go after Erin. We can't let her get away with this."

Noa shook his head. "You promised Ray last night that you wouldn't approach her again, remember?" His forehead wrinkled. "Kales, I know it's frustrating, but we've got to let the police handle this. If Erin Malone was crazy enough to murder Louana, steal Rikki's Vespa, and try to kill Luka, then she's proven just how dangerous she is. She's already furious that you've been following her around. What do you think she's going to do if you show up near her again?"

I frowned. I hated to admit it, but Noa was right. If Erin really was behind Lou's murder and Luka's attack, going after her wasn't safe. *I'm more help to Rikki alive than dead*, I thought grimly. I heaved a sigh. "I hate this."

Noa reached for my hand and squeezed it. "I know. Me too."

At that moment, my cell phone began to ring. I unhooked it from the charger and found Jamie Parker's name flashing across the screen. "Hey, Jamie," I said into the mouthpiece. "Can I call you back later? Now's not really a good—"

"Girl, you are all over the news!" my friend interrupted, her voice breathless.

"Huh?" I nearly dropped the phone in my lap.

"I was just on Facebook, and your name popped up in the news section," she replied. "You're trending! How crazy is that?"

"Less crazy than you think," I said, feeling a pit of dread form in my stomach. Unfortunately, thanks to my famous ex, I was used to being the subject of trending news stories. I'd even had a few hashtags dedicated to me on Twitter. *#HotKaley* was my personal favorite. "What is it this time?" I asked wearily.

"Your dinner date with Noa. There are pictures of you guys on *TMZ* and *Entertainment Tonight* and at least ten other celebrity gossip sites."

I felt like I'd been sucker-punched. "There are pictures of us?" I asked in a shrill whisper. "In the tabloids?" Goose bumps pricked my arms. Who had photographed us? And where?

"There are photos of y'all having dinner at Starlight on the Lagoon last night," Jamie said. "A couple of bloggers are calling Noa your 'Resort Rebound.' Want me to send you the links?"

"No," I said quickly, feeling mortified. I noticed Noa giving me a sidelong glance, and I turned to face the window so he couldn't see my burning cheeks. "Why is this happening right now?" I moaned softly. "Who could have taken those pics?"

"I think it was that nosy *Aloha Sun* reporter, Felicity Chase," Jamie said. "It looks like she was the first one to post them."

Of course. I wished I could sink through the Jeep's upholstery. I'd known that woman was trouble from the start. I pinched the bridge of my nose with my thumb and forefinger, trying to ward off an inevitable headache. "Thanks for the warning," I told Jamie.

"Anytime. Want me to kick the crap outta Felicity for ya?" she asked, her tone chipper. Despite the world of trouble I was dealing with, I couldn't help but smile at how eager she sounded to come to my defense.

"Tempting, but I think I'd prefer to handle her myself," I said, thinking of the reporter's credit card, which was still in my wallet. *A little revenge retail therapy, maybe?*

"Let me know if you change your mind," Jamie replied. "And for what it's worth, I'm really glad you took my advice about Noa." I could practically hear her grinning. "I told you I was a great wing woman."

"The best," I replied.

"What happened?" Noa asked when I ended the call.

I didn't answer, too focused on typing my own name into the Google search engine on my phone's web browser. It pulled up nearly two dozen different articles. My breath hitched in my throat as I scanned the search results. *Football Star's Ex Finds New Love in Paradise; Resort Romance for Former Mrs. Colfax; Bryan Colfax's Ex-Wife on the Rebound with Hottie in Hawaii.*

"Ugh." I slumped low in the seat and covered my face with my hands. "Don't they have anything better to report about?" I grumbled.

"Who is reporting about what?" Noa's brow furrowed. "Kaley, what's going on?"

I sighed, dropping my gaze to my lap. It was too soon to know what would happen between Noa and me. I didn't need the added stress of having the media try to define our relationship for us. "The press caught wind of our dinner at Starlight on the Lagoon," I said, my tone frustrated. "There are pictures all over the web." I opened a blog post by Felicity Chase on the *Aloha Sun's* website and surveyed the images. "It looks like Felicity camped out in the lagoon and shot pictures of us through the window." At the time, I'd been so thrilled to be seated next the gorgeous view, but now I regretted it.

"So what?" Noa shrugged, giving me a look that said it didn't bother him. "Why does it matter? Are you upset that you were photographed with me or that Bryan is going to find out about it?"

"I don't care *what* Bryan thinks," I said sourly. "We're not together anymore. Screw him and his precious image." I huffed. "I'm just angry that I can't have feelings for someone else without the celebrity gossip hounds taking to the internet to dish about it. I'm not even famous. I was only married to someone famous for a little while."

Noa grinned. "So you have feelings for me, huh?"

I blinked at him. I thought I'd made that pretty clear the night before. "That's all you got out of that?"

"That was enough for me." He took one hand off the wheel and reached over to grab mine. "It'll blow over soon anyway. By this time next week, we'll be yesterday's news." His mouth quirked. "Unless you want to do something crazy to keep 'em talking."

I felt heat rush to my cheeks. "Let's put a pin in that." There would be plenty of time to figure out what was going on between us after we found a way to get Rikki out of jail. For now, I was just glad he was there. I couldn't have made it through any of this without him.

"Where to?" Noa asked as we reached the Aloha Lagoon city limits. "Are you hungry? You should probably eat something before work." He patted his stomach. "And so should I. My lifeguard shift starts at two."

I glanced at the clock on the top right corner of my phone screen. I had an hour and a half until I needed to be at the boutique. Though I wasn't particularly hungry, he was right. "Sure."

Noa parallel parked the Jeep in an open space half a block away from the Blue Manu Coffee House. The little café was located directly across the road from the police station. I shot a furtive glance at the stucco building where my aunt was currently being held, and my hands clenched into fists. *I'll get you out of there, Rikki*, I silently promised. *As soon as I can.*

"Kaley!" called a voice that was becoming all too familiar. I turned around to find Felicity Chase hurrying toward us from about a block away. She waved. "Wait up."

This chick again? I scowled at her. I was starting to understand how Erin Malone felt about me showing up wherever she went. After her little paparazzi stunt, Felicity Chase was the last person I wanted to see. If we hadn't been across the road from the police station, I would have stabbed her with her own stiletto.

"Come on," I said, grabbing Noa by the arm and pulling him toward the café before the reporter could catch up to us. We stepped inside the coffee shop and were greeted with the lively sound of a busker performing for the patrons on his ukulele. Noa and I each ordered a cup of Kona brew. I also chose a macadamia biscotti, while he grabbed a banana and a poppy seed muffin. I paid for everything with Felicity Chase's credit card. As far as I was concerned, it served her right. If she was getting paid to post pictures of Noa and me on the web, then the least she could do was treat us to a coffee. She'd probably be able to expense the purchase to the newspaper anyway.

We grabbed a table near the back of the café. I sipped the hot beverage and studied the surfboards that lined the walls as I waited for Felicity to inevitably appear in the doorway. Sure enough, she blew into the coffeehouse just a few moments after we sat down, her chestnut hair whipping about her face. She removed her sunglasses and darted her head from side to side. The reporter spotted me and made a beeline for our table, her lips parting to show her perfect white teeth.

"Well if it isn't my new favorite couple," she said, looking from Noa to me. "I called after you just a minute ago on the sidewalk. You must not have heard me."

"I did hear you," I said sourly. "I just didn't want to talk to you. I still don't."

Felicity ignored my anger. Her lips curved in a predatory smile. "Can I get a quote from you about your aunt's arrest in the hit-and-run assault of Luka Hale?" she asked, perching in the empty chair next to Noa.

"Sure. Here's your quote." I leaned across the table, glaring down my nose at her. "No freaking comment." I might have said a different, less polite word than "freaking."

"Okay. That's fair." Felicity leaned back in her seat and then raised her eyebrows, fixing me with a quizzical look. "Have you at least given some thought to my offer from yesterday?"

"Actually, I have a different offer for you," I replied through clenched teeth. "Get rid of those photos that you took of Noa and me, and *maybe* I'll give you back your credit card." My mouth twitched. "By the way, thanks for the coffee." I dipped the biscotti in my drink and then took a bite.

Felicity flinched but recovered quickly. "You're welcome," she said sweetly, waving her hand. "What's a few bucks in exchange for the story of my career?"

I smirked. "More than a few, actually. You just bought breakfast for everyone in this café."

Her face turned as white as the napkins on the table. I was lying, but it was still fun to watch her squirm for a few moments. She totally deserved it. "I'm kidding," I said finally.

Felicity's cheeks flushed. "I knew that," she muttered. She blew out a breath. "If you won't give me a quote defending Rikki, then I'll just have to print what I know so far." Her eyes slanted, and that same sharklike smile returned. "Which is that a witness places your aunt behind the wheel of her scooter last night, running over one of her own employees." She shook her head and made a clucking noise with her tongue. "And to think, she attacked the poor boy in front of his own mother. That is straight-up evil."

I stared at her, willing myself not to reach across the table and slap the snide grin off her face. She wanted me to fly off the handle, but I wasn't going to take the bait.

Noa's shoulders stiffened. He turned in his chair to loom over her, his own expression tight with anger. "You should go," he said gruffly. "And leave Kaley alone."

Felicity cleared her throat and pushed her chair back from the table. "All right. Fine. Don't cooperate." She scowled at me. "By the way, you'll be lucky if I don't decide to write an article about your aunt's sham of a clothing shop. I want my money back for the dress I bought yesterday."

I frowned. The remark had caught me off guard. "What? Why?"

The reporter wrinkled her nose. "When I put it on this morning, the sleeve ripped."

I bit back the urge to make a comment about her fat arms. "Are you sure?" I asked instead. I found it hard to believe that a high-quality garment from the boutique could tear so easily.

Felicity huffed, blowing several strands of her chestnut hair out of place. "Of course I'm sure," she said coolly. She held out her hand. "I'd like my credit card back now, please."

I handed it to her, and she stowed it in her wallet.

"I'll be seeing you," she said, her tone making it sound like a threat.

Noa shook his head as he watched Felicity stalk out of the coffeehouse. "That woman is…" He let his voice trail off as if he were searching for the right word.

"Incorrigible," I said dryly. I drew my lips down, frowning. "She's off her rocker if she thinks that Rikki's boutique is a sham. Happy Hula has been open at the resort for years. The *Aloha Sun* even named it Aloha Lagoon's Best Place to Shop two years in a row."

Noa reached across the table and patted my hand. "She was just trying to get a rise out of you."

"Yeah. You're right." I finished my coffee and then rose from my seat. "I should probably go into the boutique a little early." Happy Hula would likely be busy thanks to the upcoming Fourth of July weekend. "Would you mind giving me a ride to the resort?"

"No problem." Noa stood and followed me back to his Jeep. A few minutes later, he pulled into the little circle in front of the main lobby, where the airport shuttles dropped off guests for check-in. "I've got a few hours until my lifeguarding shift starts, so I think I'm going to go home and start on a site for one of my new clients." A yawn cracked his mouth wide open. "Or maybe I'll take a nap." Noa leaned across the front seat and cupped my face in his hand. "Everything's going to be fine, Kales," he said softly. "Let me know as soon as they set bail for Rikki. We'll get her out of there."

"Thanks," I said, grateful for his comfort. I closed the gap between us and gave Noa a gentle kiss on the lips. "I'll call you," I promised before sliding out of the passenger seat. I crossed through the lobby and into the courtyard, feeling weighed down with worry. I hoped that Noa was right and that Aunt Rikki would be released, but I wasn't feeling very optimistic. Now that they were holding her for Luka's attack, it was probably only a matter of hours before they formally charged her with Louana's murder too.

The lunch rush hadn't begun yet when I arrived at Happy Hula. Four or five resort guests milled about the store. Sara stood behind the counter, chatting amiably with one woman as she rang up her dress and shoes. Across the sales floor, Rose was crouched low, restocking the bottom of a display shelf with several pairs of sandals.

Sara handed the customer her receipt and shopping bag. She waved when she spotted me. "Hi, Kaley." Her eyes pinched with concern when I came to stand next to her. "Is Rikki okay? Harmony said you had a family emergency this morning."

I studied her for a moment. If she knew about what had happened to Luka, her face didn't show it. The word would spread eventually, but I wasn't ready to talk about it yet—especially not while Rikki was still the prime suspect. "Everything's fine," I lied. "You should probably take your lunch break as soon as Tonya gets here to cover the register. I'm sure business will pick up this afternoon once Rose and I finish hanging all the Fourth of July sale signs."

"Sure thing." Sara smiled at me, but I could still see the sympathy behind her eyes.

"Where's Harmony?" I asked, glancing around the store.

Sara shrugged. "In the office, I think." She made a face. "When I went back there earlier, she had her feet propped up on the desk like she owned the place—and she was watching funny cat videos on her phone."

I furrowed my brow. My aunt wasn't paying her to watch funny cat videos. *I thought Rikki said Harmony was one of her best employees.* "I'll go see what she's up to," I said, turning to walk toward the rear of the shop.

Harmony wasn't in the Rikki's office. I found her in the stockroom, crouching on the floor as she sorted through a pile of garment bags. "What are you doing?" I asked, scowling down at her.

Evidently, she hadn't heard me walk up. Harmony made a startled little squeal and teetered on her heels, nearly falling backward. She recovered quickly and straightened, glaring at me. "Don't sneak up on me like that," she practically hissed.

I couldn't help but smirk. "Sorry," I said insincerely. My gaze shifted down to the black garment bags. They appeared to be stuffed full of clothes. "What are you doing?"

Harmony stepped in front of the bags, blocking them from my sight. "Nothing," she said quickly. She shook her head as if to chase away the twin spots of color forming high on her cheeks. "It's none of your business," she added haughtily. Harmony stooped to pick up the bags and slung them over her shoulder. "Now that you're here, I'm taking my lunch break," she said, walking briskly toward the door. "I'll be back."

I stared after her as she exited the stockroom, puzzling over our odd exchange. I had the impression that Harmony hadn't wanted anyone to see what she'd been doing with those garment bags.

You've got bigger things to worry about, I reminded myself. I turned and headed toward Rikki's office, my thoughts on Erin Malone. I wondered where she was right at that minute. Was it possible that she'd fled the island after attacking Luka? What if she was still somewhere on the island, waiting to make sure my aunt took the fall for her crimes? She could even be at the resort, going about her housekeeping duties as if nothing were wrong. *I need proof that she's guilty.* While I was more convinced than ever that Erin was behind Louana Watson's murder, I still didn't have hard evidence.

I stepped inside Rikki's office, leaving the door open a crack so that I could hear if Sara or Rose called for manager assistance from up front. I slouched in the desk chair, feeling frustrated. I needed something to take my mind off Erin, Luka, and my poor aunt's predicament. Since shopping is my favorite distraction, I decided to peruse catalogs for more inventory.

Opening Rikki's laptop, I discovered that it hadn't been shut down properly the day before. The screen blinked to life, displaying the web browser I'd been viewing at the end of my shift. I recognized the vendor site that I'd found on the list in Louana's computer file. I glanced at the little hibiscus flower logo with swirly lettering at the top of the website and smiled. "The Island Fashionista Online Boutique," I read aloud. "Cute."

Scrolling down the page, I clicked on the link to the boutique's full catalog. Images of dresses, capris, blouses, and more filled the screen. My gaze moved over a familiar blue ombré tankini. It was from Kate Spade's new beachwear collection. Just like the bikini I'd spied on the site the previous day, we also had that piece in stock at Happy Hula. *Louana must have done a lot of ordering from this place*, I thought, skimming through the page. I felt a frown tug at my lips when I spotted a purple and white Zac Posen maxi dress. I had placed the order for that dress myself earlier this week, though it had come from a different vendor. It had arrived yesterday.

Could just be coincidence, I told myself, but I couldn't shake the odd sensation that filled my gut. Something about this site felt fishy. One by one, I clicked on each item in the catalog, and every time, I recognized the garments as part of Happy Hula's inventory.

The very last item in the Island Fashionista catalog sent me jumping out of my chair. It was the floral Sage McKinnon blouse—the one that Rikki's local designer friend had created exclusively for the Happy Hula Dress Boutique. "This doesn't make any sense," I said out loud. I bent over the desk and tapped the laptop screen. Why would Sage McKinnon have claimed to sell Rikki an exclusive piece if she planned to supply this shop with the same blouse? Had the designer lied...or had someone stolen the blouses from Happy Hula and listed them for sale on this site?

It was that last thought that sparked through my mind, illuminating several memories. I pictured Harmony crouched on the stockroom floor with the pile of full garment bags. I'd also seen her stuffing some into the trunk of her car on Tuesday night. *And didn't Noa tell me he recently built a website for Harmony?* I was pretty sure he'd even said it was for selling clothing online. Noa didn't know our product inventory like I did, so it was entirely possible that he wouldn't have even noticed that the clothes were the same as the pieces in our shop. Was Harmony stealing from Happy Hula to supply her own store?

Another thought struck me, setting my pulse to a gallop. Louana had highlighted the Island Fashionista Online Boutique on her vendor list. Was it possible that she had also recognized our inventory on the site and had caught on to Harmony's scheme? My blood chilled. Had I been looking at the wrong people all this time? Could Harmony have murdered Lou?

Heart racing, I pulled out my cell and dialed Noa's number, groaning in frustration when the call went to voicemail. "Noa, it's Kaley," I blurted. "Call me back as soon as you get this. I want to talk to you about the website for a clothing store called the Island Fashionista Online Boutique." I paused, feeling the excitement mount in my chest. "I think I know who Louana's real killer is."

The office door creaked as I hung up the phone, causing me to jump. I cast a furtive glance across the room. Had it been my imagination, or had someone been listening on the other side? *Relax,* I thought, closing my eyes. I'd worked myself up over this new theory about Harmony, and now I was jumpy. I took a few calming breaths and then sat back down in the chair. I watched my cell phone for several minutes, waiting for Noa to call. When I didn't hear from him, I got impatient and sent him a text: *I think Harmony has been stealing from Happy Hula to supply her online shop. Louana found out, and I think Harm might have killed her.*

Felicity Chase's words from that morning echoed in my memory as I slipped the phone back into the pocket of my dress. She'd called Rikki's shop a sham after her brand-new dress had ripped. I thought back to the button that had popped off the brand-new blouse I'd picked up in the stockroom on my first full day as manager. I was past the point of believing in coincidences. Rising from the desk chair, I marched out of the office and into the stockroom. A rack of orange Donna Karen wrap dresses were hanging along the far wall. It looked like either Rose or Luka had already priced the garments and prepped them to be rolled out onto the sales floor.

On a hunch, I plucked one of the dresses off its hanger and held it up for a closer inspection. To the average shopper, the dress might appear to be made of silk, as the tag claimed, but I'd worked in fashion retail long enough to recognize that it was really a synthetic replacement. I rubbed the fabric between my fingers. Had Felicity been right? Was Happy Hula passing off cheap knockoffs as real designer pieces? It certainly seemed that way.

But Rikki would never scam her customers on purpose, I thought, biting my lip. *Could Harmony be replacing the real pieces with cheap knockoffs?* I grasped the dress's apparel label in my hand, feeling around the seams. My gut clenched. The tiniest fragment of the original tag was still there. Someone had replaced it with an authentic-looking Donna Karen label. Aside from those few small fibers, whoever had sewn the new tag into place had done a virtually flawless job.

Wait a minute. Another memory shot to the surface. I pictured the Sage McKinnon blouse with its popped button, and my throat went dry. There was someone else at Happy Hula who could have pulled this off, and it wasn't Harmony Kane.

No sooner had the realization struck me than the door to the stockroom opened. "Kaley?" called a woman's voice. "Are you back here?"

I gulped. I had nowhere to hide as Sara Thomas stepped into the room. Her gaze roved over the dress in my hand, coming to rest on the counterfeit Donna Karan tag. Sara swallowed, and her nostrils flared ever so slightly. Then her eyes snapped to my face. "So you really did figure it out, huh?" she asked, her tone suddenly bitter. Glaring, she stalked toward me. I gasped at the sight of the box cutter gripped tightly in her hand.

CHAPTER SEVENTEEN

———

"You really should stop poking your nose where it doesn't belong." Sara's dark eyes gleamed with hatred. "You've been a pain in my ass ever since you showed up."

Terror clawed at me as I pressed my back against the wall. She had me cornered. "You killed Louana," I said, fighting to keep my voice from shaking.

Sara sighed, and for a just a moment, she looked like an innocent, frightened young woman. "I didn't want it to come to this, you know," she said, chewing her lower lip. "But Lou was blackmailing me. She found my website, and when she caught me stealing from the stockroom one night after work, she figured out what was going on. I had to pay her a cut of my profits each month in exchange for her silence. When she quit her job, she demanded even more money, so I killed her." She sucked in a breath and then pushed it back out. "After Lou was gone, I just wanted to keep my head down and wait for the whole mess to blow over. The cops were looking at Rikki. They didn't have any reason to come after me." She lifted her eyes to meet mine, and her lips peeled back in an ugly sneer. "But then *you* had to go and butt in." Sara gritted her teeth. "I wish you'd never come back to the island."

"So what now?" I asked, stalling. "You're going to kill me, too? How are you going to explain that to the police?"

Sara glowered at me. "I wouldn't have to do this if you'd stayed after Marco like you were supposed to—but since I don't really have a choice but to get rid of you now, I'll have to improvise." Her forehead bunched, and her expression turning thoughtful. "I could tell them you snapped. Maybe you're just as crazy as your kooky aunt," she said.

"What about the customers out on the sales floor?" If I yelled, there had to be someone out front who would hear me and come help. "Or Rose? And didn't Tonya just arrive to take over the register while you're on lunch?" I lifted my chin. "Someone could come back here any minute. You wouldn't kill me with so many potential witnesses."

The young cashier grinned. "You're right—I wouldn't. Too bad for you that we closed the boutique early today."

My confusion must have shown on my face, because Sara's wicked smile widened.

"As soon as I heard you telling Noa that you knew who Louana's killer was, I knew I had to get you alone. So I told Tonya and Rose that you wanted to close the shop early so that you and I could roll out the rest of the inventory for the Fourth of July weekend sale." Her dark eyes glittered. "There's nobody else in the store. It's just the two of us."

Fear knifed through me. I'd been right. Someone *had* been listening at Rikki's office door when I'd called Noa. Sara didn't know I'd been referring to Harmony. She'd only heard me tell him that I had a new theory about who the killer was. That, and I had mentioned the name of the website I'd found. She'd called it *her* shop. Another piece of the puzzle clicked into place. "You've been stealing the real designer clothes from Happy Hula and selling them on the Island Fashionista site," I guessed.

Sara smirked. "I told you I wanted to run my own fashion empire someday," she said, her tone smug. "This is just the first step. I needed some quick cash to afford better materials for my own designs. I found an overseas supplier that gives me a great deal on cheap fabric. And we both know I'm a hell of a seamstress, so it wasn't hard to deconstruct a couple of pieces and figure out how to duplicate them." Sara lifted her chin, looking pleased with herself.

My mouth went dry. There was still so much I didn't know, like why Sara had hurt Luka and why she'd thrown the rock through Rikki's window last night when I hadn't given her any reason to think I'd suspected her—because at the time, I hadn't. *None of that's important now,* I thought. I'd worry about getting answers if I made it out before Sara decided to finish me off. I darted a glance around the stockroom, wondering if I could sprint past her. Sara was petite and nearly half a foot shorter than I was, but she was also crazy—and she had nothing to lose. She would do whatever it took to keep me from leaving that stockroom alive.

A loud buzzing sound came to my rescue. The phone in my dress pocket was ringing loudly. The unexpected noise caused Sara to jump and swivel her head from side to side, searching for the source. It was just the distraction I needed. I lunged forward, tucking my head down like a football player. In a move that would have made my ex-husband proud, I charged straight into Sara's midsection. She cried out in surprise, pinwheeling her arms as she staggered backward.

I wasted no time running toward the door. Unfortunately, Sara regained her footing and was practically on my heels. I pushed boxes and spare clothing racks over as I ran, attempting to block her path, but they weren't enough to slow her down. I frantically pulled my ringing cell from my pocket as I ran. The call was from Noa. "Help!" I screamed into the phone.

I looked back over my shoulder in time to see Sara clear a pile of fallen mannequins like an Olympic hurdler. She lashed out with the box cutter as she lunged toward me, bringing it down on my left shoulder.

My thoughts broke apart, red hot agony flaring in my arm as the blade sliced through muscle. My phone dropped to the floor. I howled in pain and jerked sideways, trying to pull away. Sara lost her grip on the box cutter. It fell from my shoulder, sending a spray of blood through the air as it clattered to the floor.

Sara and I both dove for the weapon at the same time. We grappled on the stockroom floor, fighting for control of the blade. For such a tiny girl, she was incredibly strong—and furious. "I hate you!" she screamed as she ripped out a clump of my hair.

Fighting through the pain, I used my good arm to block Sara's blows. I rolled over onto my stomach and jerked my elbow back as hard as I could. There was a nasty crunching sound as it connected with Sara's nose. Shrieking, she staggered backward. With my assailant momentarily preoccupied, I searched the floor for my phone. In all the chaos, we'd knocked i underneath one of the shelves. It was too far away for me to reach. I struggled to my feet, preparing to run again, when Sara rushed at me from behind. Her nails dug into my skin as she pulled me toward her.

I clenched my teeth, struggling to wrench free from Sara's grasp. With a grunt, she shoved me back down to the floor. I tried to push myself up with my good elbow only to fall again when my hand slipped in a puddle of my own blood. I rolled onto my back, groaning in pain as my shoulder continued to throb.

Sara drove her knee into my chest, pinning me down. She reached up to grab something off one of the clothing racks. Before I could pull free, Sara wrapped the garment around my neck. I caught a glimpse of something black with white polka dots before she pulled the fabric tight, cutting off my air supply. It was one of our new Kate Spade bikinis. I tore at the stringy bathing suit top, desperately trying to break free, but it was no use. I'd lost a lot of blood, and my oxygen-starved lungs were burning in my chest. Strength waning, I stared helplessly up at Sara. Her nose was gushing blood, but the look of mad triumph on her face was unmistakable. She'd won, and she knew it. Sara yanked the fabric even harder, and my vision began to blur.

This is it. I'm going to die. I thought of Aunt Rikki, still sitting in the Aloha Lagoon jail. *And Noa...* My heart ached at the thought of never seeing him again. Then a curtain of black fell over everything, and I felt my body go limp.

A dull crack sounded somewhere above me. There was a grunt, and I dimly perceived a heavy weight rolling off of my chest. The bathing suit top loosened around my neck. I choked and sputtered as oxygen rushed back into my lungs. My vision slowly returned, and I rolled over on my side, sucking in mouthfuls of sweet, precious air. Using my good arm, I pushed myself into a seated position and gaped up at my unlikely savior.

Harmony Kane stood over Sara's motionless body, gripping a plaster mannequin leg high over her head with both hands. Her brown hair was disheveled, and I could see the whites of her eyes. Chest heaving, she stared down at the slumped form on the stockroom floor beside me. "Is she dead?" she asked, her voice frantic. "*Ohmigod*—did I kill her?"

I gingerly shifted positions so that I was facing Sara. The young woman's dark hair hid her pale face. There was a large gash on the back of her head, and I couldn't tell if the blood pooling between us was hers or mine. "I'm not sure," I croaked, wincing at the pain caused by trying to talk. I lifted a hand to my throat, which was sore to the touch. It was definitely going to bruise. Squinting at Sara, I could see the faint rise and fall of her chest. She wasn't dead, only unconscious. "She's breathing." I turned to gape up at Harmony. "What are you doing here?"

Harmony's posture eased, and her shoulders sagged with relief. She lowered her arms and dropped the mannequin leg to the floor. For once, she was neither rude nor sarcastic. "I forgot my purse, so I had to come back. The front door was locked. Lucky for you that Rikki gave me a set of shop keys. They were in my pocket." She met my gaze, and I noted that her normally bronze complexion had lightened several shades. "The stockroom door was open. I heard everything Sara said." Harmony gulped. "She murdered Louana," she said, shaking her head. "I never would have thought she had it in her."

I blinked at Harmony, still not quite believing that she'd actually come to my rescue. "You saved my life."

"Well, duh." She helped me to my feet. "I may not like you, but I'm not a monster." She was beginning to sound like her usual self again.

I wrinkled my brow. "I thought it was you," I admitted, coughing when pain flared in my throat. "I thought you were stealing from the shop. All those garment bags—" My words cut off as another coughing fit came on.

Harmony's eyes narrowed. "I wasn't stealing," she said defensively. "Those were my old dresses from beauty pageants and a few other events. I brought them to the resort because Summer arranged for the laundry staff to dry clean them for me."

"What for?" I didn't understand why she would need to have the dresses professionally cleaned if she hadn't worn them in years. Was she going to try to reenter the beauty pageant circuit?

Harmony's face crumpled. "Because I'm broke," she wailed. She hung her head, looking ashamed. Harmony avoided my gaze as she spoke in a shrill whisper. "My father filed for bankruptcy last month. I've racked up a ton of credit card debt in my own name over the years, and now he can't bail me out." Her nose crinkled in disdain. "I'm poor," she said, making *poor* sound as if it were a dirty word.

I stared at her. "So you're selling your old dresses?"

"Not exactly." Harmony lifted her chin and seemed to compose herself. "I needed a quick way to make some extra cash, so I asked Noa to build a website for me. I'm renting out all my old evening wear for dances and special events. That way I don't have to part with them, and I have a second source of income." She dropped her gaze to the floor. "Kaley, I know I haven't treated you well over the years, but if you could keep the whole finance thing between us, I'd really appreciate it."

"Done." I nodded. Just an hour ago, hearing something so salacious about spoiled Harmony Kane would have made my day. Considering she'd just saved my life though, I was less inclined to revel in her misery. "I'm sorry, Harm," I croaked. The burning pain in my throat was making it harder to push out the words, but I managed. "I shouldn't have jumped to conclusions." I took a step toward the door and wobbled on my feet, the combination of blood loss and oxygen deprivation making my legs feel like a pair of wet noodles.

Harmony slipped her arm around my waist and helped me out of the stockroom. We emerged from the back hallway just as the police burst into the store. Detective Ray and three uniformed officers fanned out as they rushed toward us. Noa and Jimmy Toki were right behind them. Seeing Noa galvanized me. Feeling a renewed sense of strength, I broke away from Harmony and limped toward him as fast as I could.

"Kaley!" he cried, closing the gap between us. His face was pale. "I came back to the resort as soon as I got your message. When you answered your phone, it sounded like…" He shuddered, and his face twisted in a look of anguish. "I called the police." Noa wrapped his arms around me, and I yelped in pain as he touched my wounded shoulder. He immediately released me and stepped back, taking in my blood-soaked clothes. "Are you hurt?"

"I'll be fine," I rasped. "But Harmony didn't—"

A shriek pierced the air, and I whirled in time to see Detective Ray and his men swarm around Harmony, their guns drawn. She threw her hands up in the air and dropped to her knees. "I didn't do anything," she protested, her shoulders trembling.

"Stop!" Pain surged in my throat. The yell sapped most of my remaining strength, but it got Detective Ray's attention. He turned to look at me, his head cocked in question. "It wasn't her," I wheezed. My knees buckled, and Noa caught me before I collapsed.

"It was Sara Thomas," Harmony agreed. "She was trying to kill Kaley, but I knocked her out. She's in the stockroom." Harm made a frightened squeak when the detective and his men turned back to her. "Can you put the guns down now, please?" she asked, her voice an octave higher than usual.

"Sorry." Detective Ray motioned for his team to lower their weapons. The men filed toward the rear of the store to detain Sara.

"Are you all right?" Jimmy asked, walking over to Harmony. The beefy security guard offered her his hand.

She jerked away from him and shakily climbed to her feet. It looked as if all the blood had drained from Harmony's face. "Kaley," she warbled, teetering on unsteady legs. "Tell Rikki that I quit." Her eyes rolled back in their sockets, and she fainted.

CHAPTER EIGHTEEN

———

An ambulance arrived at the resort to take Sara and me to the hospital in Lihue. Harmony was examined when she came to, but she was cleared to go home as soon as she finished giving the police her statement. I needed stitches in my left shoulder, and Harm had whacked Sara so hard that, in addition to a broken nose (courtesy of yours truly), she also had a concussion.

When she regained consciousness, Sara confessed to murdering Louana Watson to cover up her counterfeit fashion operation. She'd been scamming Happy Hula for a couple of months, stealing authentic designer pieces whenever she could. She'd sold the clothes on her own website and had replaced them with the knockoffs she'd created in her apartment using cheap materials she'd ordered from China.

Just as she'd told me, Sara confirmed that Louana had caught her red-handed one night when she was swiping new pieces for her online shop. Lou had taken payment in exchange for her silence, but on the night she'd been murdered, she'd asked Sara to meet her in the shop after it closed. Sara had been the one to use the access road that Noa and I had discovered, meeting Louana in the back alley because she didn't have her own copy of the shop keys.

Having quit her job, Louana had decided to demand a larger cut of the profits. She and the thieving cashier had argued, and it had turned physical. Sara claimed that Louana had rushed at her. In a panic, she had strangled the other woman and had then fled the scene, leaving behind all the clothes Lou had gathered for her.

When it had become clear that the police suspected Aunt Rikki of committing the crime, Sara had thought she was off the hook. Then she'd noticed that I'd been asking a lot of questions. Realizing that I was trying to find Louana's real killer, she had panicked and tried to throw me off her trail by sending me after Marco Rossini.

Though her plan to distract me had worked, Sara had still run into trouble. With Louana out of the picture, she had thought she could continue her shady operation and keep all of the profits for herself. Unfortunately for her, Luka had caught her in the stockroom, stuffing several garments into her bag. When bribing him didn't work, she'd decided to play dirty. Luka had once confided in her about how Louana had been blackmailing him, and she'd used it to her advantage. Sara had told Luka that if he blabbed about her theft, she'd tell the police about his situation with Lou to throw suspicion on him. Then she'd told me about Luka's plight, figuring if he did cave and approach me about what he'd seen, I'd find him less credible.

Though Luka had grudgingly agreed to keep silent, Sara had begun to unravel. Convinced that he'd change his mind and would turn her in for shoplifting, she'd decided to take matters into her own hands. Sara had seen the opportunity to silence Luka while strengthening the case against Rikki.

Since Sara knew that my aunt left a spare key to her Vespa in the top drawer of her desk, she'd sneaked into the office and swiped it. While she was in there, she'd spotted her own clothing website on the open browser on Rikki's laptop. Sara had panicked, suspecting that I was catching on. She'd waited until dark and had thrown the rock through Rikki's front window. While Noa and I had been distracted by the chaos, she'd stolen the Vespa. Posing as Rikki, Sara had attacked Luka and then ditched the scooter, which the police later found hidden in the brush behind the lagoon.

With Luka unconscious in the hospital and Rikki in jail, Sara had thought she was finally in the clear. Then I'd shown up at the boutique, and she'd overheard my phone call to Noa. When I'd mentioned her website by name and said that I thought I knew who the real murderer was, Sara had decided she'd have to get rid of me too.

If Harmony hadn't stopped her, Sara would have strangled me just as she'd done to Louana. Never in a million years would I have thought I'd owe my life to Harmony Kane, but I was grateful that she had saved me—so much so that I later convinced her not to quit her job at Happy Hula and even talked Rikki into giving her a raise to help pay off some of her debt.

Noa wouldn't leave my side after the incident at the boutique, and he even insisted on riding with me in the ambulance. He held my hand as I received six stitches in my shoulder, letting me squeeze his fingers when the topical anesthesia didn't quite numb the pain.

After examining my bruised throat, the doctor informed Noa and me that I had no severe damage. He wrote me a prescription and promised that with plenty of rest, it should heal in a few days' time.

Detective Ray knocked on the door of my room as the doc was clearing me to be discharged. "How are you feeling?" he asked, stepping into the exam room.

"Like someone stabbed me in the shoulder and then strangled me nearly to death." My voice was too raspy to convey my dry tone, and I came off sounding like one of Marge Simpson's sisters.

Detective Ray's cheeks colored, and his expression turned sheepish. "I owe you and your aunt an apology," he said, shoving his beefy hands into the pockets of his chinos.

"Rikki will be released now, right?" Noa asked for me.

I smiled at him with gratitude, and he squeezed my hand.

The detective nodded. "Now that I have Miss Thomas's confession for both Louana Watson's murder and the hit-and-run that injured Mr. Hale, all charges against your aunt will be dropped." His lips turned up at the corners. "And I'm sure you'll be happy to know that Luka is going to be all right. He took a turn for the better earlier this afternoon, and he's awake now."

I exhaled a sigh of relief, wincing as my throat continued to throb. "Thank you," I wheezed.

Noa must have noticed my pained expression. His forehead puckered. "Kaley, the doctor told you to rest your voice," he scolded.

"It's a little better," I said. The numbing sensation from the lozenge the doctor had given me was already starting to take effect.

"You still shouldn't strain yourself," Noa argued.

Detective Ray took that as his cue to leave. "I should be going," he said. "I'd be happy to give you two a ride back to your car so you can come pick Rikki up from the police station," he offered.

I nodded and rose from the exam table where I'd been seated. There was just one thing I wanted to do first. "Do you know which room Luka Hale is in?" I asked, ignoring Noa's frown of disapproval.

The plump homicide detective nodded. "I'll take you by there, if you'd like."

Noa and I followed Detective Ray out of the exam room and turned down another hall, stopping in front of Luka's room. "I'll give you all some privacy," he said. "I need to make a few calls anyway. I'll be in the reception area whenever you're ready." Detective Ray shuffled back down the hall.

To my immense relief, we found Luka Hale wide-awake. His chest was wrapped in bandages, and a cast covered his leg from the knee down. I grimaced. The poor guy had to be in a lot of pain. *But at least he's alive.*

Luka's room was full of flowers and balloons. He was sitting in his hospital bed, his back resting against an oversized pillow. He looked up as we entered the room and scrunched up his face. "What are you doing here?"

I suddenly felt sheepish. The only interactions I'd had with Luka since we'd met had been filled with mistrust—from both sides. It was time to eat a little crow. "I came to see how you were doing," I said, my tone still a bit gravelly.

"Thanks." Luka's face was tight with pain. "The doctor says I've got two broken ribs and a shattered femur." His head drooped. "Guess I won't be catching any more waves for a while," he said gloomily.

"I'm so sorry," I said, feeling a mixture of sympathy and guilt. If I'd been looking for Lou's killer in the right places to begin with, I might have caught Sara before she'd hurt the poor kid. "I also want to apologize for hounding you about Louana Watson," I told him, trying to look sincere. "Her real killer was arrested today."

Luka stared at me for a few moments, his expression hard. Then his lips turned up at the corners. It was the first time I'd seen him smile. It was a good look for him. "No worries," he said, lifting his hand to make the *shaka* sign with his thumb and pinkie. "I forgive you. You were just sticking up for your aunt. I can respect that." He cocked his head to the side, brow furrowed. "So who killed Lou?"

Noa stepped forward, snaking his arm around my middle. "It was Sara Thomas," he explained. His expression darkened. "She was also the one who put you in the hospital."

Luka nodded slowly. I could practically see the gears turning behind his eyes. He clenched his jaw. "When I woke up earlier, my mom said that Rikki had done this to me, but I knew that couldn't be true. I can't remember anything about the accident, but your aunt has always been good to me." He squinted. "I caught Sara stealing yesterday, and she threatened to tell the cops that I'd killed Louana because she'd been blackmailing me." His expression turned stony. "I never should have told her about that, but I trusted her."

"I know," I said. "We all did." The quiet cashier had been there all along, hiding in plain sight. I'd known it was her dream to make a name for herself in the fashion world, but I hadn't realized how far she'd go to protect that dream. Sara had even been the one to hand me two of my biggest leads—Marco and Luka—and I'd been so focused on them that I hadn't even stopped to wonder just why she was being so helpful. She'd wanted to throw me off her trail, and she'd done a great job of it, right up until the end.

A soft knock pulled my attention to the door. Erin Malone stepped into the room, a blue teddy bear tucked under her arm. "Babe, I'm back," she said, holding up the toy. "And check out this cute little guy that I found in the gift shop—" Erin stopped talking when she spotted me. Her face turned scarlet. "You *again*?" she fumed, stalking toward me. Her free hand balled into a fist. "Now I can't even visit my boyfriend in the hospital without you showing up? This is the last straw. I'm filing a restraining order."

I held up my hands in surrender, taking a step back. "I come in peace this time, I promise." I furrowed my brow as I looked from Erin to Luka. "You two are dating?"

Luka nodded, trying to sit up straighter in the hospital bed. "Yeah," he said, wincing in pain. He shifted to make himself more comfortable. He looked at Erin. "It's okay, babe," he told her. "They came to tell me that Sara Thomas was arrested for murdering Lou—and for running me over."

Erin's glossy lips parted. "The skinny cashier chick from Happy Hula?"

Luka nodded.

Noa and I exchanged a look. "Erin, if you're with Luka, then why were you at dinner with Marco last night?" he asked.

She scowled. "That's none of your business."

"It's all right. We can tell them." Luka met my gaze. "Kaley's not so bad, after all."

"Thanks." I beamed at him.

Luka reached out to Erin, and she moved to stand next to him so he could hold her hand. "Erin was telling Marco about us," he said. "He and I are friends—well, we were, anyway. We used to be tight, but he's been kind of a dick lately." His forehead creased. "What he did to Erin wasn't cool. And with Louana Watson, of all people?" Luka shuddered. "I mean, not to speak ill of the dead, but she was straight-up cruel."

From what I'd encountered of the bellhop, I didn't think Lou was the only girl he'd cheated on Erin with. "Marco is quite the womanizer," I said.

Erin looked from Luka to me, raising a skeptical brow. When Luka nodded in encouragement, she relented. "Marco made the reservation at Starlight on the Lagoon several months ago," she said. "We were supposed to have dinner there to celebrate our anniversary. But then he cheated on me, and we broke up. I was really upset at first, but then Luka asked me out for drinks." She blushed. "It's still pretty new. We've only been seeing each other for a little over a week," she admitted. "So when Marco called me up and pleaded with me to meet him for dinner, I took the opportunity to tell him that I'd met someone else. He admitted to hooking up with a few other girls after we broke up, but he claimed that it only made him realize how much he missed me, if you can believe that." She rolled her eyes, giving me the impression that she didn't.

"I'm guessing he didn't take the news about you two very well," Noa remarked.

I nodded in agreement, recalling how angry Marco had been when I brought up Erin outside the restaurant.

"He didn't—not that I care." Erin stuck out her chin. "Marco Rossini lost the right to have an opinion about my love life the day he decided to cheat on me."

I smiled. "I'm with you on that."

Luka's mother entered the room, carrying a disposable coffee cup and a magazine. The older woman's face lit up at the sight of our little group. "Oh, Luka. How nice! You have visitors," she said brightly. She smiled at me. Her hair was a mess, and there were still dark circles under her eyes, but Nancy Hale seemed like a totally different person from the woman we'd seen in the waiting room that morning. She tilted her head as she looked at me. "You two came by earlier, right? Didn't you bring that bouquet of flowers?" she pointed to one of the arrangements on the bedside table. Mrs. Hale didn't wait for me to answer. Squinting, she asked, "What was your name again? Jamie?"

Luka shook his head. "No, Ma. That's—"

"It was great to see you, Luka," I interrupted, edging backward toward the door. "I'm glad that you're going to be all right. Everyone else from the shop sends their well wishes." I gripped Noa's arm and pulled him along with me, not wanting to have to explain to Mrs. Hale that I'd lied to her.

"What an odd girl," I heard her remark as we slipped down the hall.

Detective Ray was waiting for Noa and me in the lobby. He drove us back to the resort to retrieve the Jeep, and then we followed him to the stucco building that housed the police station.

The charges against Aunt Rikki had been dropped, and she'd been released while we were at the hospital. We found her waiting for us in the lobby, still dressed in her spandex jogging capris and running shoes, though someone—I'm assuming Detective Ray—had given her an oversized white T-shirt to wear over her neon yellow sports bra. Her black and blue hair was haphazardly pulled back from her face, and her eyes were puffy. Despite her rough appearance, my heart swelled at the sight of her. My aunt was all right, and that was all that mattered.

Rikki jumped out of her chair as soon as we walked into the lobby. Relief showed in her face as she rushed forward and launched herself at me. "Kaley! My *ku'uipo*. I knew you'd come for me." She pulled back, lowering her gaze to my bruised throat and bandaged shoulder. Her face crumpled. "Are you okay?"

"I'm wonderful." I hugged her again, not caring about the pain. Tears spilled down my cheeks. "I'm just glad it's all over." I released Rikki and stepped back. I glanced over my shoulder at Noa. He stood in the doorway, his dark eyes shining as he watched our happy reunion.

Aunt Rikki followed my gaze. "Get over here, boy," she cried, laughing. Noa joined us, and my aunt wrapped her arms around us both in a fierce hug.

I was the first to pull away. I beamed at them both, the two people I cared about most in the world. For the first time in my life, I truly felt complete. I planted a soft kiss on Noa's lips and then looped my arm through Rikki's. "Come on. Let's go home."

* * *

The Aloha Lagoon Resort held its Fourth of July luau a few days later. Though the luxury hotel hosted nightly feasts, this one was special, open to both guests and the islanders. The Ramada Pier looked like a living sea of red, white, and blue as people moved about before the dinner festivities. Adults sipped their rum punch while children zigzagged through the crowd, waving the small souvenir American flags that the resort had provided for the occasion.

"Kaley, I *love* your outfit," Jamie gushed as she slipped into the empty seat beside me at our table.

I grinned at her. "Thanks." I glanced down at my sleeveless blue and white aloha-patterned dress, which I'd paired with red sandals. A red flowered lei covered up the last remaining bruises on my neck. I smoothed a wrinkle in the skirt. "It's from a new designer named Lola Barron. The shipment just came in yesterday." My lips quirked. "Remember, Happy Hula employees get an *extra* ten percent discount at the store. Now that you're going to be working there with me, we should go on a little shopping spree to celebrate." Since we were in need of a new cashier, I'd talked Rikki into letting me hire Jamie to work part-time around her scuba instructor schedule, not that it had taken much convincing.

Jamie flashed me a toothy smile. "You had me at 'discount.'" She glanced over my shoulder, and her brows twitched. "Here comes Harmony," she warned.

I didn't even bat an eyelash. Ever since the showdown with Sara, Harmony and I had buried the hatchet. Sort of. I was grateful that she'd saved my life, and she was grateful that I'd promised not to tell anyone that she was no longer as rich as the Kardashians. Though we still didn't see eye to eye on most things, we'd learned to get along—most of the time.

Harmony took a seat across the table from us. "I'm pretty sure I just saw that reporter, Felicity Chase. She's over by the buffet," she said, inclining her head toward the large table where the feast would soon be placed. Harmony glanced at me. "I thought you said she was banned from the resort property."

I followed her gaze and easily spotted the reporter. Though she'd disguised herself under a wide-brimmed straw hat and large sunglasses, there was no mistaking her narrow face and chestnut hair. I'd agreed to give Felicity *one* interview after the events at Happy Hula, just to get the facts straight. In exchange, she'd promised to protect the shop's reputation by not including details about the knockoff designer clothes Sara had been stocking there (Rikki was working with the police to recover as much of the original inventory as she could and had begun reaching out to affected customers to make things right). Felicity had printed her story about the murderous cashier in the weekend edition of the *Aloha Sun*. Now she'd turned her attention back to celebrity sightings.

"Felicity told me she heard from a source on the housekeeping staff that Blake Lively and Ryan Reynolds are staying at the resort," I told Harmony and Jamie. I smirked. "I think she's hoping to snap a picture of Ryan in the buff."

"Can you blame her?" Jamie blurted. She bounced her eyebrows. "Where can I buy a pair of binoculars around here?"

She giggled, and I joined in. Even Harmony chuckled.

"What are you ladies laughing about?" Noa appeared at the table, taking the other empty seat next to me. "Sorry I'm late," he said, brushing his dark hair out of his face and offering me a lazy smile. He slid an arm around my shoulders and planted a soft smooch on my lips.

Out of the corner of my eye, I saw Harmony stiffen. While we'd managed to be civil the last few days, she'd been more than a little miffed that Noa had chosen me over her. Not that I cared.

I turned my attention back to Noa. "Nothing, really," I said dreamily. As far as I was concerned, Noa Kahele would beat out Ryan Reynolds as the hottest guy on the island any day of the week. I'd spent nearly every free minute with him since we'd left the hospital on Thursday.

Not only had we repaired our friendship, but we'd added a few extra (and oh-so-hot) benefits. Being with Noa felt as natural as breathing, and every time he smiled at me, I knew this was the beginning of something really special.

The luau festivities officially started a few minutes after Noa arrived. The steady beating of a drum accompanied the procession of torch bearers and the young men who filed between the tables, chanting as they carried large trays of roasted pork, fresh pineapple, poi, salads, and more. The servers set the trays down on the large buffet, and the luau's MC delivered a warm welcome to the guests before declaring that dinner was served. We rose from the table and merged into the buffet line to fill our plates. I swayed to the steel drum music being performed on the stage as I piled my own plate high with tender pork and sweet potato salad.

As the meal came to an end, the Aloha Lagoon Wahines danced their way in between tables, pulling the male guests out of their chairs to teach them how to hula. Noa declined when one of the performers approached him and tried to coax him onto the stage. He scooted his chair closer to mine and grabbed my hand. I looked to the opposite end of the table, locking eyes with Aunt Rikki. She winked at me before resuming her conversation with the woman seated next to her. My aunt was over the moon that Noa and I were close again.

When the sun finally dipped behind the ocean, the MC announced that the special Fourth of July fireworks display was about to begin. The luau staff handed out sparklers to the children, and guests left their tables to settle onto the sand for a better view of the special presentation.

Noa grabbed my hand and pulled me out of my chair, leading me toward a free spot on the beach. The sand was still warm from the hot July day as we sat down. He scooted closer to me, and I leaned my head on his shoulder. We sat there in comfortable silence, listening to the chatter of the other guests and the gentle sound of the waves lapping against the shore.

After several minutes, the first fireworks whistled through the air. Bursts of color lit up the night sky, their reflection glittering in the water below. "It's beautiful," I breathed, snuggling closer to Noa.

"*You're* beautiful." He planted a soft kiss in my hair. "I'm really glad you're back in my life, Kaley." Noa tilted his head toward mine, and I saw the bright lights reflected in his eyes. "I hope you'll stick around."

"I don't plan on going anywhere." I grinned. "I'm finally where I'm supposed to be." I leaned in and kissed him as the grand finale illuminated the sky above.

Noa reluctantly pulled away as the last sparks faded away overhead, and the crowd around us began to disperse. "That ended too fast," he said breathlessly.

A sly smile curved my lips. "In that case, come with me." I rose to my feet and dusted the sand off my knees before grabbing Noa by the hand. "Let's go home and make some fireworks of our own."

ABOUT THE AUTHOR

USA Today bestselling author Anne Marie Stoddard used to work in radio, and it rocked! After studying Music Business at the University of Georgia, Anne Marie worked for several music venues, radio stations, and large festivals before trading in her backstage pass for a pen and paper (Okay, so she might have kept the pass...). Her debut novel, *Murder at Castle Rock*, was the winner of the 2012 AJC Decatur Book Festival & BookLogix Publishing Services, Inc. Writing Contest, and the 2013 Book Junkie's Choice Award Winner for Best Debut Fiction Novel. It was also a finalist for Best Mystery/Thriller in the 2014 RONE Awards.

Aside from all things music and books, Anne Marie loves college football, Starbucks iced coffee, red wine, and anything pumpkin-flavored. She is a member of Sisters in Crime and the Sisters in Crime Guppies chapter. Anne Marie is currently hard at work on several books.

To learn more about Anne Marie, visit her online at:
http://amstoddardbooks.com

Visit the official

aloha lagoon

website!

Trouble in paradise...
Welcome to Aloha Lagoon, one of Hawaii's hidden treasures. A
little bit of tropical paradise nestled along the coast of Kauai, this
resort town boasts luxurious accommodation, friendly island
atmosphere...and only a slightly higher than normal murder rate.
While mysterious circumstances may be the norm on our corner
of the island, we're certain that our staff and Lagoon natives will
make your stay in Aloha Lagoon one you will never forget!

www.alohalagoonmysteries.com

If you enjoyed *Bikinis & Bloodshed*, be sure to pick up these other Aloha Lagoon Mysteries!

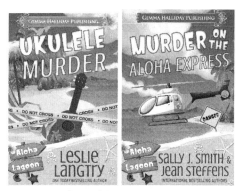

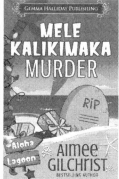

Made in the USA
San Bernardino, CA
09 November 2019